THE RED HOTEL

THE RED HOTEL

A Sissy Sawyer Novel

Graham Masterton

This first world edition published 2012
in Great Britain and in the USA by
SEVERN HOUSE PUBLISHERS LTD of
9–15 High Street, Sutton, Surrey, England, SM1 1DF.
Trade paperback edition first published
in Great Britain and the USA 2013 by
SEVERN HOUSE PUBLISHERS LTD

Peterborough City Council	
60000 0000 65971	
Askews & Holts	Jun-2012
HOR	£19.99

ISBN-13: 978-0-7278-8189-2 (cased)
ISBN-13: 978-1-84751-444-8 (trade paper)

All Severn House titles are printed on acid-free paper.

Severn House Publishers support The Forest Stewardship Council [FSC],
the leading international forest certification organisation. All our titles that
are printed on Greenpeace-approved FSC-certified paper carry the FSC logo.

MIX
Paper from
responsible sources
FSC   FSC® C018575
www.fsc.org

Typeset by Palimpsest Book Production Ltd.,
Falkirk, Stirlingshire, Scotland.
Printed and bound in Great Britain by
MPG Books Ltd., Bodmin, Cornwall.

Shadow Theater

Some people say that when we depart from this world, we leave almost nothing behind apart from our possessions, and our shadows. Every time we walked between the sun and the ground beneath our feet, or between a bright indoor light and the wall behind us, we created a negative image of ourselves – not us, but an absence of us.

Some people believe that sometimes our shadows remain here, especially if we have died without fulfilling all of our ambitions or resolving all of our differences. Long after we have gone, our shadows continue to play out the petty dramas of our lives – even though we ourselves are lying deep under the ground, where we can cast no more shadows; or when we are blowing as dust and ashes in the wind.

One afternoon, less than a year ago, shadows started to flicker along the corridors of The Red Hotel, on Convention Street, in Baton Rouge, Louisiana, and both guests and staff heard bumping and high-pitched whistling and persistent grinding noises. They said that it gave them 'the freesons', which is what people in Baton Rouge call 'goosebumps.'

Some believed that Mrs Slider had returned. Mrs Slider and her son, Shem. Because a few of the older residents in the waterfront district still harbored a strong suspicion about what Mrs Slider and her son, Shem, had done together, although nobody knew for sure, those older residents crossed themselves, and whispered a prayer for protection.

The Boy Behind the Door

The rain had been dredging down all afternoon, and both Sissy and Mr Boots had sat out on the pale-green painted verandah for the past hour or so, watching it clatter through the trees and overflow from the gutters and run in rivulets down the winding pathway that led to the road. Sissy was sitting out on the verandah because she wanted to smoke and Mr Boots was sitting out on the verandah because he was wet and he stank and Sissy wouldn't allow him into the house.

'Some summer,' said Sissy, but Mr Boots didn't make a sound. He didn't even turn around and nod, as if he were agreeing with her, which he did sometimes.

'Excuse me, cloth ears!' Sissy snapped at him, much louder this time. 'I said, "One hell of a miserable summer." What's your opinion?'

Mr Boots made a mewling noise in the back of his throat. 'Jesus,' she demanded. 'Where'd you learn that cat language? Have you been fraternizing with that mangy old tabby next door?'

She took a pack of Marlboro out of the low-slung pocket of her gray hand-knitted cardigan, but there was only one left, and that was broken in half. 'Shit and a bit,' she said, and heaved herself up off the swing seat to go into the house and see if she could find another pack, although she doubted that she had any left. She had been trying to cut down lately but it was just one of those wet, miserable days when the gray clouds were almost down to treetop height and it wasn't even worth going to the market at Boardman's Bridge because it was raining so hard and today she felt like smoking.

Sissy always said that if God hadn't meant people to smoke he wouldn't have allowed them to discover America.

She was opening the screen door when she heard the scrunching of a car in the driveway. She turned and saw the metallic-red Escalade owned by her step-nephew, Billy.

He climbed out, turning up the collar of his black hill-climber's jacket, and then walked around the hood and opened the passenger door. A girl in a shiny red raincoat and a matching red rain hat stepped down, and followed Billy up the steeply sloping steps that led to the verandah. 'Hey, Aunt Sissy!' called Billy. Mr Boots immediately barked and jumped up and started snorting and snuffling and beating his tail against the railings. Billy was a thin, pale, good-looking young man of twenty-six, with a shock of black, gelled-up hair and slightly foxy features and very blue eyes that were always wide open, as if life permanently surprised him. He was the son of Sissy's sister's second husband, Ralph, and so he wasn't really related to Sissy at all, not by blood, but for some reason they had always been as close as two conspirators.

When he was a small boy, Sissy had taught Billy complicated Atlantic City card tricks and how to predict tomorrow's weather from the behavior of garden snails – 'but mind you don't stand over a snail for too long . . . they may look innocent but country folk say that snails can suck the shadows out of you.'

There were plenty of snails around today, because it was so damp, and the verandah was criss-crossed by silvery trails.

Billy and the girl in the shiny red raincoat came up on to the verandah. Billy smacked the raindrops off his jacket and then gave Sissy a hug.

'How's it hanging?' he asked her. He nodded toward the crowded ashtray beside the swing seat. 'Still smoking like Mount Saint Helens, I see. Thought you said you were giving it up.'

Sissy coughed and shook her head. 'It was your mother who said I was giving it up. On principle I never do what your mother says I'm going to do. Never have done, since we were kids, and never will. I would have been married to a loss adjuster called Norman, if I'd done what your mother said I was going to do. Still *would* be, come to that.'

She turned to the girl in the shiny red raincoat. The girl was blonde, clear skinned and very pretty, with high cheekbones and a little ski-jump nose and green, feline eyes.

'So who's this you've brought to see me?' asked Sissy.

'This is my girlfriend, Lilian. But everybody calls her T-Yon.'

'T-Yon?'

Billy put his arm around her shoulders. 'When she was little, Lilian was brought up in Lafayette, Louisiana. T-Yon is Cajun-speak for "Petite Lilian".'

'T-Yon, how about that?' said Sissy. 'Well, good to meet you, T-Yon.'

She shook hands with T-Yon and all her silver and enamel bracelets jingled like Christmas. Sissy was an unredeemed hippy. To the despair of her family, she still wore flowing kaftans and long dangly earrings and braided her hair in a steel-gray coronet. In her day, she had been very pretty, too – one of those flower children who had skipped bare-breasted at Woodstock. Nowadays, when she looked in the mirror, she could still see the ghost of that flower child dancing in her eyes.

'Billy's always talking about you so much,' said T-Yon, shyly. 'In the end I twisted his arm to bring me up here to see you, just to see if you were real.'

Sissy held up her hand, and turned it this way and that, as if to check that she really *was* real. 'Well,' she said, 'I *think* I'm real. Most of the time, anyhow. Some days I have my doubts, I have to admit, and I almost believe I'm a ghost. It's strange, isn't it, how much your life can change from day to day? You don't know if it's the world around you that's changing, or if it's you.'

T-Yon blinked, and it was obvious that she didn't really understand what Sissy meant. But then Sissy didn't really understand what she meant, either.

'Come on in,' said Sissy. 'How about some tea? Or coffee, if you'd rather. Or Dr Pepper. Or a glass of Zinfandel?'

Billy said, 'I'm driving, so I'll stick to tea. So long as it's not that tea that tastes like grass clippings.'

'Oh, you mean my *mate de coca*? That's very good for you, *mate de coca*. And stimulating. It contains nought point four percent cocaine.'

'I don't care if it contains forty-four percent smack. It still tastes like grass clippings.'

'Well . . . if you're not having any wine, you can drive to the Trading Post for me and bring back two hundred Marlboro.'

'You want me to facilitate your death from lung cancer?'

'Put it any way you like. But please go buy me some cigarettes. In any case, death is only an illusion. I can vouch for that personally. Oh, and buy me some fresh bread while you're there, would you, and some of that Limburger cheese, and some baloney, and half a dozen cans of Artemis Holistic Dog Food for Mr Boots.'

'You're a slave-driver, Aunt Sissy, did you know that?' Billy told her; but he went back out into the rain, climbed into his SUV, and drove off down the hill. Sissy meanwhile ushered T-Yon into the house, with Mr Boots tangling himself up between their legs. Sissy snapped, 'Stay!' and shut the door on him. 'He smells like a goddamn sewer when he's wet.'

It was gloomy inside the living room because the day was so overcast, and the gloom gave the room an unnatural stillness, as if it were suspended in time – a memory of a room instead of a real room. Vases of fresh-picked garden flowers stood on every side table – yellow roses and purple stocks and scarlet gladioli – and the walls were covered with a jumbled-up variety of paintings and prints and masks and odd decorations, like a calumet covered with seashells, and a 1920s bridal headdress embroidered with white lace petals. Over the fireplace the mottled mirror reflected the blood red of T-Yon's raincoat.

'Tea?' asked Sissy. 'Here – let me take your things. They're so cute, aren't they, this hat and this coat? Little Red Riding Hood rides again.'

'I can get a glass of wine?' asked T-Yon. Her Cajun accent wasn't very strong, but it was distinctive enough for anybody to tell at once where she came from. Underneath her raincoat she was wearing a tight, gray short-sleeved sweater and tight black pedal pushers. Sissy could see why Billy had been attracted to her. Apart from being so pretty, she had very big breasts and very slim hips. Around her neck she wore a silver pendant attached to a leather cord. It was embossed with the face of a woman with her eyes closed, as if she were asleep, and dreaming.

'So tell me, how did you and Billy meet?' asked Sissy, as she came back into the living room with a frosty bottle of Zinfandel and two long-stemmed wine glasses.

T-Yon had picked up a black-bronze statuette of a dancing devil, with horns and a pointed beard and the shaggy legs of a goat.

'*Scary*,' she said, narrowing her eyes and peering into its face.

'Him? He's only scary if you believe in him.'

'But you don't? He has such a wicked face.'

'From my experience, T-Yon, I believe that ordinary people are a whole lot wickeder than devils. Human beings – now *they're* scary.'

T-Yon carefully replaced the statuette and sat down on the floral-covered couch. She watched as Sissy poured her a glass of wine.

'Billy and me, we met in bakery class. I was supposed to be making choux pastry but every time I tried to do it I ended up with this big dry lump. Billy came over and showed me how to beat the flour into the water and the butter, and that was how we got together.'

'Billy's a great personality,' said Sissy. 'Never seems to lose his cool. So you're at Hyde Park, too? How's it going for you?'

'It's OK. It's good. I think if we stay together Billy and me will open our own restaurant when we graduate. My whole family, they've always been in that kind of business. Restaurants, hotels. It's just that – you know.'

Sissy sipped her wine and waited for T-Yon to say more. It had sounded from her intonation as if she wanted to say more. *It's just that – you know –* what, *exactly*? T-Yon looked back at her, saying nothing, but then she gave a quick, nervous laugh.

'Go on, T-Yon,' Sissy encouraged her. 'What are you worried about? *Something's* eating you, isn't it?'

'You can tell that?'

'I think I've been living on this planet long enough to sense when a person has something on their mind. You don't have to tell me if you don't want to, but that's the reason you're here, isn't it?'

T-Yon blushed. 'Billy's always talking about you and I wanted to meet you so much. I've been nagging him for weeks to bring me here. But now that I *am* here, I feel like I'm wasting your time.'

'Oh for God's sake, don't you worry about *that*,' said Sissy, flapping her hand. 'Time is something I have plenty of, in abundance. Ever since my Frank was taken away from me, all those years ago, it's just me and Mr Boots, and the days go by so slow, they're like windmills turning when there's scarcely any wind.'

T-Yon said, 'Billy told me all about your fortune-telling. You know – the cards that you use.'

'The DeVane cards, yes.'

'He said they're like Tarot cards? I never heard of them before.'

'They're kind of like Tarot cards, yes. But for starters, they're very much bigger, and each individual card is a whole lot more complicated than any Tarot card. For instance, the DeVane cards won't just tell that you're going to meet the man of your dreams, they'll tell you that you're going to hate his brother, because his brother is unkind to animals, and that his mother cooks so badly that you sometimes wonder if she's trying to poison you.'

'Wow,' said T-Yon.

'Well, yes, *wow*. They're amazing, if you know how to read them, but they're not at all easy to read if you don't have the facility. Me, for some reason, I've always been able to read them without any trouble at all, ever since I was ten or eleven years old. Don't ask me how, or why, but I can see what's going to happen tomorrow afternoon just as clearly as I can remember what happened yesterday afternoon. With the help of the cards, of course.'

T-Yon said, 'Would you read them for me? I know that people usually pay you to do it, and I can pay you.'

'You'll do no such thing. You're Billy's girlfriend.'

'I know, but I don't want you to think that I'm taking advantage.'

Sissy stood up and went over to the carved walnut bureau that stood underneath the window. The rain was still gushing noisily over the guttering, where the downpipe was blocked with last fall's leaves. Frank had always been good at maintenance. He would have been up there months ago with his ladder and his trowel, clearing it out. But the long dead can't clean out gutters, any more than they can hold us in their arms and tell us how much they used to love us.

She opened the left-hand drawer and took out the worn cardboard box that contained the DeVane cards. On the front of the box there was a picture of a clown with a red hat and a deathly white face, holding up a complicated key in his left hand and a glass ball in his right. He had an extraordinary expression on his face, the expression of somebody who is still laughing a loud and artificial laugh, but is right on the edge of screaming with fury. '*Oh, you think that's funny, do you? You think that's so–o–o fricking funny?*'

The curly circus-style lettering above the clown's head said *Images d'Amour*, meaning *Pictures of Love*, but Sissy knew from years of experience that the cards didn't necessarily predict love that had a happy ending. They could show you a passionate love affair, but a love affair that might be brought to a bloody conclusion by a jealous husband rushing into the bedroom and stabbing both of the lovers with two enormous kitchen knives. They could show you a beautiful new baby girl and her doting parents, and then foretell that the baby would drown in a garden pond before she reached the age of two, surrounded by ducks.

Sissy always thought that the DeVane cards showed life as it really was, without any false hope. In the DeVane cards, Death stood patiently by the window, staring at the rain, but knowing that sooner or later the time would come for him to turn around.

'Here they are,' said Sissy, coming back across the living room and showing T-Yon the box. 'They were engraved and printed in France in the eighteenth century, and this is the only pack I've ever seen. There *are* others, so I'm told, but I don't think anybody uses them to tell fortunes, the way I do. Probably because they don't know how, or else they *do* know how but they're scared to. Like I told you,' she added, tapping her forehead, 'you have to have the facility.'

T-Yon touched the box with her fingertips, as if for luck. 'They're *huge*. And that clown. He's real creepy looking, isn't he?'

'He's called *Le Serrurier Riant*, the Laughing Locksmith. He's showing you that he can unlock the future. Key in one hand, you see? Crystal ball in the other.'

Sissy sat down and slid the cards out of the box. 'Before I start, T-Yon, I really need to know why you wanted me to tell your fortune so badly. It's a hell of a drive from Hyde Park to here, especially on a day like this. Forty miles at least.'

T-Yon didn't answer at first, so Sissy said, 'You didn't come here just to find out if you and Billy are suited for each other, did you, or if you're going to make a real career out of your cookery?'

T-Yon raised her left hand in front of her face, looking at Sissy through her fingers. Sissy knew exactly what it meant, when people did that. They were about to tell her something that they couldn't hold in for very much longer, but which made them feel confused, or guilty, or deeply ashamed.

'I've been having these dreams,' she said, so quietly that Sissy could hardly hear her.

'You want to speak louder, sweetheart?' Sissy asked her. 'I'm a little deaf in my left ear. And whatever it is that's upsetting you, it won't be cured by whispering.'

'Sorry,' said T-Yon, and took her hand away from her face. 'I've been having these dreams about my older brother, Everett. Not dreams, really, nightmares. But worse than any nightmares I've ever had before. I know I've only just met you but after what Billy told me about you—'

'Go on,' Sissy coaxed her. 'It's like I said. You can tell me if you want to but you don't have to tell me if you don't.'

'Well – Everett has just restored this old hotel in Baton Rouge. That's what he does, him and his business partner, he finds these run-down hotels and he restores them and gives them all of their glamour back. They've done two so far, the Shenandoah Suites and the Denham Palace, and The Red Hotel is their third.'

'Sounds like he's pretty successful, your brother.'

'He is. He has been. But about three weeks ago, not long

after he'd opened The Red Hotel, I started having these night-mares about him.'

'OK . . .'

T-Yon said, 'They're really embarrassing, but they're horrible, too. And they're always the same, night after night. I haven't told anybody about them, not even Billy. But I've been beginning to think that if they don't stop soon, I should maybe go talk to my doctor.'

'Instead, you've decided to come to me,' said Sissy. 'So let's see if I can help you.'

T-Yon paused again, but then she took a deep breath and said, 'I'm lying in bed in this hotel room. For some reason I know that it's The Red Hotel, but it's not like The Red Hotel the way it is now. I mean, Everett and his partner have remodeled it completely, so that it's all red-velvet drapes and gilt-framed mirrors. You know, like old-style Baton Rouge. But in my nightmare the room is all brown and green, with a nineteen sixties TV and a nineteen sixties telephone with a dial on it. And it *smells*, too. I've never been able to smell anything in a dream before, but this hotel room has a very strong smell like lavender furniture wax and bug spray. I can still smell it even after I've woken up.'

Sissy raised her eyebrows. 'That's highly unusual. Most of us can *hear* things in dreams, you know – like people talking, or singing, or the ocean crashing on the shore. And most of us can *feel* things, too. But to *smell* your dream, that's very rare, although my late husband once woke me up in the middle of the night because he swore that he could smell smoke, when there was no smoke. But anyhow, carry on. What happens in this nightmare?'

T-Yon said, 'I'm lying on the bed, like I said, and the thing is that I'm not wearing anything at all except for a black garter belt and black nylon stockings. I've never worn a garter belt and stockings in my life, *ever*, which makes this so weird. The door opens and my brother Everett walks in. He's wearing a Mardi Gras mask – dead white, with very black slanty eyes – but I know at once that it's him. He's not wearing anything, either, except for long black socks, and I've never known him to wear long black socks – like, *never*, ever.'

'OK,' said Sissy. Outside, it had suddenly stopped raining, and the room gradually began to fill with light.

'Everett doesn't hesitate. He comes across to the bed and he climbs on top of me. I know what he's going to do but I don't try to stop him. In fact I feel like I want him – not because I love him but because I feel that he's going to make it worth my while. It's like I'm a prostitute, rather than his sister. It's really hard to explain. He starts to have sex with me and even though he's my older brother I don't resist him at all. On the other hand I'm not too enthusiastic either. I just lie there and watch TV and let him do it.'

'What's on the TV?' asked Sissy. 'Is it any program you recognize?'

'Is that important?'

'I don't know. It could be.'

'It's in black and white . . . something like *The Lucy Show*. The TV is slowed right down, so I can't hear what anybody's saying. All I can hear is Everett panting underneath that mask.'

'I hope you don't mind me asking you this, but don't you feel even the least bit turned on?'

Sissy could tell that T-Yon was taken aback by her directness, but before she consulted the DeVane cards it was important for her to know as much as possible about T-Yon's nightmare – what she could hear, what she could see, and how she was feeling. Sometimes the smallest detail could unlock the whole secret of a frightening dream. A face glimpsed high up at an attic window. A tatty old crow, perched on a distant gatepost. A small child sitting by the roadside, sobbing his heart out.

'Turned on?' said T-Yon. She thought about it, and then she added, 'No, I guess I'm not – not really. I can *feel* him making love to me, physically. I can feel him inside me, but it's not really exciting.'

'Does it go on for long, this love-making?'

'Some nights it seems to go on for hours. Other nights it's over in just a few seconds. But it always ends the same. Everett makes love to me faster and faster and then he suddenly stops, and bunches up, and lets out this terrible *aaahhhhhhhh*! At the same time I have this sliding feeling in my stomach.'

T-Yon ran her fingertip down in a vertical line from her breastbone to her waist. 'It's the most horrible sensation you can imagine. It's like somebody's cutting me open with a really sharp scalpel – right through my skin and my muscles and all the layers of fat and everything.'

She stopped for a moment, and took two or three steadying breaths. Then she said, 'Everett, he's making this kind of a whimpering noise. You know – like a puppy when somebody's run it over. It's muffled, because he still hasn't taken off his mask. I'm too shocked to make any sound at all. I lift my head and look down at my stomach and it's gaping wide open. Everett's still on top of me, and *his* stomach is gaping open too.'

'My God,' said Sissy. She was really craving for a cigarette now, and she wished Billy would hurry back from the store. On the other hand, she was anxious to hear the rest of T-Yon's nightmare before he returned. She didn't want T-Yon to hold anything back, which she might very well do if Billy were here. Hearing that his new girlfriend was having nightmares about sex with her own brother wouldn't be the greatest aphrodisiac of all time.

'I look down. I've seen it night after night and it's always the same, but it still gives me the fremeers, every time, without fail. All of our intestines are tangled up together, Everett's and mine, so that I can't tell where his begin and mine end. They're like spaghetti, and they're so twisted and knotted that I know that we could never untangle ourselves. The only way to separate us would be for somebody to cut us apart, slice right through our intestines, and I know that would kill us.'

'Does anybody try?'

'No, that's pretty much the end of the nightmare. I hear a clock striking and that's when I always wake up. Well – almost.'

'Almost?'

'Yes . . . before I do, I see the door open. Only three or four inches, but enough to see that there's a boy standing outside – a boy with red curly hair and a very white face.'

'Does he *say* anything, this red-haired boy? Does he move? Does he come into the room?'

T-Yon shook her head. 'He doesn't speak and he doesn't move at all.'

'Do you recognize him from anywhere?'

'No. He just stands there staring at us, me and Everett, lying on the bed with our intestines all mixed up together. I can't be sure, but sometimes I think he's smiling at us. He really frightens me. My grandma would have called him a *possedé*, that's Cajun for a really bad child. Like, you know, *possessed*.'

'But *then* you wake up?'

'Yes,' said T-Yon. 'Always shaking and sweating and always feeling so nauseous. I mean I actually feel as if my insides have been dragged right out of me and all jumbled up and then crammed right back inside of me, for real. It's like I've been quickly sewn back up again only a second before I open my eyes.'

'Well,' said Sissy. 'That's one hell of a nightmare.'

T-Yon sat right on the edge of the couch with an imploring look in her eyes, her hands clasped tightly together, as if her nightmares were a sin and she was praying for Sissy to absolve her. Sissy took another two or three thoughtful sips of wine before she said anything. She needed time to think what these nightmares could possibly mean, because they were crowded with so many signs and innuendoes.

Sissy had learned from years of fortune-telling that recurring nightmares were almost always a warning, but in T-Yon's case it was difficult to say exactly what she was being warned about. Her waking relationship with her brother Everett was obviously healthy and non-sexual, and yet her nightmare about him was grossly incestuous. It not only suggested a carnal relationship, but something much more – a visceral entanglement. Their destinies were so closely twisted together that they were like conjoined twins, who shared even their intestines.

Yet there were so many more questions to be answered. Why was she wearing stockings and a garter belt, which she never wore in real life? Why was Everett wearing a Mardi Gras mask? What was the significance of the black-and-white comedy on TV, if any? Why did T-Yon feel that having sex with Everett would be 'worth her while', and what exactly did that mean? Who was the red-haired *possedé*, peering in through the door?

Sissy was still trying to answer all of these questions when they heard Billy honking his horn outside, immediately followed by Mr Boots barking.

'Listen,' she asked T-Yon, 'do you have time to stay for the rest of the afternoon? You can even stay the night if you don't want to drive back to Hyde Park today. Sherlock Holmes used to talk about a "three-pipe problem" which would take him at least the length of time to smoke three pipes to sort out. I think this nightmare of yours might be a three-reading problem.'

'But what's your first impression about it?' asked T-Yon. 'Do you think I need to be seriously worried about it, or do you think I'm just being dumb and letting my imagination run away with me? Maybe if I change my diet? Or give up drinking – not that I drink a whole lot? Or stop stressing out so much?'

Sissy shrugged one shoulder and tried to give her a reassuring smile. 'Maybe, yes, sure, it could be something like that. It could be that you're allergic to some food additive, or that you're pushing yourself too hard at college. But let me read your cards for you, T-Yon. Then we'll soon see what we're up against.'

T-Yon said, 'Thanks, Ms Sawyer. I so much appreciate it.' She glanced toward the kitchen to make sure that Billy wasn't listening, and then she added, almost mouthing it, 'I can't tell you how desperate I've been.'

'Call me Sissy, for God's sake,' Sissy told her.

T-Yon stood up and went through to the kitchen to help Billy with the groceries. Sissy stayed where she was, with a furrow in her forehead. She didn't like the sound of this nightmare at all – especially not the way in which it kept repeating itself, night after night. That didn't sound like a food-allergy nightmare or a nightmare related to worry or overwork. Sissy's years of experience with the DeVane cards had given her a psychic sensitivity which very few other fortune-tellers could match, and T-Yon's nightmare had made her feel deeply uneasy.

It reminded her of one particular DeVane card, *La Cuisine De Nuit*, the Night Kitchen, which was a card that cautioned against futile self-sacrifice. She very much hoped that this card wouldn't turn up when she read T-Yon's future.

One other disturbing detail was the clock that T-Yon could hear striking. That meant that whatever catastrophe these night-mares foretold, it was imminent. It was going to arrive in days, rather than weeks.

Mother and Son

Before she started her first reading, Sissy took Billy and T-Yon out on to the verandah so that she could smoke a cigarette and drink another glass of wine. She filled a yellow ceramic bowl with her home-made Parmesan cheese straws, sprinkled with sesame seeds, and brought out a jug of celery sticks, too, which they could dip in her extra-hot home-made salsa.

Billy popped open a can of Schlitz and sat with his feet up on the railing. 'So did T-Yon tell you all about her nightmares?'

'She did, yes,' Sissy nodded. The sky had cleared now, and the sun was shining, so that everything sparkled. Mr Boots was lying at her feet, panting.

'She won't tell *me* about them,' said Billy. 'If I've asked her once I've asked her a million times, but she flat out refuses.'

'That's because you would take them all the wrong way,' said T-Yon.

'How do you know I would, unless you tell me?'

'Because I just do.'

'I think you misunderestimate me, as George W. Bush used to say.'

'No, I don't. It's just that I know how touchy you can be. Look at that time Daniel was showing me how to make that Béarnaise sauce. You totally lost it.'

'He didn't need to cup his hand around your boob. There's nothing about *that* in the recipe for Béarnaise sauce.'

'He didn't cup his hand around my boob. He was showing me how to stir, that's all.'

'Oh, that's what you call it. It sure looked like *he* was pretty stirred, I can tell you.'

'You see? That's exactly why I wouldn't tell you about my nightmares.'

When Sissy had crushed out a second cigarette, she said to T-Yon, 'Come on, sweetheart. Come back inside and I'll give you a reading.'

'Can I sit in?' asked Billy.

'No, you can't, Billy-bob. Not this time, anyhow. You can peel some potatoes for me. I think I'll make us one of my potato and mushroom bakes for supper.'

'Slave-driver.'

Sissy and T-Yon went back into the living room. T-Yon sat down on the couch and said, 'I don't know why I'm feeling so nervous.'

'*Relax*,' Sissy told her. 'The more you open your mind, the clearer your reading will be. The DeVane cards pick up on your thoughts and your emotions, and they tell you in pictures what your thoughts and emotions mean, and where your life will be taking you next. But it makes it harder for them to give you a full and accurate prediction if you deliberately hide anything that you're embarrassed about, or ashamed of. So – please. Do try to let yourself go. I'm not going to judge you. The cards are not going to judge you. We're just going to show you what your future has in store for you, that's all.'

She picked up the deck and sorted through them until she found a card called *La Sorcière Blanche*. She passed it across to T-Yon and said, 'This is your Predictor card. In other words, this is the card that represents *you*. Lay it down on the coffee table and place the palm of your hand on top of it.'

T-Yon held the card up and frowned at it. 'This is me?'

'The White Witch,' Sissy translated for her. 'I could have chosen the Pastry Maker for you, or the Cook, but I think this suits you better.'

The card showed a disturbingly beautiful young woman standing in a cave, stirring a three-legged witch's cauldron with a long-handled ladle. She was wearing a tall, white conical hat with her blonde hair braided on either side of her head into two buns, like Princess Leia; but apart from that she was naked. In place of pubic hair, however, she had a purple flowering hydrangea.

Peeping out of the broth that was bubbling in the cauldron were several grotesque fish, and a spiny lobster; and also a very tiny girl, or maybe she was only a doll.

The expression on the White Witch's face was riveting, as if she were daring whoever looked at this card to turn away.

Behind her, clearly visible through the mouth of the cave, three poles were standing in a sloping field, arranged like the crosses on Calvary. On one of them was impaled the severed head of a donkey. On the other two, the severed heads of a reindeer, complete with antlers, and a Chinese-looking woman.

Beyond the field rose dark pine forests, and distant mountains. High up in the sky, among thundery clouds, a kite was flying with its tail on fire.

'This is *seriously* weird,' said T-Yon. 'What about these heads, stuck on these sticks? What do they mean? And what about this tiny little girl, inside of this cooking pot?'

'It depends what the other cards come up with,' Sissy told her. 'Everything that you can see on this card has a meaning, but the meaning always varies from one person to the next. That burning kite could mean that you're prepared to take risks to be a high-flyer in your catering career. But it could also mean that your time is running out – that the kite itself is going to start burning soon, and drop to the ground. It's like that little girl. She may be a doll but she may be a real child. We'll have to see.'

She shuffled the remainder of the cards and then she laid them out like a Cross of Lorraine, almost the same as most fortune-tellers would lay them out for a Tarot reading. Then she arranged three more cards above them, face down, in a fan pattern.

T-Yon placed her Predictor card on the coffee table and pressed the flat of her hand on top of it.

'OK,' said Sissy. 'Now I want you to ask the cards a question. Don't tell me what it is. Think hard about it, and they'll answer it for you.'

T-Yon closed her eyes and frowned in concentration. Then she opened them again and said, 'Right. I've done it. I've asked them.'

'You're ready for this?' Sissy asked her.

T-Yon nodded. 'Ready as I'll ever be.'

Sissy turned over the first card. It was called *La Châtelaine*, and it showed a cross-section of a four-story town-house, like a dolls' house with the front open. In each of its nine rooms stood a thin, narrow-shouldered woman in a pale gray gown – the same woman in every room, unless she was nontuplets. Her black hair was pinned up tight, and her face was pinched, as if in disapproval. She wore a white floor-length apron over her gown, and around her waist hung a chain with nine keys dangling from it.

'The Mistress of the House,' said Sissy.

T-Yon peered at the card with a frown. 'She doesn't look too happy, does she?'

'I'm not surprised. Take a closer look at each of those rooms.'

In the living room, a man was sitting cross-legged in a high-backed armchair, holding up a newspaper. He had a high wing collar, but no head. In the parlor next door, a maid in a mob cap was kneeling in front of the fire, prodding it with a poker. The scene looked normal enough at first glance, until T-Yon saw that a young woman's head was hanging upside down out of the chimney, her hair in flames and her face blackened with soot.

The scene in the kitchen was even more disturbing. A bald, stocky cook in a bloodstained apron was chopping up meat with a cleaver. On the chopping block in front of him was a grisly mixture of rabbits' heads and pigs' trotters, as well as human hands and knee joints.

Behind him, a red-haired kitchen maid was setting out a row of pies to cool on the window sill. Out of the crusts of each of the pies, human fingers were protruding. A fat man with a walrus moustache was standing right outside the window, holding up a pocket watch.

In every room, something gruesome and strange was happening. Even the portraits that hung on either side of the staircase depicted people with empty eye sockets, or people with their backs turned, or people whose faces were distorted in expressions of alarm.

In the smaller bedrooms, three of the beds looked at first as if they were covered with coarsely woven gray blankets, but then T-Yon saw that they were actually swarming with heaps of gray rats. On one bed, from underneath a tangle of rodents, a woman's hand was dangling down; and on another bed, a child's bare foot was protruding, but these were the only visible signs of what the rats were feasting on.

To begin with, T-Yon could see nothing horrific in the master bedroom, until she noticed the congealing blood that was sliding out from underneath the wardrobe doors, and the bloody red handprint on the white chamber-pot below the bed.

'This is just *horrible*,' she said, handing the card back to Sissy. 'Like, what does it all mean? How can this have anything to do with me and my nightmares?'

'I don't know yet,' Sissy admitted. 'But *La Châtelaine* is the very first card and this means that it's an indicator of everything that's going to happen to you next in your life.'

'I'm going to see people having their heads cut off, and being stuffed up chimneys, and eaten by rats?'

'No, no. The card isn't telling you that. But it *is* saying that your nightmares have their origins in a house someplace, a house in which some very upsetting things happened, and where things like that are very likely to happen again. Not necessarily people getting chopped to pieces and baked into pies – but things which led to people being seriously hurt, either physically or psychologically.'

'You're making me feel frightened now.'

Sissy gave her a serious, sympathetic look. 'I'm sorry, T-Yon. That's the last thing I want to do. But I've never once known the DeVane cards to be wrong. Not substantially, anyhow.'

'But this woman, this chatelaine?' T-Yon persisted. 'I've never known *anybody* who looks like that. Well – maybe my old math teacher, Miss Berthelot, just a little. Is she a real person, or what?'

'Yes,' said Sissy, 'I'm pretty certain that she is. Or *was*. Let me put it this way: she's more than just a sign, or a metaphor.

Now, you see this fat fellow with the big moustache standing outside the kitchen window – *he's* a metaphor. I'd say that he's what amounted to an officer of the law in the year seventeen something or other, and as soon as those pies have cooled off, he's going to be opening them up to see what's inside them, and if he finds fingers and ears, he's going to be making an arrest on a charge of cannibalism.'

'You can tell all that, just from this one card?'

Sissy smiled. 'I did tell you, T-Yon. I have the facility. To me, these cards are like a picture book; or maybe a three-D movie. I pick them up and they come alive, and I can understand almost at once what they're showing me.'

'So what are they showing you about this chatelaine?'

'To be honest with you, it's not entirely clear, not yet. We'll have to look at some more cards. But I do think that she's the instigator of all of this. I don't fully understand *how* or *why*, not yet, but, in some way, this woman is the root cause of your nightmares.'

'Is she good or is she evil? I mean – do you think she's giving me a warning about something, or is she trying to scare me?'

'Again, T-Yon, I'm not entirely sure. She doesn't look particularly *shocked* by what she's found in each of these rooms, does she? This guy with no head reading the newspaper and all of these chopped-up people in the kitchen. I get the feeling that it's the *mess* that's upsetting her the most. All of this blood, and all of these arms and legs, and all of these rats doing their droppings. Look at her. She's not flinging up her arms in horror, is she? She's not screaming. She's just standing there, looking distinctly pissed.'

T-Yon looked at the chatelaine more closely. 'You're right. She does look angry, doesn't she? I don't think I like her at all.'

Sissy said, 'Anyhow – let's see if the next card can throw some more light on the subject, shall we?'

'OK. But let's hope it's not quite so horrible as this one.'

Sissy turned the second card over. It carried the picture of a boy, maybe eight or nine years old, wearing a floppy brown leather hat that covered the back of his neck, like the hats once worn by colliers or icemen. His shoulders were narrow and his face was pinched, like that of the chatelaine. Apart from his floppy hat, he was wearing a baggy brown jerkin and knee britches. His boots had no laces in them and looked very shabby and run down.

He was standing in a grassy field, under a sky filled with billowing white clouds. Behind him, six or seven naked young women were dancing in a line. They were all wearing immense hats piled up with apples and pomegranates and game birds and feathers, and one of them even had a large fish coiled around the brim.

In one hand the boy was holding up a lantern with a dazzling white light inside it, even though it was daytime; and in the other hand, a long metal spike with a T-shaped handle. The caption said *La Piqûre de Guêpe*.

'The Wasp Sting,' said T-Yon. 'This card is really so strange.'

'Stranger than you think,' Sissy told her. She pointed to the ground around the boy's feet and said, 'Look at the grass. Stare at it, until your eyes go slightly out of focus.'

It appeared at first as if the wind had randomly ruffled the grass into swirls and waves, but as she continued to stare at it, T-Yon could gradually see patterns forming, and these patterns weren't random at all, but human faces, with hollow eyes and noses and wide-open mouths. Human faces, scores of them, formed out of nothing more than windswept grass.

What was more, they were all individual faces, all different. Some of them were obviously men but many more were women. All they had in common was that they were screaming, as if they knew that they were trapped in this field forever and could never escape.

Red Stain

Everett was winding up his conversation with the mayor's office when his deputy manager, Luther Broody, rapped at his open office door and mouthed the single word, '*Problem.*'

Everett said, 'That's fine, sir. That's terrific. So long as his honor can be here by three. Thank you. Thank you again. Yes. Thank you. Goodbye.'

He tossed his phone on to the heaps of correspondence on his desk, tilted his chair back and looked up at Luther with a self-satisfied beam. 'That's it, L.B. Everything's sorted. The mayor has agreed to cut the ribbon and make a short speech and even better than that he's going to bring his daughter, Lolana, along, too. If the reigning Miss Teen Baton Rouge doesn't pull in the media, I don't know what the hell will.'

'We have ourselves a problem,' Luther repeated. Luther was a bulky African-American with a glossy bald dome like a mahogany newel post and bulging wide-apart eyes and a look about him that always led people to ask if he was Samuel L. Jackson's younger brother. They never said 'Samuel L. Jackson's younger but enormously fatter brother' but Luther could tell what they were thinking by the way they looked at his belly overhanging his belt. Luther had never been able to say no to a king shrimp po'boy.

'OK,' said Everett. 'What's gone wrong now? You sorted out that elevator problem with Kone's, didn't you?'

'We have a stain on one of the bedside rugs in Suite Seven-Oh-Three.'

Everett blinked at him. 'A *stain*? What kind of a stain? Can't Clarice deal with it? For Christ's sake, just change the rug. Don't tell me we don't have any spare rugs.'

'I think you should come take a look at it first.'

'L.B., I'm up to my neck at the moment. I have a meeting in about five minutes with Paul Artigo for which I'm already going to be late and then I have a lunch date with Theresa Overby and after that I have a conference call booked with the bank.'

'It looks like blood.'

'It's *blood*? How much blood?'

'A whole lot of blood. At least half a body full, I'd say.'

'You're kidding me.'

'I wish I was, Mr Everett, sir. But I think we may have to consider calling the poh-lice.'

Everett stood up. 'OK, let's check it out. Shit, this is all I need.'

He drew back the sliding window that connected his office with his personal assistant next door and said, 'Bella, I'll be back in five. Can you tell Raymonde that the mayor is coming for definite? And can you ask Olivia what's happening with those revised media releases? She promised me she'd have them all done by this morning.'

Bella was a handsome fifty-year-old woman with her hair fixed in a gray French pleat and a sharp line in pale gray suits. 'Yes, sir, boss,' she replied, without looking up. Everett knew that she would do it. She was the most efficient PA he had ever employed. She would even remind him when it was the doorman's daughter's birthday.

Everett lifted his cream linen coat from the back of his chair and shrugged it on. He straightened his bright red necktie in the mirror beside the door, and then followed Luther out of his office and across the hotel lobby.

Several guests were gathered around the fountain in the center of the lobby, talking and laughing. Although the hotel would not be officially opening until Friday afternoon, its refurbishment was ninety-nine percent complete and Everett had been taking reservations for more than a month. All that needed finishing off now was the decorative tiling in the sauna and the planting of camellias on the roof garden.

'Who found it, the rug?' asked Everett. 'It wasn't a guest, was it?'

Luther shook his head. 'Housekeeper, making the room ready for this evening. The guests are coming in from Cincinnati and they don't touch down at BTR until eight oh five, so they won't be checking in before nine at the earliest.'

'That's one mercy. We do have an alternative suite free, in case?'

'Seven-Oh-Nine. It's not up to the same specification, of course, but if we have to alter their booking, I guess we could offer it to them gratis.'

Everett looked at him sharply, so he added, 'Or, you know, at a ten percent discount.' Another sharp look. 'Or maybe five.'

The elevator arrived with a soft chiming sound and they

stepped aside to let out a party of six or seven elderly men wearing Kiwanis baseball caps. Everett nodded and smiled to them and said, 'Have a great day, gentlemen. Good to have you stay with us.'

'Fine hotel!' said one of them. 'Can't believe how great you've fixed it up! I stayed here once in nineteen seventy-nine and it was the *pits*, I can tell you! You could hardly get near the bar for all the women of easy virtue.'

'I'm sorry to tell you that the women of easy virtue have all moved on,' Everett told him.

'Damn shame!' piped up another Kiwanis. 'I didn't bring my wife with me on this trip! Don't know any good phone numbers, do you?'

'Sure,' said one of his companions. 'Southside Gardens Retirement Community. Plenty of women there, Martin – and all of them a darn sight sprightlier than you!' and they all wheezed with laughter.

Everett and Luther went up in the elevator to the seventh floor. In the three mirrored walls, where they could see six more Everetts and six more Luthers, Everett thought how tired he looked, or maybe it was just the lighting. He was tall and rangy, with dirty-blond hair that stuck up straight no matter how much he tried to wax it down, and he had the same pronounced cheekbones as his sister, as well as the same green eyes, although his chin was squarer, like his father's. His girlfriend, Zelda, always complained that he looked as if he worried too much and didn't eat enough, and she was right: he did, and he didn't.

When they reached the seventh floor they turned left and walked along the corridor to the very end. The corridor was quietly carpeted in crimson, and there were gilded antique-style lamps all the way along it. Their interior designer had been given the brief of 'plush Southern boudoir.' Everett and his partner, Stanley Tierney, had wanted their guests to feel as if they were back in the nineteenth-century Baton Rouge of paddle-wheel casinos, piano bars, and saloons like the Rainbow House, with its wines, liquors and 'segars'.

Clarice Johnson, the head housekeeper, was waiting for them outside the open door to Suite 703, along with one of her maids. Clarice was a small, round African-American woman with a huge pompadour fastened at the back with a bright red bow, but although she was small she was tireless and dynamic, and had a relentless eye for detail. If a toilet roll hadn't been folded into a point and fastened with a Red Hotel sticker, the offending maid would be made to feel that she was the laziest, most shiftless girl that Clarice had ever had the misfortune to employ, and that she had let down not only herself, but her family, and The Red Hotel, and the entire Louisiana hospitality industry.

'Hi, Clarice,' said Everett. 'And this is . . .?'

'Ella-mae,' said Clarice. 'She started working here only two days ago.'

Ella-mae was hugging her shoulders with her thin black elbows sticking out, and her eyes were darting from side to side as if she were looking for a way to escape. Everett said, 'Hey, Ella-mae. There's nothing for you to fret about. Just tell me what happened.'

'Go on, Ella-mae,' Clarice encouraged her.

'Just as soon as I goes into the bedroom I sees it right there,' said Ella-mae, in a high, unhappy whine.

'You mean the rug beside the bed?'

'That's right. It's supposed to be white but it ain't white it's all this blood color. I don't know how it could have gotten that way so I goes up close and I kneels down and I touches it with my finger. And it's wet, and on my glove it's all red like it really *is* blood. I runs right out of the room and I calls for Ms Johnson.'

'Thanks, Ella-mae,' said Everett. 'You did just the right thing. You can go now, but please don't leave the hotel yet, OK? I may need to talk to you some more.'

And the cops may want to question you, too, he thought, but he didn't tell her that.

He turned to Luther and said, 'Come on, L.B. Let me check this rug out for myself.'

Clarice ushered Ella-mae away to the service elevator, her arm around her shoulders. Everett pushed open the door to Suite 703 a little wider, using his elbow, in case there were fingerprints on it.

Inside, the suite was furnished in grandiose nineteenth-century style, with buttoned armchairs and a red-velvet couch that was heaped with cushions. The drapes were red velvet, too, and drawn back from the windows with gold silk cords. In spite of the period effect, the room smelled very new. New plaster, new floor-sealant, new paint. A gilt-framed antique mirror hung above a mock marble fireplace, but on the facing wall there was a fifty-inch plasma TV screen.

Off to the right, the door to the bedroom was wide open. Everett could see the end of the bed with its red-satin bedspread and the overhead chandelier shining. He crossed the living room slowly, checking the polished wood floor for footprints or any other marks, but all he found was a yellow duster that Ella-mae must have dropped as she came running out of the bedroom in a panic. He left it where it was.

The bedroom was decorated in the same rococo style as the living room. It was dominated by a king-size tester bed with heavy, red brocade curtains, another red-velvet couch, and a gilded dressing table that could almost have doubled as an altar.

The stained rug was lying on the floor right in front of him, slightly askew and rumpled up in the middle. It was a large rug, at least seven feet long and four feet wide. As Ella-mae had said, it was supposed to be white, but, except for one small triangular corner and half of one edge, it was soaked through with glistening crimson.

'You see?' said Luther. 'Sure *looks* like blood, don't it, even if it ain't?'

Everett got down on the floor on his hands and knees next to the rug and leaned right over it. He sniffed, but it didn't smell of anything distinctive, like paint. If this really *was* blood, it was fresh, and hadn't yet acquired that rusty tang that blood did when it dried.

He knelt up straight and looked around the bedroom with a frown. 'I don't get this. I mean, I really don't get this at all. Where the hell did this come from? And who the hell would have wanted to put it here? And why?'

'You can search me,' said Luther. 'Even if it *is* blood, maybe it ain't *human* blood. Maybe somebody killed some animal on this rug. Some goat maybe. You know like those Muslims do, when they cut their throats and hang them up to bleed to death. What do they call it? *Halal.* Or maybe some voodoo priestess sacrificed two or three chickens.'

Everett stood up and brushed the knees of his pants. 'Get a grip, L.B. This suite hasn't been occupied yet, has it? Not by anyone?'

'No, sir, it hasn't. Tonight's guests are going to be the very first.'

'Nobody has stayed here and even if somebody *did* manage to get in, how did they smuggle in a human sacrifice, or a live goat, or enough chickens to produce this much blood? And how did they do it without making any noise? And why is the blood only on the rug, and not splattered all over the floor and up the walls?'

Luther looked thoughtful. He sniffed, and then he said, 'Supposing that it *is* blood, and it comes from some person, or some animal, or however many chickens, then they was killed on it someplace else, and the rug was brung in here afterward.'

Everett nodded. 'Exactly. That's the only explanation, isn't it?'

'Sure. But it still don't tell us who done it, or *why* they done it.'

'There's something else it doesn't tell us, and that is what we're going to do about it. We could throw the rug into the incinerator, and not say anything more about it. That's the simplest solution.'

'Well, sure it is,' said Luther. 'But what if the person who done this comes back when we have guests staying here? Whoever it is, he or she has acquired themselves a key card to let themselves in. Maybe even a master key. What if they come back and do harm to one of our guests?'

'You can change all the security codes, can't you?'

'Of course I can, for sure. But that still ain't no guarantee, is it? If any of our guests got themselves killed or injured and the police found out that we incinerated this rug then we would both be in serious doo-doo, wouldn't we, on account of destroying material evidence?'

'How are they going to find that out? You and me, L.B., we're the only people who know about it.'

'You and me and Clarice and Ella-mae and anybody else that Ella-mae has told already. Apart from that, we both have a conscience, don't we?'

'OK. You win.' Everett had forgotten that Luther used to be a sergeant in the Baton Rouge PD, apart from being a lay preacher at his local Baptist church. He knew that Luther was right, and that they should really call the police, but – Jesus – he had so many other problems to deal with, like a critical shortage of kitchen staff and a series of inexplicable glitches in the hotel's computer system. This mysterious blood-soaked rug was just about the last thing he needed.

He took his cellphone and flipped it open. 'This is going to give us some grade-A publicity for our grand opening ceremony, wouldn't you say? "Cops probe inexplicable blood-stain at Red Hotel." Folks are going to start asking if it's safe for them to stay here even before we're officially open for business.'

Luther said, 'Wait up, Mr Everett. We don't have to rush into nothing. First off, before we do anything at all, I'll have the security team search the whole building, top to bottom. Maybe that will give us a clue as to who brung this rug in here. If there's anybody staying here who didn't ought to be, we should find them for sure.'

'And if we don't? Then what?'

'I can't say for certain. Let's don't cross that bridge before we reaches it.'

Everett checked the time on his cellphone. He was ten minutes late for his meeting with Paul Artigo, the president and CEO of the Baton Rouge Convention and Visitors Bureau, a man he was anxious to schmooze, not antagonize.

'OK,' he said, 'why don't you instigate a search and get back to me later? I really have to go.'

He turned to leave the bedroom. Just as he did so, however, the front door of Suite 703 slammed shut, as if somebody had banged it in a temper.

'What the *hell* was that?' he said. He hurried to the front door, opened it, and stepped outside into the hallway. He looked to the right, toward the elevators. There was nobody in sight, which there should have been, even if the door-slammer had immediately run away.

He looked to the left, and as he did so, he saw the briefest flicker of a shadow at the very end of the hallway, next to the window. It was a tall, attenuated shadow which reached almost to the ceiling – not quite the shadow of a man but nothing like the shadow of one of the curtains. It vanished almost at once, but, as it did so, Everett had the strangest sensation of *compression*, like the window of an automobile being closed at speed. A moment of temporary deafness.

Luther came up behind him.

'What's up, Mr Everett?'

'Nothing. I don't know. I'd better get going.'

'Don't you start worrying yourself about this rug, Mr Everett. No matter what happens, no matter how weird it seems to be, there's always an explanation for everything. My Aunt Epiphany told me that, and she's a real genuine authentic voodoo queen.'

Everett continued to stare at the wall by the window where the shadow had been dancing. 'OK . . .' he said, slowly, although he couldn't understand why his skin felt so *prickly*, as if he had brushed up against poison ivy.

The Night Kitchen

Sissy had now turned over all of T-Yon's cards, except for the three cards arranged in a fan shape.

Some of the cards were bizarre. One showed a horse-drawn carriage being driven at breakneck speed by four monkeys in powdered wigs. On another, two hugely obese men were sitting under a sky that was black with rooks, greedily cramming their mouths full with struggling brown toads.

Yet another depicted a dead man lying in an open coffin while seven women in bird-like masks danced around him, all of them lifting up their voluminous petticoats to show that they were wearing nothing underneath.

'For some reason, this card is very, *very* meaningful,' said Sissy, holding up *Sept Putains De Danse*.

'You don't know why?' asked T-Yon.

'Not yet, I have to admit. But that's not unusual. Everything will fall into place, I promise you, like a jigsaw. It always does. Sometimes you get the answer before you get the question, and I think this is one of those times.'

'Seven women exposing themselves to a corpse? If that's the answer, I can't begin to imagine what the question is.'

Sissy looked down at all the DeVane cards that she had already turned over. 'Don't you worry, sweetheart. It's all beginning to come together. Like I said, your nightmares about your brother have definitely been set off by this woman, *La Châtelaine*. I don't yet know where her house is located, but if *this* reading doesn't tell us, we'll probably find out in the next.'

'But who is she? And why is she giving me these nightmares?'

'Again, I'm still not sure. But – here – look at this next card.'

The card depicted a gloomy prison cell, in which a woman and a boy were sitting on a bale of dirty straw, both in leg irons. The caption read *La Récompense Est Des Chaînes*, The Reward Is Chains.

'Look at their hands,' said Sissy. 'Blood red, halfway up to their elbows. That means that they've committed some really terrible crime, probably murder. In this reading, the woman is almost certainly the chatelaine and the boy is the same boy who was wearing the floppy brown leather hat. I'm almost one hundred percent sure that he's her son. So whatever they did, they were both caught and brought to justice and punished.

She swallowed some more wine, and thought for a while, lightly drumming on the prison card with her fingertips. Then she said, 'They *were* locked up, but I can sense that both of them are free now. They may have served their time, but I'm not feeling that. I'm feeling that maybe they're dead. All the same, I get the strongest sense that they're making a comeback. In fact I'm sure of it.'

'How can they do that, if they're dead?'

'Well – they shared a very powerful telepathic bond between them when they were alive and they would still have that same bond in the spirit world. That kind of psychic togetherness can sometimes develop between parents and their children, although it's usually much closer between mothers and sons – not so much between fathers and daughters.'

'But what do they want?'

'The cards tell me that they've come looking for two things. One is to settle some old scores. You see this double-headed ax at the side of this picture? That's the symbol for revenge. The other is to pick up where they left off. There they are, walking along a country road, with their backs to us. They're headed for that tall house in the distance, which looks pretty much like the same house in the chatelaine card. They're going back to the place they consider to be their home.'

'But why are they giving *me* nightmares? I don't know anybody like that. I never have.'

'You never knew them but they obviously know you. Or *of* you, anyhow.'

T-Yon shivered. 'They know me? Now you're *really* scaring me.'

Sissy reached across and squeezed her hand. 'It's better to be scared than to let yourself be caught unawares. In your heart you know that, don't you? I think that's why you came here to me looking for help, rather than go to your doctor. A doctor would have done nothing more than give you a prescription for Xanax and tell you to stop worrying so much.

'*Me*, on the other hand, I'm telling you exactly what your immediate future has in store for you, and I won't lie to you, T-Yon – your immediate future looks very strange, and maybe a little dangerous, too. We need to find out who these spirits are and why they're giving you such terrible nightmares, and we don't need to be wasting any time.'

'So how do we do that?'

'See this card – *Le Retour Effrayant*? This means that you'll soon be going on a long journey, although I doubt you'll be traveling by pony and trap, like the girl in the picture.'

'*Le Retour Effrayant*? What does that mean?'

'Literally translated, The Frightening Journey Back.'

'Oh, no. The Frightening Journey Back to where?'

'Someplace familiar, I would say, even if it *is* frightening. Look at the girl. She's holding up a hand mirror in front of her face, because she doesn't need to see the road ahead. She knows it already. All she wants to do is study her own expression. Now see here – there's a monk in a brown hood standing by the side of the road and he's leaning on a long red walking stick. Now, if *that* isn't a clue . . .'

T-Yon turned to Sissy wide-eyed. 'A red stick. Of course. That *has* to mean I'm going to Baton Rouge.'

Sissy smiled. 'I told you how much these cards could show you, didn't I? Now let's see who you're going to be visiting in Baton Rouge, as if you didn't know already.'

Sissy turned over the next card. 'This is *L'Asile De Mon Frère*.'

'*L'Asile*? Doesn't that mean . . .?'

'Yes. It means "asylum". This is your brother's madhouse – according to the cards, anyhow.'

T-Yon studied the card intently. After a while, she said, 'It's the same house, isn't it? It's the same house as the chatelaine's house. I'm sure of it. What do you think?'

'You're right,' said Sissy. 'They do look alike.'

The house in the asylum card was seen from the point of view of somebody standing very close to it, and looking up, so that it almost appeared to be collapsing on top of the artist who was drawing it. Above it, the sky was swirling like a Van Gogh painting, with crows and hats and sheets of paper being blown around the rooftops in a gale-force wind. It wasn't one hundred percent identical to the other two houses, because it was painted gray, but it had the same number of windows and the same kind of gambrel roof.

'I don't understand any of this,' said T-Yon.

Sissy touched all the cards again, her fingertips dancing from one to the other. Then she said, 'As far as I can work out, the cards are telling us that sometime in the past this woman used to be in charge of your brother's hotel. It's the same building.'

'But this house doesn't look like The Red Hotel at all.'

'Of course not. The Red Hotel wasn't even thought of when these cards were first drawn. But it *symbolizes* The Red Hotel, in the same way that this chatelaine and her son symbolize the real people who are causing your nightmares.'

'So this scary thing you were talking about . . . you think that's where it's going to happen? At The Red Hotel?'

'I would say so, almost certainly. That's unless somebody does something to stop it.'

'And that somebody, that's me?'

Sissy said, 'It could be. I'm not entirely sure. Let's take a look at these last three cards. Maybe they'll fill in some of the gaps.'

She picked up the left-hand card and turned it over. 'This card tells you *why* you're facing such trouble.'

The card was almost totally black, with only a pair of yellow eyes glowering in the darkness. It was called *L'Ombre Qui Siffle,* The Shadow Who Whistles.

'Every time this card comes up, it means that there's some individual in your life who's waiting for you,' said Sissy. 'For some people, it's a long-lost friend, or a lover. For other people it's somebody who means them to do them harm. He's hiding in the shadows, but he's very patient, he'll go on waiting for as long as it takes. That's why he's called "the shadow who whistles", because he'll amuse himself by whistling until you show up.'

'How do you know it's a "he"?'

'I don't. It could equally be a "she". Usually the cards give me quite a definite feeling one way or another, but this time they're kind of ambivalent about it.'

'Maybe it's the two of them,' T-Yon suggested. 'The mother *and* the son, both.'

'You could be right. But let's see what *this* card has to tell us. This is what is going to happen to you today.'

She turned over the next card. It was *Le Drapeau Rouge,* The Red Flag. The picture showed a young woman in a kitchen, cutting out pastries. Outside the open window, a sunny meadow sloped down toward a river, and beside the river stood a wooden watchtower. A young man was standing on top of the watchtower waving a large scarlet banner, and obviously calling out, because he had one hand raised to his mouth.

Underneath the watchtower, scores of brown pelicans were clustered; and all around the window, white magnolias flowered, so beautifully engraved that Sissy could almost smell them.

'I believe that young woman in the kitchen is you and that young man on top of that tower is your brother,' Sissy told T-Yon. 'See those brown pelicans? The brown pelican is the state bird of Louisiana, and the magnolia is the Louisiana state flower. You're going to talk to your brother today, and he's going to tell you something important. It's something to do with the color red, I imagine. Maybe it's just about The Red Hotel, but I get the feeling that it's more than that. I get the *distinct* feeling that he's worried. In fact I'd say that he's *very* worried.'

'Maybe I should call him now,' said T-Yon. 'My God, I hope he's OK.'

'Let's just turn this last card over, shall we?' said Sissy. 'This will tell you what's going to happen tomorrow, and the day after, and the day after that.'

She took hold of the edge of the card and she was about to turn it over when she hesitated. She could feel which card it was even before she looked at it, and she was reluctant to show it to T-Yon in case it upset her too much. She could turn it over and lie about what it meant, but the DeVane cards were very unforgiving if anybody tried to distort what they were saying. It had happened to her once or twice before, when a really terrifying card had come up, and she had pretended to her client that its message was relatively harmless. The cards had gone cold for weeks on end, and it was only after she had laid them out again and again and kissed each card and expressed her heartfelt contrition that they had gradually come back to life. The DeVane cards were always complicated, and sometimes obscure, but they invariably told the truth, no matter how unpalatable that truth might be; and they expected anybody who used them to do the same.

'I – ah – yes,' said Sissy. 'Why don't you call your brother now? He's an hour behind us, isn't he, so maybe you'll catch him before he goes for lunch.'

T-Yon looked down at the card in Sissy's hand. 'Aren't you going to turn it over? I think I'd like to know what tomorrow's going to bring.'

'Same old, same old, I shouldn't wonder.'

T-Yon waited for a moment, and then she said, 'You don't want to show me, do you? You know what it is and you don't want to show me.'

'All right. You're right. I don't want to show you. Why don't you go call your brother?'

'Is it that bad?'

'It depends on your interpretation. Like I said, you can turn up the same card for two different people and it will have two totally different meanings.'

'So what does this one mean for me? Come on, you just told me I had to face up to my future. "Better to be scared than caught unawares", that's what you said.'

'It could be a mistake,' said Sissy. 'Let's wait until I do a second reading.'

But T-Yon reached across and picked up the card herself. It was the one card that Sissy had feared would come up: *La Cuisine De Nuit*, the Night Kitchen.

T-Yon studied it for a few long moments, and then she said, 'Oh my *God*. Oh God! This is worse than my nightmare.'

The card showed a woman standing in front of a stove in a huge, gloomy kitchen. High up behind her there was a small, circular window, through which a full moon was shining, and apart from a single candle on the table beside her, this was the only illumination. The walls of the kitchen were hung with copper saucepans and colanders and ladles, and the table was crowded with bowls and jugs and sauce boats, as well as vegetables – cabbages and cauliflowers and carrots.

The woman looked about twenty-five years old, with a pale, almond-shaped face and very large sad eyes. She was wearing a white bonnet with wings, rather like a nun's wimple.

At first, in the gloom, it was difficult to make out what she was doing. She was holding the handle of a large iron skillet in one hand, and a fork in the other, and she was prodding what looked like heaps of sausages. It was only on closer inspection that it became clear that her dress was unbuttoned all the way down the front, and that her stomach had been split open, all the way up to her breastbone. She was standing in front of the stove, frying her own intestines.

T-Yon stared at Sissy in total shock.

'I'm sorry,' said Sissy. 'Now you can understand why I didn't want you to see it.'

'But you said that the DeVane cards always tell the truth.'

'They do, T-Yon, they do. But like you've seen with most of these other cards, they're symbolic rather than literal. The Night Kitchen card means that you might be tempted to make a sacrifice on somebody else's behalf, and it's advising you that it might not be the right thing to do.'

'You're sure of that? I'm not going to be cut open and have my insides fried?'

'Of course not. Of *course* not. I'm sorry.'

T-Yon stood up and went to the window. Her blonde hair shone in the sunlight. Sissy sat and waited and said nothing. She was sure that T-Yon wasn't in any danger of meeting the same fate as the girl in the Night Kitchen, but she also couldn't be certain that something equally grisly might not happen to her. At the same time, she could sense the cards' disapproval that she wasn't being honest. It was like a chilly draft up the back of her neck, as if Billy had left the back door open.

After a few moments, however, T-Yon turned around and said, 'No, Sissy, you shouldn't be sorry. I asked you to tell my fortune and you did. It's not your fault that it turned out so scary. At least you've warned me about it. My God.'

'Let's do another reading later on,' Sissy suggested. 'There's still so much that the cards haven't explained. I think you'll find that your future isn't going to be quite so terrible after all.'

'Do you know what I asked them?' said T-Yon.

'You don't have to tell me. It's between you and the cards.'

'I asked them if my brother was in trouble. I asked them if he needed me.' She paused, and then she said, 'He does, doesn't he? And I think he needs *you*, too.'

The Whistler

When Everett came back from his lunch with Theresa Overby, Luther was waiting for him in his office, with one vast buttock perched on the edge of his desk. Luther's expression was unusually somber.

'Well?' asked Everett. 'You look like you lost a ten spot and found a nickel.'

'What we found was more blood,' said Luther. 'Or what looks like blood.'

'Shit. Where?'

'Seventh story stairwell.'

'Shit. Why didn't you call me?'

'Didn't see the point. I knew you'd want to check it out for yourself, before we called in the cops.'

'All right. Let's go take a look at it. Jesus. What the *hell* is going on in this goddamn hotel?'

Bella slid back the window between their offices and said, 'Hi, boss! Enjoy your lunch? Mr Tierney says he can meet you at seven at the Kingfish Lounge, OK? And Olivia's bringing round those media releases around five thirty. She said that Frank Thibodeaux hadn't finalized all the dinner menus, that's what held her up.'

'OK, Bella. Thanks. I'll catch up with you in a minute.'

Everett and Luther took the elevator back up to the seventh floor. This time they turned right when they left the elevator car and walked along to the door which led to the emergency staircase. Everett pushed it open and they stepped inside.

The staircase was all concrete, with red-painted tubular handrails. It was hot and humid in here, because it wasn't air-conditioned, and they could hear banging and clattering from the third floor down below them, where an ice-making machine was being installed.

Luther said, 'There,' and pointed across to the opposite side of the landing.

On the bottom two steps that led up to the roof, Everett saw two broad smears of reddish-brown, and another smear on the floor just below them, in an elongated S-shape. There was also a random pattern of reddish-brown marks on the wall, like squashed moths, as if somebody with bloody hands had repeatedly lost their balance and had reached out seven or eight times to steady themselves.

Everett went across and examined the stains more closely. 'If this *is* blood, and not paint, or rust remover, I'd say that something pretty nasty happened here.' He leaned to one side and peered upward. 'You check out the roof?'

'Of course. We checked the *en*-tire building, roof to parking garage. Every guest room, every storeroom, every closet, but this is all we found.'

'OK. Looks like it's time to call in the law. But I hope that won't be a serious error of judgment.'

Luther said, 'Think about it this way, Mr Everett, sir. If it *ain't* blood, then we don't have nothing to worry about. At least we'll know for sure.'

'What do *you* think it is? I mean, seriously?'

'I think it's blood.'

'Yeah. Me too, damn it.'

Detective Slim Garrity stood and stared at the crimson-stained rug for over a minute without saying anything, although his jaws kept working on a large wad of Big Red chewing gum. He was a thin, angular man with black slicked-back hair, and the impression he gave of a Southern card sharp was accentuated by his bolo necktie and his shiny, black narrow-shouldered suit.

Beside him, his partner Detective Kevin Mullard was hefty and disheveled. He had sandy hair and sandy eyebrows and freckles and his red rubbery lips seemed to be permanently smirking at some private joke. His green linen three-piece suit looked as if he had bought it from a thrift store and got change out of a twenty, and never pressed it.

'So . . . your cleaner was the first one to see it?' asked Detective Garrity. He spoke with an unmistakable Baton Rouge accent, but without any expression in his voice at all, as if he were reading from a teleprompt. 'And there was nobody else here in the suite when she came in to clean? No guests, no hotel staff? No unauthorized visitors?'

'Nobody, so far as I know,' said Everett. 'You can talk to her in a minute, if you want to.'

'Very well. OK. But the first thing we have to decide is what this stain is really constituated of. The crime-scene boys'll be here in a few minutes, and they'll be doing a presumptive test, which will tell us for certain if it *isn't* blood.'

'They can tell if it isn't, but they can't tell if it is? How does that work?'

'The presumptive test can only tell us if it's probable. It's not one hundred percent foolproof, because there's other factors which can give you a similar reaction to human blood. Interferences, we call them. Some plant and animal materials, they can affect a test for human blood, and so can some metals, like copper and iron. That's why we have to be careful when we're testing for blood outdoors, where there's a whole lot of vegetative life, or in any kind of vehicle.'

'I see. What if it probably *is* blood?'

'Then they'll take the rug back to the CSI laboratory and put it through some further tests for human-specific enzymes or human-specific DNA.'

'My guess is it's blood,' put in Detective Mullard, still smirking. 'It sure *looks* like blood, don't it? And what else could it be? Red-eye gravy?'

'Let's not go leaping to any premature conclusions, Kevin,' Detective Garrity admonished him, out of the side of his mouth. 'Quite apart from that, we don't want to upset these good people here more than we necessarily have to, do we.'

Everett said, 'I'm not squeamish, Detective. I just want to know for sure that nobody's been murdered here.'

'Of course you do, sir, and believe me we'll be expediting our investigation as quick as conceivably possible.'

Everett led the two detectives to the stairwell, so that they could look at the stains on the steps, and the floor, and the patterns on the wall.

'Again, it's hard to tell for sure if that's blood or not,' said Detective Garrity. 'You'd be surprised the number of times we've come across suspicious-looking stains at some crime location or another, and they've turned out to be totally innocent. Look at these here. My partner here mentioned red-eye gravy, and it's perfectly possible that these here stains in this stairwell are just that. Red-eye gravy is made with ham grease and coffee, isn't it, and that could give you this reddish-brown coloration.'

Everett said, 'You don't seriously believe that this *is* gravy, do you?'

Detective Garrity's jaws continued to chew gum. He looked at Everett with eyes as black and hooded as a turtle. 'No, sir. To be truthful to you, I don't seriously believe that this is gravy.'

Two crime-scene specialists arrived, one tall African-American woman and one short, bullish-looking white man with rimless spectacles and a blue shaven head. They unpacked their kits, taking out Sangur strips for the rug and BlueStar Forensic liquid for the polished wooden floor that surrounded it, to see if there were any blood spatters that might have been washed or wiped away.

The African-American woman moistened a Sangur strip, which was like a large cotton bud, so that it turned pale yellow. She wiped it against the stain on the rug, and almost immediately it turned a bright greenish-blue. She held it up without a word, so the two detectives could see it.

'Probable for blood,' said Detective Garrity, flatly.

The bullish-looking CSI turned to Everett and said, 'Maybe you can give us some elbow room now, sir, so that we can check out the rest of the room.' The way he said it, it didn't sound like a request.

'Sure,' said Everett. He had plenty of work to be catching up with downstairs, even though he hardly felt like carrying on as if it was business as usual. Luther was waiting for him outside in the corridor.

'Well?'

'Worst case scenario. They believe that it's blood.'

'We need to work out how we're going to present this, Mr Everett, sir. I mean, like, media-wise.'

'I don't have any idea. "Copious bloodstains have been discovered on the seventh story – but don't panic! We haven't found any corpses yet! So far as we know, nobody has actually been murdered at The Red Hotel, so we trust that you all enjoy your stay with us – sweet dreams!"'

They went back down to the ground floor. In the elevator, a pretty young brunette in a tight turquoise T-shirt kept smiling at Everett and batting her eyelashes, but Everett found it impossible to give her anything in return but a quick, sick grin. Jesus, if somebody *had* been killed, right here in The Red Hotel, he could be ruined.

He returned to his office and slid back the glass partition. 'Bella, how about a *very* strong cup of coffee?' In fact, he could have used a double Jack Daniel's, straight up, but he wanted to try and stay clear-headed.

'Oh, boss – you're back!' said Bella, brightly. 'Your sister just called you! I told her you were tied up. She gave me her number . . . someplace in Connecticut, she said. She didn't leave a message but she asked if you could call her back asap.'

'OK, fine. Thanks. Do you want to get back to her for me?'

He sat down at his desk. His press officer, Olivia Melancon, had left him her latest media release, with a color photograph of himself and his partner, Stanley Tierney, and the mayor of Baton Rouge, George Dolan, all standing in front of The Red Hotel beaming with pride and holding up their thumbs. Her headline proclaimed: *THE FUTURE IS RED – New Lease Of Life For BR's Bijou Hotel.*

The future is red, he thought. Well done, Olivia. You don't know just *how* red. Red bloodstains and red balance sheet, both.

His phone warbled. He picked it up and it was T-Yon.

T-Yon said, 'Thanks, Bella,' and then, 'Everett? It's me. Everett – is everything OK?'

'Where are you? Bella said you were someplace in Connecticut.'

'Allen's Corners, it's just outside of New Milford. We came here to see Billy's aunt Sissy.'

'OK. What are you calling me for? You sound kind of upset.'

'It's a really long story but we came to see Billy's aunt

because she can tell fortunes, and tell you what your dreams mean, stuff like that.'

'Oh, yeah?'

'She's fantastically good at it. She uses these special cards like nothing you ever saw in your life. They all have these really strange pictures on them, like witches and peculiar children and people getting baked into pies.'

'Really? Jeez.' Everett was trying to read Olivia's media release at the same time as talking to T-Yon.

'She told me my fortune.'

'And, like, what? She told you that some horrible fate is going to befall you? You know I don't believe in any of that hooey.'

'Everett, she said that you were worried. In fact she said you were *very* worried. She said that it's something to do with The Red Hotel, and it's red.'

Everett abruptly leaned back in his chair. 'Say that again? It's something do with The Red Hotel, and it's red?'

'That's right. The color red. She didn't exactly know what, but it all seems to be connected to a woman who used to run The Red Hotel way back whenever.'

Everett paused for a moment, and then he said, 'That would be . . . what was her name? Vanessa something. I know – Vanessa Slider. I remember the name because it's like slider turtles. So far as I know she was the only woman who ever ran this hotel.'

'When was that?'

'Oh, who knows – way back in the late nineteen eighties, I think. Luther told me all about it. She and her husband used to manage it together but then her husband died and she took over. She ran it for a while – maybe three or four years – but then she was found guilty of assaulting a call girl who had come to the hotel to service one of the guests. Tried to strangle her, that's what Luther said.'

'It's *her*,' said T-Yon. 'Whatever you're worried about now, it's all to do with her. What did you say her name was?'

'Vanessa Slider. But I haven't told you that I *am* worried.'

'You are, though, aren't you? Sissy said that these cards know everything, and they never lie.'

'T-Yon, it's all baloney. They're *cards*, that's all.'

'It's not just the cards, Ev. I didn't want to tell you, but I've been having nightmares, too. Nightmares about us – you and me. That's why I came here to see Sissy in the first place.'

'Nightmares? What kind of nightmares?'

'They're just terrible. I mean like really, *really* horrific. I'll tell you all about them when I see you. I can't describe them over the phone. But they started when you opened The Red Hotel, and Sissy is sure that there's some link between my nightmares and this woman who used to run it – this woman and her young son.'

Everett said nothing. He didn't know if he ought to tell T-Yon about the bloodstains or not. Even though Detective Garrity had said that they were probably human, he was still holding out hope that they had come from some animal; or that they were paint, or dye, or even red-eye gravy, goddamnit.

T-Yon said, 'Sissy thinks that this woman is looking for revenge. She doesn't know all of the details yet. We're going to do another reading this evening. But she says that we could be in real danger – both of us, you and me.'

'How can she be looking for revenge? If she was running The Red Hotel in the nineteen eighties she must be getting on for eighty by now – that's if she's still alive.'

'Sissy believes that people can still come looking for revenge, even after they've passed over.'

'Oh, spare me! Come on, T-Yon, when people are dead, they're dead. We never hear from Momma, do we, and *she* had plenty to be vengeful about, the way Poppa left her to bring us up all on her ownsome.'

'That's different. And anyhow, Momma never bore a grudge against anyone. She wasn't that kind of a person. She was sweetness and light, God bless her.'

'T-Yon,' said Everett, 'thanks for your call but I really have to go now. I'm up to my ears.'

'So you're telling me that you're not worried about anything at all?'

'Right now – apart from finding myself three qualified sous-chefs before tomorrow lunchtime – no.'

'Cross your heart?'

Everett was just about to answer when he was almost deaf-
ened by a piercing whistle. Immediately, he took the phone
away from his ear, but the whistling continued, rising and
falling like a high wind whistling through a gap in a window.
T-Yon was still talking, but he could barely make out what
she was saying.

'T-Yon?' he shouted. 'T-Yon? There's some kind of interference on the line, I'll have to call you back!'

'*What?*' she said.

'I said there's some kind of interference on the line! Can't
you hear it? Like somebody whistling!'

'*Can't . . . hear . . . anyth—*'

'I'll call you back, OK?'

He switched off his phone and went over to the sliding
glass window. 'Bella, can you get me that number again,
please? T-Yon's number in Connecticut?' He stuck his
finger in his ear and screwed it around. 'The phone started
making this really loud screeching sound. Damn near deaf-
ened me.'

She had started to punch out the number again when Luther
knocked at the door.

'Just had a complaint from five-one-two.'

'What was it? For Christ's sake, Luther, can't *you* deal
with it?'

'I been up there already, Mr Everett, sir, and I sure don't
know what to make of it. Thought you'd want to come hear
it for yourself.'

'*Hear* it? What do you mean by that?'

'It's a whistling noise. Like somebody whistling, only real
loud. I can't work out where it's coming from, or what's
causing it.'

Everett turned back to Bella and said, 'Bella – forget that
call for now. I'll be upstairs on five if anybody needs me.'

He could hear it as soon as they stepped out of the elevator.
Only three of the rooms on the fifth floor were occupied, out
of twenty, but five guests were standing in the corridor with
their fingers in their ears, looking distinctly unhappy. The
whistling sound was overwhelming – the same hurricane-force

whistle that Everett had heard on the phone. It rose and fell in both volume and pitch, and at its highest it made it almost impossible to think, let alone hear anything.

'*What is it?*' a young man shouted. Although it was only mid-afternoon, he was wearing only a hotel bathrobe, white with *The Red Hotel* embroidered in red on the pocket. Everett recognized him and his pretty blonde partner as a honeymoon couple who had booked in only about three hours ago. 'It's even making the TV go on the fritz!'

Everett walked down to the end of the corridor and looked out of the window. There was nothing outside the hotel that could be making a whistling noise as loud as this. There was no wind blowing, no helicopters hovering, no emergency vehicles parked in the street, no construction sites with klaxons or hooters.

Luther yelled, 'Could be the plumbing, what do you think? You know – air that's gotten trapped in the pipes, something like that? My Aunt Epiphany's house used to rumble something terrible when she got air trapped in her pipes.'

'I don't have any idea!' Everett yelled back at him. 'Just get Charlie Bowdre up here with his maintenance crew!'

The honeymooner came up to them. 'We can't stay here with this noise going on! Like, if you can't fix it, you're going to have to find us another room!'

An older man quavered, 'It's playing all hell with my hearing appliance! Like somebody screaming, right inside my head! If I suffer a perforated eardrum, because of this, I tell you, I'm going to sue your ass!'

'OK, OK, everybody please calm down!' Everett shouted. 'I'm going to call for our maintenance guys to come up here as quick as they can. Like my deputy manager says, it's probably nothing more serious than some air in the water pipes, or maybe it's an a/c problem. Whatever it is, we'll get it sorted asap. Meanwhile, if you'd all like to come down to the Showboat Saloon, we'll give you complimentary cocktails and snacks until you can return to your rooms.'

Even though the whistling was now even higher – so high that it was right at the upper edge of human hearing – the guests appeared to be satisfied with Everett's offer, and they returned to their rooms to change into clothes that would suit the Showboat Saloon.

Luther meanwhile called Charlie Bowdre, their maintenance engineer, on his headset and told him to get up to five as fast as humanly possible.

Luther paused, and then he said to Everett, 'Charlie says he's all tied up.'

'What the hell does he mean he's all tied up? This is a goddamned crisis!'

Luther talked to Charlie Bowdre again. When Charlie Bowdre answered him he raised his eyebrows and said, '*Damn.*' That was about the coarsest expletive that Luther ever used, so Everett knew that it had to be serious.

'What is it?' he asked. The whistling had subsided a little, but it had changed to a low, plaintive, quavering sound, like a chorus of desolate ghosts.

'Charlie says that there's a loud whistling noise down in the basement and he's real concerned that the boiler may blow.'

'Jesus. I don't believe this. I'm going down there myself. You wait here, OK, until all of these people are ready, and escort them down to the Showboat.'

The whistling rose and fell, rose and fell. Luther looked up at the ceiling, and then all around him.

'Sure sounds spooky, doesn't it?'

'Bloodstained rugs and spooky whistling, I seriously don't need stuff like this.'

He left Luther and went to the elevator. As he pressed the button to go down to the basement, the whistling abruptly stopped. He turned back and looked at Luther in bewilderment. The total silence was almost as unsettling as the whistling that had come before it.

They waited and waited, but the whistling didn't resume.

'What shall I do, Mr Everett, sir?' asked Luther.

'Give them their free drinks anyhow. Don't want them to think we're cheapskates, do we? I'll meet you in my office, OK?'

The elevator arrived and its chime made him jump. As the doors opened, he saw the reflection of a young woman in the mirrors; a young brunette woman in a cream-colored dress with her back turned to him. When he stepped into the elevator car it was empty.

He turned around and around. There was nobody else in the car but him, and his own reflections. The young woman must have been an optical illusion, a trick of the lights, and the mirrors. He must have seen nothing more than an image of himself, in his own cream linen coat.

He held the doors open and looked back outside. There was no girl walking away from him in the corridor, only Luther patiently waiting with his hands clasped in front of his crotch.

Shit, he thought. *I'm losing it. I must have been working too hard.*

But then he thought about his telephone conversation with T-Yon.

'Sissy believes that people can still come looking for revenge, even after they've passed over.'

Ghost Dance

Sissy went into the kitchen to make her potato and mushroom bake, while Billy and T-Yon took Mr Boots for a walk up the road. The sky had cleared now, and even though it was cool for an August evening, Sissy could leave the kitchen door open.

She could hear the repetitive whistling of a whippoorwill from somewhere in the woods. She always thought whippoorwills sounded as if they had lost their mate, like she had, and were hopelessly whistling for them to come back, over and over.

She sliced parboiled potatoes and laid them in a buttered dish. Then she covered them with sliced mushrooms, rosemary, chives and garlic, followed by another layer of potatoes. She poured cream over the top of the potatoes and seasoned them lavishly with ground black pepper; and then slid the dish into the preheated oven.

Frank had always complained when she made potato and

mushroom bake. 'A man needs his meat,' he used to say. 'You want to see me wasting away in front of your eyes?'

But Frank had never had the chance to waste away: he had been shot by a nineteen-year-old drug addict called Laurence Stepney, when he had tried to stop him from breaking into a station wagon outside the Big Bear Supermarket, near Norfolk. That was nearly twenty-five years ago now, and Laurence Stepney was now a free man. Frank, of course, was still in his casket.

'*Pretty woman, walking down the street,*' Sissy sang, under her breath, as she took off her apron. Frank had often sung that for her, even though it had usually come out in a low, off-key growl. He had never been good at paying her compliments, so he had recruited Roy Orbison to do it for him. And in spite of his complaints, he had always finished his potato and mushroom bake, and scraped the plate.

She poured herself another glass of Zinfandel and went back into the living room. She knew that she needed to give T-Yon a second reading if she was going to answer all of the puzzles and uncertainties that her first reading had raised. But the final cards that she had turned up had given her such a strong sense of danger that she wondered if it was a good idea to take the readings any further.

If T-Yon was convinced by her card readings that her brother, Everett, was at risk in any way, then she would obviously consider flying to Baton Rouge to try and protect him. The cards had predicted that she would. But Sissy was having second thoughts about the wisdom of T-Yon doing that. It was strange that T-Yon was the one who was having the nightmares, not Everett – not as far as she knew, anyhow. It was possible that T-Yon could make matters worse. Maybe Vanessa Slider was using her nightmares as way of getting herself back into The Red Hotel, as if T-Yon were carrying her in, like an infection. Or maybe she had some other reason for wanting T-Yon back there.

Shit and a bit, thought Sissy. *And here I was looking forward to a quiet feet-up weekend, and maybe a few glasses of wine and a game of gin rummy with my old friend, Sam.*

She had Googled *Vanessa Slider* on her laptop, but she had

found only two, sparse entries, neither of which had given her very much more background than Everett had told T-Yon on the phone.

Wikipedia said that Vanessa and her husband Gerard had jointly managed what was then called the Hotel Rouge until 1985, when Gerard had died and Vanessa had taken over. In 1988, Vanessa had been arrested for the attempted homicide of a prostitute called Evangeline Doucet, for reasons which she refused to explain in court. She had been jailed for a minimum of fifteen years at the Louisiana Correctional Institute for Women, while her son, Shem, had been sent to the East Baton Rouge Juvenile Detention Facility.

There was no information on Vanessa's release date, or whether she was still alive. But as Sissy had told T-Yon, she had an intuitive feeling that Vanessa was dead, and that maybe her son Shem was, too, although she couldn't be one hundred percent sure.

It wasn't always so easy, telling the difference between the dead and the living. Some people who visited Sissy to have their fortunes read gave her a chill like a winter wind blowing across a graveyard, even though they were still alive. *Abominable snowpersons*, Sissy called them. On the other hand, she had been to funerals where her natural sensitivity had shown her that an aura still lingered around the person lying in the casket – usually blue, or gold, or pink – even though their hearts had long stopped beating.

She took out a cigarette and flicked her Zippo alight, but then she snapped the Zippo shut and tucked the cigarette back into the box. She had tempted death quite enough for one day, she thought to herself. Sometimes you have to turn around and look him in the eye and say, no, you can wait.

Billy and T-Yon came back into the house, and brought Mr Boots in, too. 'He had a swim in the pond, didn't you, boy? But he's dried off now, and he doesn't smell quite so bad.'

'I sometimes wonder why I don't have him put down,' said Sissy. 'He costs me a fortune in food, and he's such an unresponsive mutt these days.'

Mr Boots lay down on the floor and looked up at Sissy with sad, appealing eyes.

'You won't have him put down because you love him,' said
Billy. 'And you know that he'd come back to haunt you. That's
the trouble with being so psychic. Your friends die, your pets
die, but you can never get rid of them. What was the name of
that cat you used to have? The one you saw sitting on the
window sill looking in at you, about three years after he had
died?'

'Oh, Smokey,' said Sissy, with a flap of her hand. 'I saw
him two or three times after that. At least those goddamned
goldfish never came back.'

'Something smells good,' said T-Yon. 'Is that your potato
and mushroom bake?'

'It'll be ready in a half-hour,' Sissy told her. 'Hope you're
ravenous; I made three times too much, as usual.'

'Does that give us time to have a second reading?'

'You're really sure you want to?'

'Of course, yes. If there's any kind of problem at The Red
Hotel, I really want to know about it. I don't want anything
to happen to Everett.'

'I suppose you want me to kick my heels outside?' said
Billy.

'No, Billy-bob, you can stay here for this. I'd like to see
what *you* think of the cards that come up.'

'OK. But those DeVane cards, they always give me the
heebie-jeebies. They always did, even when you used to tell
my fortune when I was a kid. I guess they were always right,
though. They said that I was going to be working a kitchen,
didn't they, even when I was sure that I was going to be a
Navy Seal?'

Billy went into the kitchen to fetch himself a can of Schlitz
and then flopped down in the armchair opposite and popped
the top. 'So – you've done one reading. What's the story so
far?'

Sissy quickly told him all about Vanessa Slider and The
Red Hotel, and how the cards had predicted that she and her
son, Shem, were trying to get back to the hotel to exact
their revenge. She confessed that she wasn't sure *why* they
wanted revenge, or what for, although she suspected that it
was linked in some way to all of the gruesome goings-on

depicted in *La Châtelaine* card – all that chopping up of humans and animals and baking them into pies, as well as the beds heaped up with ravenous rats, and the man with no head.

She didn't tell Billy about T-Yon's nightmares; and neither did she tell him about the Night Kitchen card, with the girl frying her own entrails. She didn't want to spoil Billy's relationship with T-Yon by telling him that she had dreamed about sleeping with her brother, and neither did she want him to think that something terrible was going to happen to her, and panic. They had to interpret the cards calmly, and rationally, and analyze what they were really trying to say, even though some of them were so enigmatic and some of them were so gory, and most of them were both.

Billy listened, and nodded, but when Sissy had finished he shook his head and said, 'No. No way, José. I can't see any of this happening for real.'

'But you said yourself that the cards were always right,' said T-Yon.

'They are. They are. I'm not disputing that. But even if they're right, they're not always, like, *literal.* You can't take them at face value, can you? Because it's like they're hundreds of years old, right, and most of the things they're predicting about, they didn't have them in those days. So you have to *interpret* them. This guy with no head, for example, reading the newspaper. He could be some reporter, giving The Red Hotel a bad write-up, because he's stupid. No head, see? No head equals no brains. It doesn't literally mean that some guy's going to get his head cut off in real life.'

T-Yon turned to Sissy and said, 'Is that right? I mean, I *hope* it's right.'

Before Sissy could answer, however, Billy added, 'Don't get me wrong. I do believe the cards are giving you the heads up that Everett's in for some trouble. But it's not going to be, like, death-and-destruction type trouble. I don't know. Maybe the Baton Rouge planning authorities are going to give him a hard time about his fire doors. Or – look at these rats. Maybe he's going to have mice running around in some of the bedrooms and he has to call in the rodent exterminator. It could be that his restaurant gets some one-star reviews. You know, maybe some of the guests are going to get food poisoning or something.'

He picked up some of the cards, and said, 'Look at these pictures. You don't seriously think that anybody is going to be baking human fingers into pies anytime soon? It's *symbolic*. That fat guy outside the kitchen window, maybe he's a local cop who wants a kickback for protection. Pie, fingers. You know – getting his fingers into the pie.'

'But what about Vanessa Slider and her son?' T-Yon asked him. 'The cards specifically say that they're looking to get their revenge.'

'Yes, but – *again*,' said Billy, 'you don't even know if this chatelaine woman is really her. She could represent one of her relations, or some attorney who thinks that Vanessa Slider was done out of her share in the business when she was sent to the pokey, and is trying to claim it back. A writ can do as much damage as a double-headed ax, don't you think? *More, probably.*'

He paused. 'All I'm trying to say is, this is the twenty-first century, and even if what these cards predict is always spot on, you have to interpret them according to the way life is today, not like it was back in eighteen-oh-when.'

Sissy collected up all the DeVane cards and slowly shuffled them. 'There's a lot in what you say, Billy,' she admitted. 'In fact I taught you most of that myself, when I first showed you how to use them.'

Billy spread his arms wide and said, 'It's logical, right? Like, for instance, even if T-Yon *does* go back to Baton Rouge, there's no way she's traveling there in a horse and buggy. Jesus. It would take her the next six months.'

'Well,' said Sissy, 'we'll have to see what the cards tell us next. Here's your Predictor card, T-Yon. Ask your question. In fact, you can ask more than one question, if you want to. But again – don't tell me what it is.'

T-Yon laid the card on the coffee table, closed her eyes for a moment, and then opened them up again and said, 'Done it. *Three* questions, actually.'

Sissy laid the cards out in the Cross of Lorraine pattern, with three cards in a fan shape at the top. Billy leaned forward in his armchair so that he could see better, and said, 'Go, Aunt Sissy! Let's see you unravel the mysteries of the future, right before our very eyes!'

Sissy looked at him sharply. 'I hope you're going to take this seriously, Billy-bob. Otherwise you *can* go kick your heels outside. And your ass, too, while you're at it.'

'Sure, Aunt Sissy. Sorry. I just think the DeVane cards are really cool, that's all. Scary as all hell, but really cool.'

Sissy took hold of the edge of the first card and she was about to turn it over when she felt a strange prickling sensation in her fingertips, as if the card had given her a very mild electric shock. She let go of the card and looked around the living room, frowning.

'What's up, Aunt Sissy? Aren't you going to turn over the cards?'

Sissy could feel some disturbance around her. She wasn't at all sure what it was. For some reason it put her in mind of the last time she had visited Florida, and the foyer of her hotel had been hung from floor to ceiling with light gauzy drapes, which had silently lifted and fallen in the breeze which blew in from the ocean.

'Something's wrong,' she said, in a very quiet voice. 'Well, maybe not *wrong*, but different.'

'What is it?' asked T-Yon.

'A draft. A very soft draft. Can you feel it?'

T-Yon lifted her head. 'I don't know. Maybe something. How about you, Billy?'

Billy pulled a face. 'I don't feel nothing. Come on, Aunt Sissy. I think you're just spooking yourself out.'

'Yes, maybe I am. But let's just see what this first card has to tell us. This is going to be like *La Châtelaine* card, T-Yon . . . whatever it is, it's going to influence all the rest of the cards which follow. You do realize that?'

'Whatever, it's OK with me,' said T-Yon. 'I'd rather know the worst.'

On the back of this card, like every other card, there was an engraving of a peacock sitting in the center of a frame of decorative leaves. Sissy turned it over, but to her bewilderment the front was exactly the same.

She thought for a split second that two cards must have somehow become stuck together, face-to-face. But then she felt that soft draft, rising again, and she sensed that this was no accident. She quickly turned over the next card, and the next, and the next. All of them were identical, with the same pattern on the front as there was on the back. All of the pictures of chatelaines and chefs and terrifying kitchens – all of the pictures of rats and monks and screaming faces in grassy fields – they had all disappeared. Both sides of every card showed the same peacock in the same leafy surroundings, but that was all.

Outside, the wind was rising again, and the trees began to thrash restlessly at their roots, like tethered stallions.

Billy dropped down on to his knees and shuffled through every single card in the pack.

'They've *gone*,' he said. 'I can't believe it! Every single one of them. Even my favorite, *Les Moulins À Vent Pourpres* – The Purple Windmills.'

He turned them over again and again, almost frantic, but it made no difference. Every one had the same peacock pattern on both sides. No Wasp Stings, no Wizards, no Frightening Journeys, no Clowns.

'What's happened?' said T-Yon. She was breathless and panicky. 'It's not a trick, is it? Sissy – please – tell me it isn't a trick!'

Although she was determined not to show it, Sissy was probably as frightened as T-Yon was. She stood up, and as she did so she felt a chill crawling through her bones, all the way down her spine, one vertebra after another, and all around her pelvis, like a frozen girdle, and down her thighs. Even her skin felt as if it were shrinking.

From the direction of the kitchen, off to her right, a faint white figure appeared. It was almost an exaggeration to call it a figure, because it was less substantial than a wisp of smoke. Yet it appeared to have a smudgy face, with hollow eyes, and it moved as if it were trying to walk along a verandah in a high wind, with its right hand held out sideways for a non-existent railing, and its left hand clutching its collar close to its neck.

All of these details were blurred; and they came and went as the figure made its way across the living room.

T-Yon looked up at Sissy and said, 'My God! What *is* that? Is that a *ghost*?'

But Sissy raised her hand to caution T-Yon that she should stay quiet, because a second figure had appeared, and then a third. They were both as indistinct as the first figure, but somehow Sissy could see that they were different. The second figure had its head bent and both hands clasped to its neck; the third was walking with a much stronger stride, as if it were determined to face up to this unfelt hurricane without holding on to anything for support.

Each of these smoky white images silently flapped and silently curled, which gave Sissy the impression that they were women, with wind-blown dresses. They walked toward the window, through which the last pale light of the day was shining, and as they approached it they melted away.

Four or five more of them materialized and flickered across the room, while Sissy and Billy and T-Yon watched them in silent disbelief. Then the last of them vanished, as if they had never existed. A twist of white smoke, and then nothing at all.

Billy stood up and said, 'Christ on crutches, Aunt Sissy. What were *they*?'

Sissy bent down and picked up a card from the coffee table. It was *La Châtelaine*. The image had returned to the face of the card; and so had all of the images on all of the other cards. Billy picked some up, too, to make sure, and then dropped them again.

Sissy was shaken to the core. She opened her mouth but she couldn't speak. With her DeVane cards, and her natural facility to read them, she had always felt that her psychic influence was stronger than anybody's. Anybody that she had ever met, anyhow, and she had met more than a few – at psychic fairs, and seances, and so-called magic shows. Gypsies and mediums and general purveyors of hocus-pocus.

But something or somebody had passed through her living room this evening and whoever or whatever they were, their influence had overwhelmed hers like a psychic tsunami. It had mocked her by defacing all of her DeVane cards, and then it had trailed in front of her a procession of spirits, white and transparent, although Sissy for the life of her couldn't think why.

She sat down, abruptly. T-Yon said, 'Are you OK, Sissy? You're looking real pale.'

'I'm, ah . . . yes, I'm OK. Just get me another glass of wine, would you, sweetheart?'

She took out a cigarette and lit it – took two puffs and then crushed it out in the ashtray.

T-Yon came back from the kitchen with a glass of wine for her. 'What were those things? I never saw anything like that in my life, *never.*'

'No,' said Sissy. 'Me neither. But I'll tell you something for sure. You and me, we're off to Baton Rouge.'

'You're *what*?' said Billy. 'You can't go to Baton Rouge! What are you going to do in Baton Rouge, for Christ's sake?'

Sissy looked up at him. 'I wish I could tell you, Billy-bob. But I can see it right here.'

She tapped her forehead with her fingertip. 'I can see it and I can even *hear* it. I don't think I was ever supposed to. What we saw here tonight, those spirits or ghosts or whatever you want to call them, they were a warning. I was being told to stay away and mind my own business.'

'By who?'

'My guess is, Vanessa Slider.'

Billy shook his head in exasperation. 'Come on, Aunt Sissy. You don't have proof of any of this. You can't go all the way to Baton Rouge based on some half-assed card reading and some optical illusion of some spirits or whatever they were. Hey, they could have been smoke, blown in from next door's bonfire, and because we were all hyped up for that reading, we thought they were ghosts.'

'You really think that? Did they *smell* like smoke?'

'No, OK, they didn't smell like smoke. But even supposing you're right, and this Vanessa woman *is* warning you off, don't you think the prudent thing to do would be to stay right here? If she can wipe all of the pictures off of your DeVane cards, and then put them back again, do you think that's somebody you're any match for?'

Sissy said, 'T-Yon came to me, Billy-bob, asking me for help. When people come asking me for help, I never say no, and I'm not going to say "no" now.'

Billy opened his mouth, but before he could speak, the kitchen door slammed so loudly that all three of them jumped in fright.

The Missing

Detective Garrity appeared in the open doorway of Everett's office with a toothpick protruding from the side of his mouth. Everett was talking on his headset to Charlie Bowdre, his chief maintenance engineer.

'So you checked all the plumbing, yes? And you checked the a/c vents? And what? You found nothing at all? How about the Wi-Fi system? No – I know you don't have Wi-Fi in the boiler room, but I'm trying to consider every possible option here. Like, maybe it was some kind of radio interference. Yes. No. Well, how the hell should I know?'

He beckoned to Detective Garrity and said, 'Come on in. How's it going up there?'

Detective Garrity took out the toothpick. 'The CSIs are pretty much done. I'll have their report in tomorrow sometime and, if there's anything more I need to ask you, I'll get back. They're taking the rug with them for chromatography and DNA tests.'

He paused for a moment, looking at Everett with those black turtle eyes. Then he touched his ear to imitate Everett's headset and said, 'Don't mean to be intrusive, sir, but it sounds to me like you got yourself even more problems.'

'Well, yes, but we're not even sure what's wrong yet. Didn't you hear anything, up on seven?'

Even longer pause. 'Hear anything like what?'

Everett blinked. 'OK. Obviously you *didn't* hear it. You would know for sure if you had, believe me.'

'So what was it, this thing that I didn't hear?'

'If you didn't hear it, Detective, it really doesn't matter.'

'I think that I can be the judge of that, sir.'

Everett thought: *shit. As if I don't have enough of a head-ache. This is just going to get weirder and weirder and more and more out of my control, and if I can manage to open this hotel on Friday without any more shit hitting any more fans, it's going to be a miracle.*

'We, uh – we had some kind of a whistling sound, up on five. I don't think it was anything serious.'

'Whistling sound. What kind of a whistling sound?'

Everett shrugged. 'Kind of like, whistling, that's all.'

'But it's stopped now, right?' said Detective Garrity. 'Although you don't have any idea what caused it.'

'Well, that's right. That was Charlie Bowdre, my chief maintenance guy, I was talking to just then – to see if he could find out what it was.'

'Doesn't sound dangerous or nothing? Not like nothing's going to blow up?' These were questions, and very pointed questions, too; although Detective Garrity spoke so flatly that they didn't sound like it.

'No, no. Nothing like that. It's probably like I was saying to Charlie, Wi-Fi interference. We have Wi-Fi in every room. *Free* Wi-Fi as a matter of fact, if you're interested, unlike many of the major hotels in downtown BR.'

'I'm not fixing on staying here, sir. I came down here to see if I could talk to the maid who found the rug.'

'Ella-mae? Oh, sure.' He pressed the button on his speak-erphone for housekeeping and asked to speak to Clarice.

'Clarice? Can you bring Ella-mae to my office, please? Detective Garrity wants a few words with her, but don't tell her that. Just bring her.'

'Ella-mae went to the bathroom.'

'OK, bring her as soon as she comes back.'

'Come to think of it, Mr Everett, sir, she's been gone for more than ten minutes. Maybe even longer than that. I can't say that I've been keeping my eye on her.'

'You don't think she's snuck off home, do you?'

'I don't rightly know, Mr Everett, sir, but I'll go take a look in the ladies' room. I'll get back to you directly.'

Everett raised his eyebrows and said, 'Staff! You got to believe it! One word from me and they do what they like.'

Detective Garrity remained expressionless. 'You have the girl's home address, if needs be.'

'Oh, sure. But she's probably still around the hotel some-place. I did ask her to stay.'

They waited for a minute or two. Everett was about to ask Detective Garrity if the CSI team had found any more traces of blood in Suite Seven-Oh-Three when his speakerphone buzzed.

'Mr Everett, sir! This is Clarice! You better come quick. I went to the women's restroom and there's blood all over.'

'What about Ella-mae?'

'No sign of Ella-mae, noplace.'

Grim-faced, without hesitation, Everett hurried out of his office with Detective Garrity close behind him. As they speed-walked across the lobby, trying not to break into a run in case they alarmed any of the guests, Detective Garrity took out his cellphone and spoke to Detective Mullard.

'Kevin, I'm down on the first floor. Haul your ass down here pronto and bring those two forensics with you. No – tell them to drop whatever it is they're doing and get on down here now. The staff restrooms on the first floor. The women's. Reception will tell you.'

Then he called the second precinct for backup. 'No, I don't know for sure. Possible fatality, but no cadaver yet. Whatever it is, we're going to need all the help we can get.'

The women's restroom was halfway along a corridor in the first-floor annex which housed most of The Red Hotel's live-in staff. Six or seven of them were milling around, whispering to each other, looking shocked. The restroom door was halfway open and Clarice Johnson was standing outside it, trying to appear calm and in control, but Everett could tell at once that she was just as shaken as the others. She kept twisting her black bead necklace as if she were trying to strangle herself.

Everett introduced her to Detective Garrity. Clarice said, 'I'm so sorry, Mr Everett, sir. I had no idea nothing like this was going to happen.'

Detective Garrity said, 'Of course you didn't, ma'am. How could you.' Then he said, 'I understand how upset you are, but how about trying to describe what you saw when you first walked in there.'

Clarice twisted her necklace one way, and then the other. 'I push open the door and call out, "Ella-mae, girl, you *still* in here? What's the matter witchew?" But then the very first thing I saw was blood, and it was all over. Up the wall, all across the floor. Even on the *ceiling*, Lord help us.'

'Did you go in any further?'

'Well, for sure, to see if Ella-mae was hurt. I walk in and I'm having to go on my tippy-toes because of all the blood on the floor. I push open the cubicles one by one but there ain't no Ella-mae. If that blood is hers, I don't know how she could have gotten out of there because anybody who lose that much blood must be dead as a doornail. I don't know. Maybe somebody carry her out, or drag her out.'

Detective Garrity looked up and down the corridor, with its gold-carpeted floor. 'However she got out of there, whether she walked or whether she was carried, she couldn't have come this way. There isn't a single spot of blood on this carpet.'

He looked down at Clarice's feet. She was wearing only white socks.

'What happened to your shoes, ma'am? The shoes you were wearing when you walked into the restroom.'

'I took them off. They was all bloody on the bottom so I took them off.'

'You still got them? You didn't wash them or nothing?'

'No, sir. I got them in a shopping bag.'

'Good for you. Our forensics people will want to examine them, to compare your footprints.'

'What with?'

'Anybody else's footprints, obviously. Ella-mae's, if that was Ella-mae in there, and whoever attacked her and subsequently disposed of her.'

Clarice shook her head. 'I didn't see no other footprints, sir. That restroom floor, that was shiny like a red mirror.'

'You're sure about that?'

'I can see it in my mind's eye, sir. Clear like day.'

'OK, ma'am,' Detective Garrity told her. He nearly rested a reassuring hand on her shoulder but then he drew it back. 'If you can stick around for a while. I may need to talk to you some more.'

'I ain't going noplace,' Clarice reassured him. 'I live here.'

Detective Garrity took a pair of fawn latex gloves out of his inside coat pocket, and made a fastidious performance of snapping them on. His voice may have been flat but all his gestures were very showy. He pushed the door of the restroom wide open, so that they could see right inside. Everett said, '*Jesus.*'

There was a small vestibule and then a second door, which was also wide open. Beyond that, Everett could see the edge of the wall beside the washbasins, part of a washbasin, and about a quarter of one of the mirrors. There was bright red blood all the way up the wall, in loops and spatters and squiggles, and even blood across the ceiling, as Clarice had told them. The mirror was smeared with blood as if somebody's hair had been forcibly pressed against it and then wiped from side to side. There were even two or three handprints on it.

Clarice had been right about the floor, too. The white tiles were covered from one wall to another with glassy red, with only a few erratic footprints in it. From the size and pattern of the footprints, which looked like a sneaker about size 6.5, it didn't seem likely that anybody else had stepped into it but her.

Detective Mullard arrived, with the two CSIs, his pants flapping noisily as he came toward them.

'Where we at, Slim?'

Detective Garrity nodded his head toward the open restroom door.

'*Blood,*' he said. 'That's where we're at.'

Everett had only just returned to his office when his phone rang. He picked it up and Bella said, 'Your sister again.'

'T-Yon? Hi, T-Yon. What is it now?'

'I'm coming down to BR. In fact we're *both* coming down to BR. Me and Billy's Aunt Sissy.'

'T-Yon, it's always great to see you, but why? You're right in the middle of your cookery course. And why are you bringing this old lady with you?'

'You're in danger, Ev. I know it. You're in danger and only Aunt Sissy knows what kind of danger.'

'T-Yon, I don't have any problems that I can't deal with by myself. I'm opening up a hotel, for Christ's sake. You always get teething troubles.'

'The red, Ev. It's blood.'

'What? What did you say?'

'You know that Aunt Sissy said that you were worried, and that it was all to do with The Red Hotel, and that it was red?'

'Oh, come on, T-Yon. I'm having a hard time finding the exact right shade of red velvet for the cushion covers for the lobby, that's all. You have no idea how many different kinds of red there are. Crimson, cerise, candy apple, magenta.'

'You're lying to me, Ev. Aunt Sissy is absolutely sure that it's blood.'

Everett sat up straight. 'T-Yon, the distance between wherever you are in Connecticut and Baton Rouge has got to be more than a thousand miles. Be serious. How the hell can this Aunt Sissy or whatever the old biddy's name is tell from over a thousand miles away that it's blood?'

'Because she's sensitive to things like that. Because she can.'

'T-Yon, forget it. There is no need for you to come down here and there is definitely no need for you to come down here and bring some elderly whackjob with you. I'm sorry.'

'She heard that. I have my speaker switched on.'

'All right then, sorry. Tell her I apologize. I don't even know her.'

There was a few seconds' pause, during which Everett could hear nothing but clicking and scratching sounds, as if T-Yon had her hand held over the phone, with all of her rings on.

Then she said, 'Grover.'

'What?'

'Wait up a second. Aunt Sissy says, does the name "Grover" mean anything to you?'

'No,' said Everett. 'The only Grover I know is that screechy blue monster from *Sesame Street*. Please, T-Yon, I'm real busy right now. I *do* have problems but they're practical problems. You know, like down-to-earth problems. I can't get my head around all of this psychic gibberish.'

'We're still coming. We're booked on the thirteen-fifteen Continental flight from La Guardia, tomorrow afternoon. We have to connect at Houston but we should be with you for six thirty.'

'What about Hurricane Debby?'

'I checked with the airline. It's pretty much blown itself out.'

'T-Yon—'

'There's nothing you can do to stop me, Ev. I'll see you tomorrow, OK?'

With that, she switched off her phone. Everett was tempted to call back but then he said, '*Shit*,' and dropped his phone on to his desk. He knew T-Yon better than that. Once she had made up her mind to do something, she always did it big, no matter what it was.

He was about to call Bella about his scheduled breakfast tomorrow morning with Bobby Lamb from *The Baton Rouge Advocate* when Detective Mullard knocked and stepped into his office before he could say, 'Come on in.'

Detective Mullard sniffed loudly and said, 'Just to let you know that we've checked through all of the hotel staff on your duty roster today and Ella-mae is the only one not accounted for.'

'I see. Do your CSIs have any idea what happened in that restroom?'

'They're leaning toward the opinion that somebody got themselves pretty comprehensively killed.'

'But you're still not one hundred percent sure who it was? Or where their body disappeared to?'

'Not yet, sir, no. We've already sent two officers to Ella-mae's home address in order to check that she simply didn't get bored with waiting around here. And if she's not there, alive and well, or if her folks don't know for certain where she is, then those officers have been instructed to bring back a hairbrush so that the CSIs can check for DNA.'

'All right,' said Everett. 'What else?'

'We're going to have to tape off the door from your main lobby to the staff annex.'

'Tape off? What do you mean – "crime scene do not cross"? Jesus, that's going to be great for business, not. Can't you just lock the door so nobody can get in?'

'I'm sorry, sir. Has to be done. Procedure.'

Everett closed his eyes for a moment. *Please God let this all be a nightmare. Please God let me open up my eyes and discover that none of it ever happened. No blood-soaked rug. No eerie whistling in the corridors. No restroom turned into a human abattoir.*

Detective Mullard's cellphone played *Hey, Fighting Tigers*, the theme tune of the LSU Tigers. 'Pardon me,' he said, and answered it.

Everett waited impatiently while Detective Mullard said, 'Sure thing,' and 'sure thing,' and 'gotcha', and 'great.' In the end he slid his cell shut and said, 'Nobody knows where Ella-mae could possibly be right now. She didn't go home, and she hasn't been in touch with any of her friends. As a rule, she's texting and tweeting every five minutes or so.'

'So what now?' asked Everett.

'We start searching for her. Mr and Mrs Grover have given us some recent pictures of her, and what we'll do is circulate them, here inside the hotel if we can count on you to cooperate with that, and anyplace else she might have gone to. Or been taken to.'

'Mr and Mrs *Grover*?'

'That's right. That's her parents. That's her name, Ella-mae Grover.'

'Shit,' said Everett.

Detective Mullard frowned at him and said, 'Sir? Is there anything wrong?'

'I don't know,' Everett told him. 'I truly don't know. Suddenly I don't even know the difference between wrong and right.'

Flight to Red Stick

Hurricane Debby had almost blown itself out, but the first two hours of the flight from New York to Houston were still wildly turbulent. Sissy and T-Yon had to keep their seat belts fastened as the 737 jolted and bumped through thick cloud cover, and Sissy had to hold her glass of wine tight to stop it from spilling across her tray. She was tempted to ask the flight attendant if they could make an unauthorized stopover at Washington, DC, so that she could smoke two or three cigarettes to steady her nerves.

'I just hope that Everett isn't *too* mad about my taking you down to meet him,' said T-Yon. She was wearing a gray silk headscarf and absolutely no make-up, but she still looked striking. 'He has a very short fuse, but I guess that's what makes him a really good manager.'

'Don't you worry,' said Sissy, patting her hand. 'I believe that he's going to be extremely relieved to see us. He didn't want to upset you, that's all, but I can tell you for sure that he's deeply worried.'

'Do you still think that what you saw was *blood*?'

Sissy nodded. 'Absolutely,' she said. 'No doubt about it whatsoever.'

She had read her own cards, and she had been overwhelmed with red: drowned in it, almost. Red skies, red flags, red ribbons, cardinals dressed in red and cups overflowing with human blood. After she had done that, she had turned to her Alphabet Cards, which had the same latent force as a ouija board, except that the answers they gave were always proper names. She had learned long ago that finding out who you were going to meet in the future was equally valuable as knowing what was going to happen to you – if not more so, in many cases.

When she had dealt out the cards, two names had come up: SLIDER and GROVER. The name SLIDER she already knew, so she shuffled the cards and put them back in the pack. But the name GROVER meant nothing to her, so she dealt out the cards again. The letters G – R – O – V – E – R had come out in sequence, but sometimes the Alphabet Cards made deliberate mistakes, and a name would be spelled wrongly, like PERSONA instead of PEARSON; or they would give her a clue to a name rather than the name itself, like TENOR for the name SINGER. The cards weren't simply being mischievous; they were subtly giving her more information about the people she would soon encounter, and how to deal with them.

But GROVER had come out again, and then again, spelled exactly the same way. That told her nothing, except a name. Eventually, she had tried collating all six cards together, still in the same order, and picking out different cards at random. Now at last the cards had started to speak to her – or rather, to whisper in her ear. Card number three had been V, when it should have been O. Card number five had been R, when it should have been E.

The cards had been telling her something critical. Whoever GROVER was, he or she was no longer in one piece. GROVER, like the six cards that made up GROVER's name, was all cut up, disassembled, either metaphorically or literally. That was why she had told T-Yon to mention GROVER when she was talking on the phone to Everett, to see how he had reacted.

The flight attendant brought Sissy another miniature bottle of wine, and an orange soda for T-Yon.

'Don't you miss the South?' Sissy asked T-Yon. 'I've visited Savannah a few times, to stay with my old school friend Ruth, and every time I've been there I've never wanted to leave.'

T-Yon shrugged. 'I *do* miss it, but then again I don't. When I'm in BR, I always feel like the days are sliding past and the next thing I know I'm going to look in the mirror one morning and I'll be old and I won't have done anything. At least in New York I feel awake all the time, and that I'm getting on with my life. You know – like actually doing something, instead of dreaming my life away.'

'You were born in Lafayette, though?'

'Even dreamier, Lafayette.'

'When did you move to Baton Rouge?'

'My parents split up. Well, my Poppa walked out on my Momma. He was a teacher at Lafayette High. He left her for some older woman, I never really found out why. My Momma was beautiful. I mean she was really, *really* beautiful. But she was left to bring up me and Everett by herself, and she had to struggle so hard.

'She had plenty of men wanting to court her, especially one of her cousins, who was called Sam Boudreaux. He was disgusting. It would be an insult to pigs to call him a pig. All greasy hair parted in the middle and red face and white suits with sweaty patches under his arms. He kept coming around almost every day and one evening I think he raped Momma or at least he tried to rape her. She would never talk about it. Whichever it was we packed up the very next day and left Lafayette and moved to BR.'

The plane was flying more steadily now, and suddenly the sun broke through the windows. Sissy's wild gray hair shone silver, and all of her necklaces and bangles sparkled.

'You *lost* your Momma, though, didn't you?' she asked T-Yon. 'When was that?'

'Everett was twelve and I was five. First of all Momma got a job at a grocery store and we lived in back of the grocery store and we liked that even though the rooms were so shabby. But then something happened, I don't know what, and the manager accused Momma of stealing groceries and she lost that job. Maybe he came on to her and she said no.

'She managed to get another job for a cleaning company and we lived in this one room, but the worst thing was that she was out for most of the night and she was sleeping for most of the day and we hardly ever got to see her. Then she got really sick and they took her into hospital and me and Everett had to stay at this children's home. Then one afternoon when we came home from school they told us that Momma had died. We never even got to say goodbye.'

'I'm sorry,' said Sissy. 'I know it was a long time ago but it must still hurt.'

T-Yon looked across at her and smiled but there were tears in her eyes. 'Yes, it does. I have pictures of her and it wasn't just my imagination that she was beautiful.'

She paused for a few moments, wiping her tears with the back of her hand. Sissy could have offered to get in touch with her late mother's resonance, but she didn't think that now was the time. They had other, more immediate problems to deal with first. Like blood.

T-Yon said, 'About six months after Momma passed, we were taken into foster care by George and Renée Savoie. They were the couple who started the Red Bean Restaurant chain, and they had never had the time to have children of their own. Great people. Great, great people. Warm, loving, very hard-working but always cheerful. After a year they adopted us; and that's how we became Everett and Lilian Savoie.'

'That's wonderful,' said Sissy. 'I always like a happy ending.'

'Oh God,' said T-Yon. 'Let's hope this all turns out happy.'

Luther was waiting for them as they came out of the baggage claim area. He was wearing mirror sunglasses and a very white short-sleeved shirt. The air conditioning inside the airport was ferocious but outside Sissy could see the glare of a hot Louisiana afternoon.

'Where you at, Ms T-Yon? And you Ms Sawyer, correct?'

'That's right,' said Sissy. 'But why don't you call me Sissy? I've never been one for formality. By the way, I'm sorry about your loss.'

Luther had taken the luggage cart from T-Yon and had started pushing it toward the entrance. It had one squeaky wheel. 'My *loss*, ma'am?' he asked.

'You lost a pet quite recently. A dog, wasn't it?'

'That's right. My old bloodhound, Hooker. Named him for John Lee Hooker. But how'd you know that?'

'Because you still miss him, that's why, and if there's one thing that nobody can ever hide, it's grieving. Of course it's always more pronounced if it's a *person* that you've lost, rather than a pet, but it's grieving all the same.'

'Well, brush my feet,' said Luther. 'You and my Aunt Epiphany ought to get together. She's all into this mind-reading and fortune-telling and spellificating. She even perdicted the exact day and the exact hour when my grandpa was going to breathe his last, and he did. Five after eleven in the morning on the twenty-first of February, nineteen ninety-seven. I'll never forget it.'

They walked out into thirty-three degree heat and eighty-percent humidity. There was only one cloud in the sky, a long thin wisp of cirrus that looked as if an angel in tattered robes were sailing past, high above them, heading for someplace far to the north. Luther led them across to the curb, where a white Ford S-Max was parked, with *The Red Hotel* logo on the side of it in sloping red italics.

Luther stowed their luggage, and then they climbed in and drove south on Veterans Memorial Boulevard to join Interstate 110, which would take them into the center of Baton Rouge.

'This mind-reading stuff,' said Luther, his eyes floating in his rear-view mirror. 'Is that something you naturally born with, or can you learn it?'

'Bit of both, I think,' Sissy told him. 'Some people have the facility but never use it because they don't understand what they've got, and some people never use it because they're scared to. I have to admit, it can be pretty scary at times.'

Luther twisted himself around in the driver's seat. 'Scary? Let me tell you, Ms Sissy, when you find out what's been happening at The Red Hotel, scary don't even get anywheres close.'

'Give me a for-instance,' said Sissy.

'Well, I'm not sure that I should. I gave my solemn promise to Mister Everett that I wouldn't discuss with you none of what's been going on, not till he has the chance to talk to you himself.'

'All right, please yourself.'

Luther frowned at her for a moment, but then he said, 'Still and all – I guess it wouldn't hurt. Like, even the poh-lice are involved right now, so it's more or less out in the public domain.'

'OK,' Sissy told him. 'But I really would prefer it if you kept your eyes on the road ahead of you while you're driving. You don't have to be psychic to predict a fatal rear-end collision.'

Luther turned back round so that he was looking where he was going. 'I'm sorry. The thing is that I believe that something seriously weird is going on, but Mr Everett is trying his darndest to play it down because we're all ready for the grand opening tomorrow and he's worried we might have to postpone it, or even scrub it altogether.'

'The blood,' said Sissy.

'The blood? You know about that, too? How the *heck* you know about that?'

'I've seen it in the cards, Luther. Red, red and more red. When the cards come up with that much red, that means blood. Plain and unequivocal.'

As they circled around the on-ramp to join the interstate, Luther started to tell them all about the bloodstained bedside rug and the smears of blood on the walls of the staircase, and the inexplicable whistling noise, and the disappearance of Ella-mae Grover, with all the blood in the ladies' restroom.

'Ella-mae *Grover*?' said T-Yon, looking at Sissy with her eyes wide.

'That's right. Ella-mae Grover. Why you sound so surprised?'

'Because Sissy saw that name in her Alphabet Cards. And she predicted that somebody called Grover would be all chopped up.'

Luther stared at Sissy in his rear-view mirror. He was still staring at her when a huge red semi thundered past them in the inside lane, blaring its air-horns. Luther swerved, and then straightened up, and said, 'Sorry – *sorry*! Jesus. I'm real glad that you've taken the trouble to come down here, Ms Sissy. I mean that. I think we sorely need the services of somebody like you, and we need them urgent.'

'Let's just get to The Red Hotel in one piece, shall we?' said Sissy. 'I might be able to contact the spirit world, but I'm not quite ready to go there. Not yet awhile.'

The Presence of Terror

When they arrived outside The Red Hotel, they saw that half of Convention Street along the 200 block was cordoned off by yellow police tapes. Five squad cars were parked facing the curb, as well as a dark blue panel van from the forensic unit, and assorted cars and vans from WAFB 9 and WBRZ television stations and WJBO radio. The sidewalks were crowded with onlookers.

A warm breeze from the Mississippi, only a block to the west, set the police tapes flapping like applause, so that the atmosphere sounded almost festive.

'So much for playing it down,' said Sissy.

'The poh-lice put out a statewide media appeal for Ella-mae,' Luther told her. 'And you know what folks are like. If something horrible has happened, they got to come along and gawp, even if they never get to see nothing. Look at them. You'd have thought they had something better to do.'

A police officer unwound one of the tapes for them so that they could drive through and park on Lafayette Street, next to the hotel's side entrance. Luther heaved himself out of the driver's seat and led them inside. They crossed the lobby, where police and reporters were milling around, as well as several unhappy-looking guests, and made their way to Everett's office. Compared to the street outside, the inside of the hotel was icy cold, and Sissy couldn't help herself from giving one quick shiver.

Everett was talking to Detective Garrity when Sissy and T-Yon and Luther came into his office. His red necktie was loose and his shirt was crumpled and his hair was even more mussed up than usual. His eyes looked puffy, too, as if he hadn't slept well.

He came around his desk and gave T-Yon a hug and a kiss.

'So, *pischouette,* you came here anyhow! As if I didn't know you would!' Then he turned to Sissy and said, 'Hi there. Welcome to The Red Hotel. You must be my sister's boyfriend's psychic aunt.'

'Got it in one,' said Sissy, holding out her hand. 'I'm pleased to meet you, Everett, regardless of the circumstances. You can call me Sissy. It's easier than saying "my sister's boyfriend's psychic aunt" every time.'

Detective Garrity came over and clasped her hand too. 'Detective Garrity, Baton Rouge Police Department,' he announced himself. 'Mr Savoie here tells me you're something of a fortune-teller-slash-clairvoyant-slash-medium type.'

'That's roughly about right,' said Sissy. 'One of those fortune-teller-slash-clairvoyant-slash-medium types that you're extremely suspicious of, considering your past dealings with such people.'

Detective Garrity's little black turtle eyes seemed to shrink to pinpoints. 'Oh, yeah. And how would you happen to know that?'

'Because I'm a fortune-teller-slash-clairvoyant-medium type, and because I'm very good at reading people's auras. Everybody has an aura, and the moment you saw me and realized who I was, Detective Garrity, your aura went as dark as the sun going down.'

'Oh yeah. And what did you surmise was the significance of that?'

'It told me very explicitly that you don't hold psychics in very high regard, and the most likely reason for *that* is because sometime in the not-too-distant past you have had an unpleasant or humiliating experience involving a psychic. Or fortune-teller-slash-whatever.'

Detective Garrity stared at Sissy with those little pinpoint eyes for a very long moment. Then he gave her a very thin smile and said, 'Good. You're good. Even if you're right, and I don't hold psychics in very high regard.'

T-Yon said, 'Luther told us what's been happening here. I really think that Sissy can help you to find out who's responsible. Or *what*.'

Everett glanced sharply at Luther, but Luther pulled a face and said, 'They was going to find out sooner rather than later, so why not? Trying to keep a lid on it ain't going to make one smidgen of difference, is it?'

'You don't think so? Detective Garrity has just been telling me that we may have to evacuate the entire hotel.'

'I'm afraid that's right,' said Detective Garrity. 'Even though we haven't discovered any cadavers yet, the amount of blood that we've encountered makes it highly probable that we're dealing with more than one act of homicide. It would be foolhardy in the extreme to allow guests to remain here in the hotel until we know for sure.'

'Terrific, isn't it?' said Everett. 'We haven't even officially opened and they're closing us down.'

'How many guests are we talking about?' asked T-Yon.

'Fifty-seven. But the last time I checked we had one hundred three booked in for tomorrow, and it could be more by now. Every single one of whom we will have to contact and tell that they can't stay here for our gala opening ceremony, complete with The Ralph Dickerson Jazz Ensemble and The Back Bayou Zydeco Quintet and enough crawfish to feed the entire population of Baton Rouge for the next six months, as well as appearances by his honor, Mayor Dolan, and his delectable daughter, Lolana, who happens to be Miss Teen Baton Rouge, and a stand-up comedy routine by the very pricey Jerry Lake, who will expect us to pay him whether he appears or not.'

'Don't look on the black side just yet awhile,' said Detective Garrity. 'Right now we're regarding the entire hotel as a crime scene, but once the forensics people have finished checking for bloodstains and fingerprints and any other circumstantial evidence, we may be able to give you a partial all-clear. For the guest rooms and the public areas, anyhow.'

At that moment, Bella slid back her window and said, 'Excuse me, boss. Sorry to interrupt but I've just had a call from Nesta at reception. She has at least thirty guests lining up to check out and cancel the rest of their reservations, and demanding a refund.'

'Shit,' said Everett.

'Looks like you won't have to evacuate the hotel after all,' said Detective Garrity. 'Looks like your guests are doing the evacuating for you.'

Everett sat down behind his desk. 'That's it. We're finished. We're totally wiped out. How the hell are we going to get over something like this?'

Luther said, 'Plenty of hotels have murders in them, and they don't go out of business.'

'Oh yeah? Name one.'

Sissy came up to his desk and said, 'I imagine that you've searched the whole building?'

Everett looked up at her as if he were tempted to say something deeply sarcastic, but then he said, as courteously as he could, 'Yes, Sissy. You did say your name was "Sissy", didn't you? Yes, we've searched the whole building. First of all our security team went through it, and now the police have gone through it, and what they found was absolutely zilch.'

'All the same, there *is* something here.'

'What do you mean? Something like what?'

Detective Garrity was leaning against the filing cabinet with his arms folded and a toothpick in his mouth. He took out the toothpick and said, 'I think Ms Sissy here is talking about a spirit, if I'm not mistaken. That's what I was told when I was out looking for a woman who was supposed to have been strangled in a house on Spain Street in the Garden District.'

'A *spirit*?'

'That's right. There was no trace whatsoever of a cadaver, but this psychic gentleman swore to me that her spirit was still in the house, and that he could hear her talking to him. On the basis of that and some circumstantial forensics we arrested her former husband and charged him with homicide. Whereupon the strangled woman herself appeared at the precinct and said that she had never felt healthier.'

Sissy turned and gave him a smile. 'I'm sorry for what happened to you, Detective. I'll admit that there are plenty of so-called psychics who simply take advantage of people's need and gullibility. But there are some sensitives who really know their stuff.'

'So how do we know which kind are you?'

'You don't. Not until I get results. It's the same for detectives, wouldn't you say? You get your highly competent detectives but you also get your so-called detectives who mostly get by on bluster and bluff. I know. I used to be married to a cop.'

Detective Garrity plainly didn't like that response. Still leaning against the filing cabinet, he said, 'When you say "results", what kind of "results" are you talking about?'

'I'm talking about finding out what's going on here, and as quickly as possible, before anybody else gets hurt. If people have been murdered here, we need to know who did it, and why, and how they managed to get away with it.'

'And how do you propose to do that, exactly?'

Sissy turned back to Everett. 'With your permission, I'd

like to search through this entire hotel until I've found what I'm looking for.'

'You mean like spooky voices in the walls,' said Detective Garrity. 'And what makes you think that I'm going to authorize you to wander around a crime scene listening for ghosts?'

He cupped one hand to his ear, and said, 'Hallo. Is there anybody there?' He meant it as a joke, but his voice was so flat and his eyes were so humorless that nobody so much as grunted.

The Night Visitors

Everett took Sissy and T-Yon into the Showboat Saloon so that they could have a drink and something to eat. The saloon was decorated like the interior of a turn-of-the-century paddle steamer, with a wide staircase and a galleried landing running all the way around. Eight sparkling chandeliers were suspended from the ceiling and the room was furnished with red plush banquettes. There was a long mahogany bar with engraved mirrors behind it and bottles of every kind of liquor. Sissy could almost imagine Clark Gable coming down the stairs with a white bow-tie and a cigar.

As they sat down, Everett explained that a jazz quartet would usually be playing on the small stage at the end of the saloon, and the tables all around them would be packed. This evening, however, there was only the three of them, apart from two waitresses and a barman, and the room was almost completely silent.

'You can pretty much order what you like,' Everett told them. 'I've kept on three chefs in the kitchen because we still have to feed the maintenance crew and all the security guys, plus we'll have at least fifteen cops in the building until the crime-scene people are done with what they're doing, and they're going to get hungry.'

T-Yon asked for a vegetable omelet with hash brown potatoes and biscuits, while Sissy chose a crab asiago bisque, which was a rich soup made with lumps of crabmeat, butter and cream. She was supposed to be on a diet. She was *always* on a diet – spinach, mostly. But she doubted if she would ever visit Baton Rouge again in her life – that's if she survived *this* visit – so she decided that she might as well indulge herself.

Even as she ate, however, she couldn't shake off the feeling that there was a *presence* in this hotel. She had never felt such cold hostility in any building before, and it wasn't just the frigid air conditioning. It was almost as if somebody were covertly watching them, and narrowing their eyes with jealousy and hatred at every move they made. She couldn't help herself from turning her head around, now and again, to see if she could catch anybody looking their way, but there was nobody there, apart from the bartender. All of the other tables were set with cutlery and glasses, but deserted.

'Something wrong, Sissy?' asked T-Yon, after a while. 'You don't like your soup?'

'Oh goodness, no!' said Sissy. 'The soup is heavenly. But what I was saying before – about there being some kind of *atmosphere* here – I can still sense it very strongly, even now. In fact stronger than ever. I don't know how else to describe it. I hesitate to call it a spirit.'

Everett was forking up rice and red beans. 'I'm sorry, Sissy. No disrespect meant. But I really don't believe in spirits.'

'You don't feel anything yourself?'

'I feel angry. I feel frustrated. I feel devastated that we may not be able to open tomorrow.'

'But you don't feel anything else? You don't feel when you walk around this hotel that somebody is resentful about you being here? Because that's the feeling that I'm picking up on.'

'Oh, come on, Sissy, who could possibly be resentful? Stanley and me, I think we've done an amazing job, remodeling. We've improved the whole district. We've given jobs to over a hundred seventy local people, of all ethnic backgrounds. I think we've brought something back that the riverside district has been missing for years. All of the other hotels are state-of-the-art modern. But The Red Hotel, it's fun, it's flamboyant. You should see some of the reviews we've had already. Four stars and we're not technically open yet.'

'Good for you,' said Sissy. 'But I'd still like to take a look around, if you'll allow me. I mean, it's quite possible that I'm mistaken, but I really don't think so. I'm convinced that there's something here that the crime-scene technicians just won't be able to see, no matter how much Luminol they spray around.'

'You'll have to wait until the cops say it's OK,' Everett told her, wiping his mouth with his napkin. 'But, well – my stubborn little sister has taken the trouble to bring you all the way down here, and I guess you can't do any harm. That's so long as you don't let on to anybody else what you're doing . . . especially the guests, if and when we get them back in. I'd rather they weren't aware that you're looking for some kind of evil manifestation.'

'Now, then,' Sissy corrected him. 'I never said for sure that it was evil. Sometimes the most bothersome spirits are the spirits who are trying to do good, and to make amends for transgressions they committed when they were still alive.'

'In that case, *phew*,' said Everett, mopping his forehead in mock relief.

'But don't let's count any chickens,' Sissy cautioned him. 'If that blood *is* human blood, then the chances are that this spirit or presence or whatever it is *does* have malign intentions. Not just malign, but murderous, too.'

'But why?' asked Everett.

'Because many people who have passed over harbor deep feelings of envy for people who are still alive; and a few of them actually want to do them harm.'

'You mean dead people want to murder live people?'

'That's about it.'

Everett said, 'I can't believe I'm having this conversation. Like I told you before, Sissy, I don't believe in *any* of it. Spirits, after-lives—'

'Not even God?'

He shook his head, emphatically. 'Not even God. I was brought up a Baptist, but with a little bit of Roman Catholicism thrown in. Our Momma always made sure we went to church on Sundays; and when she died, and we were adopted by the Savoies, they still insisted that we went to church. You want to hear me sing *Oh, Happy Day*?'

'No, no. You don't have to do that. I'll take your word for it.'

At that moment Detective Garrity came across the saloon, with Detective Mullard close behind him. Detective Mullard was vigorously blowing his nose.

'Hi folks,' said Detective Garrity. 'Not too bad news. The forensics team are done checking the second and third floors, so if you need accommodation for yourselves tonight, those are the floors to head for. No guests tonight, Mr Savoie, but it looks like there's an outside chance that you may be able to reopen and hold your opening ceremony tomorrow, as planned.'

'So the CSIs didn't find anything?' asked Everett.

Detective Garrity shook his head. 'Nope. Not on either of those two floors, anyhow. And believe me they have more than a dozen technicians up there, dusting every door handle for fingerprints and checking every inch of carpet for blood spatter.'

He looked across the table at Sissy, as if he expected her to challenge him, and ask, *How about spirits? Did they check for spirits?* But Sissy knew when it was important to keep people on side, and she thought that it was better for her to say nothing at all. *The time might well come when I need your help, Detective Garrity, and I'm not going to put your back up just to score a point.*

'OK,' said Detective Garrity. 'We've carried out another thorough search of the entire hotel – floor by floor and room by room – and this time we brought in the tracker dogs, too, just to make sure. We even checked the a/c vents and the laundry disposal chutes. We're now one hundred percent sure that Ella-mae Grover is no longer in the building; and neither are any unauthorized personnel. If somebody murdered Ella-mae, which is still the likeliest scenario, he or she somehow managed to take her cadaver out of the hotel and dispose of it elsewhere.'

'All the same, the hotel will be guarded by officers from the BRPD throughout the night, as well as your own security people, and I'll come back to see you tomorrow morning, Mr Savoie, sir, and discuss the situation with you then.'

'So we may be able to hold our opening gala after all?' asked Everett.

'Unless some dramatic new evidence turns up, maybe you will. Enjoy your meal, folks. And *dormez bien*.'

They stayed in the saloon, drinking and talking, until well past midnight. T-Yon tried to explain to Everett about the reading that Sissy had given her with the DeVane cards, and how she had seen *La Châtelaine*, the woman she took to be Vanessa Slider, and her son, Shem. She told him about the distressed faces that she had seen in the grass, and the blood, and how she had seen Everett himself waving a red flag for help. She even told him about the ghostly apparitions that they had seen in Sissy's living room, the blurry white images that had flickered in front of them, and then faded.

Everett said, 'You told me you were having nightmares, too. What was that about?'

T-Yon blushed. 'I'll tell you later, when it's just you and me.'

'You know what I think?' said Everett. 'I think this catering course of yours is putting a whole lot more pressure on you than you realize. You're in a strange place, far away from home. You've found yourself a brand new boyfriend. That's why you're having nightmares. You're, like, disoriented. Your brain is still trying to make some sense of it all.'

'If it's all in my head,' T-Yon retorted, 'how come the DeVane cards came up with all of those predictions about Vanessa Slider, and this hotel? How come Sissy feels that there's some kind of atmosphere here? How come she knew Ella-mae's name was Grover? Sissy never met me before. She never even knew who I was.'

Everett shrugged, and took a mouthful of Heaven Hill whiskey. 'Don't ask me, boo. Like I said, I don't disrespect anybody who believes in the supernatural, and fortune-telling. I check my own horoscope every morning in the *Advocate* – not that it ever turns out to be the remotest bit accurate. But what's been happening here – the bloody rug, the whistling, Ella-mae going missing – there has to be some rational explanation for it. Maybe it's going to take some lateral thinking to find out who's behind it. But, so far as I'm concerned, it's a *who*. It's a real person. Not a spirit, not a ghost. A real, genuine, living and breathing person. Vanessa Slider, come on, T-Yon. Be serious.'

Sissy drained her glass of wine, and stood up. 'We'll have to see, won't we, Everett? To be honest with you, I very much hope that you're right. At this particular moment, though, I think I badly need to get some sleep. Do you think you can show me where my room is?'

'I'll join you,' said T-Yon. 'I'm exhausted.'

Everett went to his office to check which rooms they had been allocated, and then took them up in the elevator to the second floor. One of the hotel's security team was sitting opposite the elevator doors, reading *Sports Illustrated,* a huge African-American in a red shirt and black pants. He stood up when they appeared, but Everett said, 'It's OK, Samuel. Just make sure that you keep your eye on these ladies for me, that's all.'

'Sure will, Mr Everett, sir.'

Everett showed them to rooms 209 and 211, which were adjacent to each other at the end of the second-floor corridor.

Before they went inside, T-Yon hugged Everett tight and said, 'You're really not mad at me, are you, Ev, for bringing Sissy?'

'Of course not. It's great to see you. And, like I say, I can't see Sissy causing us any problems, so long as she doesn't tell anybody that this is more than a social visit.'

'My lips are sealed,' Sissy promised him.

Sissy found that her case had already been brought up to the room for her. She unpacked, and then she undressed and put on her long cotton nightdress with the tiny pink rosebuds on it. The room wasn't large, but it was lavishly furnished, with heavy velvet drapes and a marble-topped dressing table and a bedspread with scarlet and gold embroidery.

She went into the bathroom to start running herself a bath and to let down her hair. Maybe it was tiredness, but when she looked at herself in the mirror over the washbasin she thought she was looking very old, with papery skin and eyes that were losing their blue. She could still remember how pretty she had been, but that seemed like a long, long time ago.

She thought about Frank, too. She could remember how his hand had felt, when he stood behind her and put it on her shoulder, and then kissed the nape of her neck. They had been married for thirty-seven years, but now that seemed like a distant memory, too, dwindling smaller and smaller with every passing day.

'Frank,' she said, just to hear his name.

T-Yon opened her eyes. Her room was almost completely dark, except for the glow of the standby light on the TV and the illuminated numbers on the bedside clock. It was 2.43 a.m.

She lay there for almost a minute, not moving. She was sure that she had heard a noise, or felt something bumping into the bed, and that was what had woken her up. She listened and listened, straining her ears, but all she could hear was the echoing sound of traffic on Convention Street and the rumbling of a jet at BTR, seven miles away.

No, she thought, *I must have been dreaming. At least I wasn't having that nightmare about Everett.* She turned over, plumped up her pillow and closed her eyes, but almost as soon as she had done so, she heard a rustle, and a whisper.

She froze. She was sure that she could hear somebody breathing – quick, suppressed breaths, like an anxious child. *Maybe it's my own breathing,* she thought. *Maybe that rustle was nothing more than the amplified noise of the sheet against my ear.*

She held her breath and listened even more intently. Only the sounds of the city outside. No rustling, no breathing. *I'm doing it again. I'm letting my imagination run away with me. Maybe I'm asleep right now, and I'm dreaming this.*

But then she heard a soft bump, like somebody accidentally walking into a chair. She leaned over sideways and reached for the old-fashioned lamp on the nightstand, but at first she couldn't find it. She swung her arm from left to right, knocking the bedside clock on to the floor, and then tipping the lamp over. It fell against the wall and she heard the bulb shatter.

She sat up, pulling the bedcover right up to her neck. She was wearing only a T-shirt and she felt terrifyingly vulnerable.

'*Who's there?*' she demanded, trying to sound angry rather than afraid, but her voice came out breathy and broken.

Nobody answered. She strained her eyes, but now that the bedside clock had dropped on to the floor, the room was almost totally dark.

She began to shuffle herself over to the opposite side of the bed, where there was a second lamp, but before she could reach it she heard another rustling sound, and she stopped, and stared into the darkness even harder. She gradually made out two shapes that were even darker than the darkness itself, like two ghosts draped in black sheets rather than white. One was quite tall, but the other was small, like a child.

'*Who's there?*' she repeated, even though her throat was so constricted that she may not have been audible to the two dark figures standing in the middle of the room, if they were real, and not just a nightmare. '*Who are you? What do you want?*'

The figures said nothing, but continued to stand there, and all T-Yon could hear was the sound of their breathing.

Sleep Talking

S issy was dreaming that she was walking along the shore of Lake Candlewood with Frank. It was early fall, and the trees were turning, and their rusts and crimsons were perfectly reflected in the water. There was no wind, and the horse's tail clouds were unnaturally motionless.

For some reason, Frank stayed close behind her, so that she couldn't see him properly, although she could hear his footsteps crunching on the shingle path and she could hear him talking.

He said, 'We ought to bring out the sailboat, at least one more time before winter.'

Sissy stopped, and tried to look back at him over her shoulder, but he stayed tantalizingly out of sight. 'I *sold* the sailboat, Frank. Don't you remember? I sold it about six months after you died.'

That was what she had always found so strange about dead people, when they appeared in dreams. They never realized that they were dead.

She was about to carry on walking when she heard a frantic banging sound, and a girl's voice screaming out, '*Sissy! Sissy! Open the door! Sissy!*'

She woke up. The banging was real, and it was frantic.

'*Sissy! Open the door! Sissy!*'

Still half dreaming, Sissy climbed out of bed and groped her way across the room, her arms waving in front of her like a sleepwalker. She found the light switch and turned on the overhead lights. Then she drew back the security bolt and opened up the door. T-Yon came bursting in and immediately slammed the door behind her.

'Why, T-*Yon*! What on earth is the matter?'

T-Yon's hair was all messed up and her eyes were wide with panic. 'I saw them! They were in my room! I heard a noise and it woke me up and they were just *standing* there, at the end of my bed!'

'Here, hush, calm yourself down,' said Sissy. She took hold of T-Yon's arm and led her across to the bed.

T-Yon sat down and said, 'I've never been so scared in my life. Like, *never.*'

Sissy sat down next to her. 'My, you're shaking! Who were they? Don't you worry, I'll call that Samuel fellow.' She stood up again and went back toward the door.

'No!' said T-Yon. 'Don't open the door! They might still be out there!'

'But *who*, sweetheart? Who were they? This whole floor is supposed to be secure.'

'I know! I don't know how they could have gotten into my room! I had the chain on the door and everything!'

Sissy sat down again and put her arm around T-Yon's shoulders. 'Come on, hush, whoever they were and however they got into your room, they didn't hurt you, did they?'

T-Yon shook her head. She was quaking uncontrollably, as if she had been out without a coat on a bitter winter's night.

'Did they say anything to you?' asked Sissy. 'They didn't threaten you or anything? They didn't ask for your money, did they, or your jewelry?'

'They didn't speak,' said T-Yon. She tilted her head sideways so that she could wipe her eyes on the shoulder of her T-shirt. 'But I know I wasn't having a nightmare. At least I don't think that I was. I could hear them breathing, and one of them bumped into the chair.'

She turned to Sissy and said, 'I couldn't see who they were. Both of them were wearing these black sheets over their heads. One of them was quite tall, about my height, but the other was only about so high, like a child.'

'I think I *should* call that Samuel,' said Sissy. 'Whoever they were, they shouldn't have come into your room, even if they were only playing some kind of a sick joke.'

'Oh, God,' said T-Yon. 'You don't think it was Ev, do you, trying to scare me?'

'Your brother? Well, you know him a whole lot better than I do. Would he really do anything like that? He came across as much too serious-minded.'

'No, you're right, he wouldn't. Like, he was always teasing me, when we were growing up, but I can't see him doing anything as mean as that. Besides, he's far too busy, isn't he? And he's desperately worried about tomorrow.' She held up both hands. 'My God, look at me. I'm still shaking like a leaf.'

Sissy didn't have to call for the security guard. There was a knock at the door, and a deep voice said, 'Security, ma'am. Is everything OK?'

Sissy opened the door and Samuel was standing outside, holding a long black nightstick.

'Sorry if I'm bothering you, ma'am. I thought I heard some kind of disturbance, and the door to Two-Oh-Nine is open and there ain't nobody in there.'

'Ms Savoie here thought she saw some people in her room,' said Sissy. 'Apparently they were both wearing black sheets, an adult and a child.'

'They was wearing what?' asked Samuel, peering over Sissy's shoulder at T-Yon.

'Well – maybe they weren't sheets,' said T-Yon. 'They might have been cloaks, with hoods. I don't know. I couldn't see too well. It was dark, and I was scared out of my mind.'

'So, an adult, and a smaller individual, all dressed up in black? Did they speak to you?'

'No. Not a word.'

Samuel smacked his nightstick into the palm of his hand and looked back up the corridor with an exaggerated frown, his lips pursed, as if he were trying to think what to say to the boss's sister without suggesting that she had simply been dreaming.

In the end, he said, 'I have to tell you that I didn't see nobody coming along this corridor tonight, ma'am, big or small.'

'You're sure?'

'Positively positive, ma'am. 'Cause even if they didn't use the elevator, they would have had to pass by me to get to the stairs. And there's no way that nobody can climb out of none of these windows, not even a kid.'

'Could be they're still here, in another room,' Sissy suggested. 'If they could get into Ms Savoie's room, maybe they have a master key.'

'But I had the *chain* fastened,' said T-Yon. 'It was still fastened when I was trying to get out of there, and I had to slide it open myself.'

'You're sure you fastened it yourself, before you retired?' asked Samuel.

'I fastened it as soon as I got into the room. I always do.'

'Hm. Well. I'll tell you what I'll do. I'll go take a look in each unoccupied room, just to make sure there ain't nobody hiding in none of them.'

'You don't believe I saw anybody at all, do you?' said T-Yon.

'I haven't come to no conclusions at all, ma'am. My job description is security, not coming to conclusions. I'll go check, and then come back and give you the all-clear. OK?'

'I guess so,' said T-Yon. 'Thanks.'

'Don't mention it,' said Samuel, and went off jangling his keys.

They stayed up and talked until Samuel came back. He knocked at the door, and when Sissy opened it, he said, 'Nobody hiding in none of the rooms, ma'am. If those two individuals was here, I don't think they're still here now. But what I'll do is, I'll move my chair up closer so that I can keep an eye on your door.'

'All right,' said Sissy. 'Does that make you feel happier, T-Yon?'

T-Yon looked up at her, her eyelashes spiky with tears. 'Would you mind if I stayed here with you for the rest of the night? I'm really scared to go back to that room.'

'For sure, if that's what you want. And if you don't mind my snoring. Frank always said that I snored like a buffalo.'

Sissy turned to Samuel, and shrugged, and Samuel shrugged, too. 'Seems like that's settled, then,' he told her. 'Hope you sleep good.'

They climbed into bed and Sissy switched off the light. She lay there for a while, with her eyes open, wondering who it was that T-Yon had seen in her room. Unlike Samuel, she believed that T-Yon's black-sheeted visitors had been real, in the sense that T-Yon hadn't been dreaming, or hysterical. If the security chain had still been fastened, then it was likely that they had been spirits, or presences. Sissy had encountered enough of those in her life to know that the human soul can go on making itself felt long after the physical body has been buried, or cremated.

However, it was more logical to assume that they had been living people, and that somehow they had found a way to enter a locked hotel room. Sissy had known several stage magicians, and she had seen them apparently walk through walls and even plate-glass windows. The question was, why should anyone want to visit T-Yon in the middle of the night, whether they were living people or not?

After ten minutes or so, she heard T-Yon breathing slow and deep.

'T-Yon?' she said, very softly, but there was no answer.

T-Yon was asleep. Sissy turned over and closed her eyes. She hoped she didn't dream any more tonight, even if she dreamed about Frank, and Candlewood Lake. She knew that Frank's spirit was at peace, wherever he was, but sometimes she wished that he would let her go. He was never going to come back, not in the flesh, and she found it quite wearing these days, carrying around all of those memories of him, as happy as most of them were.

She fell asleep herself. Outside, Convention Street was almost completely silent, in that hour-long hiatus before sunrise and traffic started up again.

'Where have you *been*, Momma?' said T-Yon, quite loudly.

Sissy opened her eyes. It was beginning to grow light. It took her a few seconds to remember that T-Yon was sharing her bed, but when she did she turned her head and looked at her, to check if she was awake. T-Yon still had her back to her, so all that Sissy could see was her shoulder, in her pale gray T-shirt, and the back of her neck, and her tangled blonde hair.

She waited for a while. If T-Yon was simply talking in her sleep, she didn't want to wake her up. She was just about to turn over again when T-Yon said, 'Why do you always leave us alone at night, Momma? It's so *scary*.'

Another pause, and then T-Yon started speaking again, but this time in a different voice, huskier, with a much more pronounced Cajun accent.

'I have to, *beb*, you know that. We have to keep body and soul together somehow. Money doesn't grow in the garden.'

'But what do you *do* all night, Momma?' said T-Yon, reverting to her own voice. 'I don't understand.'

'I do cleaning, *beb*,' she replied, in that huskier tone. 'I clean buildings where people work, so that when they arrive first thing in the morning, their offices are all dusted and their washrooms are all sparkly.'

'I don't believe you, Momma. I think you do something *dirty*, not clean. All my friends think that you're a *salope*.'

'That's a terrible thing to say to me. Come on, now, that's enough. Give me *un p'tit bec*. It's time for you to *fais do-do*.'

'Why won't you tell me what you really do, Momma? Are you ashamed?'

'Watch a slap, T-Yon!'

With that, T-Yon suddenly jerked her head sideways, as if she had been smacked across the face, very hard. Then she sat up, one hand pressed against her cheek, blinking in bewilderment.

'T-Yon?' said Sissy. 'T-Yon, are you all right?'

T-Yon turned and stared at her. 'I thought . . . I thought I was talking to my Momma. I thought she slapped me. I really thought it was real.'

She took her hand away from her cheek. 'It *was* real. I can *feel* it. It *hurts*. How can that be?'

Sissy reached over to the nightstand and found her spectacles. When she put them on, she clearly saw that there were red fingermarks on T-Yon's left cheek, even though that was the cheek which had been pressed against her pillow.

'You were talking in your sleep,' she said. 'It sounded like you were talking to your mother and then your mother was talking back to you. It was like ventriloquism. I mean, you actually put on a different voice.'

T-Yon said, 'I was calling my mother a whore. I never said anything like that to her, *ever*. Why was I doing that? I never thought she was a whore. My God, no wonder she slapped me.'

'She didn't slap you,' said Sissy. 'Nobody slapped you. Nobody real, anyhow.'

'But I felt it. I can *still* feel it.'

Sissy pushed back the covers and climbed out of bed. She went across to the window and drew back the red-velvet drapes, and the bedroom was immediately filled with sunlight. She looked down into the street below, and saw that the police crime-scene tapes were still in place, and that five white squad cars were still parked by the curb. She didn't say anything to T-Yon, but she was sure now that what was happening at The Red Hotel could never be solved by Detective Garrity and his team, no matter how good they were.

She glanced at the bedside clock. It said 6.25 a.m. 'Go look in the mirror,' she told T-Yon.

T-Yon got out of bed and went to the bathroom. 'That's so scary. I actually have a handprint on my cheek.'

Sissy said, 'I need to talk to your brother, Everett, T-Yon – and urgently. Those two people you saw in your room last night, and that argument you just had with your mother. They're both *signs*, T-Yon, like a weathervane swings around when there's a storm coming. Something's brewing in this hotel, something that could be disastrous, or even fatal, and believe me it's going to happen real soon.'

She came up to T-Yon and gently touched her cheek. 'These fingermarks on your face, they're what we call psychostigmata.'

'Psycho-*what*? What are *they* when they're at home?'

'Psychostigmata are the impressions that a psychic experience can make on your physical body. Like people who have puncture wounds in the palms of their hands after they dream about the crucifixion, or even bleed. Or people who dream that they're fighting with demons, and wake up covered all over with bruises.

'The marks on your face – that's all the proof I need that something is about to happen here. To misquote Sherlock Holmes, if you eliminate the improbable and the highly unlikely and the plain insane, whatever remains must be the answer, even if you think it's totally crackers.'

'I'm sorry, Sissy,' said T-Yon. 'I really don't understand what you're talking about.'

Sissy was rummaging in one of the drawers in the closet, trying to find herself a pair of knee-length nylon socks.

'What I'm saying to you is that my gut instinct about you and your brother and The Red Hotel has been right all along. There's a very powerful presence somewhere in this building, and it's angry about you being here, for whatever reason, and it means to do you and your brother considerable harm. I believe it gave you those nightmares about Everett, and I believe it did it for the sole purpose of making sure you came here to Baton Rouge, where its influence is much stronger. It wants you and Everett together – *close* together, intertangled just like you saw in your nightmares – so that it can take its revenge on both of you. Maybe simultaneously, just like it happens in your nightmare.'

'So what can we do? Can we, like, *exorcize* it?'

Sissy found a sock, took it out of the drawer and stretched it. 'If you mean is it worth us bringing in a priest and asking him to sprinkle the hotel with holy water, then the answer is categorically no. Waste of holy water, especially at five dollars the four-ounce bottle. This isn't a religious possession, T-Yon. Nothing to do with Satan, or demons.'

She paused, and looked at T-Yon with a serious expression on her face, like a mother warning her daughter about all the evil in the world. 'I'm almost sure from what we saw in your cards that Vanessa Slider and her son, Shem, are behind all of this. In fact my feeling is that those two people you saw in your room last night, that's who they were. Not them in person, of course, but their *resonance*. Or their spirits, if you prefer.'

'This is really creeping me out,' said T-Yon.

'Well, let's go downstairs and find ourselves some coffee and some breakfast and let's go talk to Everett about my searching the hotel for whatever it is that's hiding here. I need to go on a spirit-hunt, T-Yon, or the Lord alone knows what shit is going to come raining down on us, and I mean it.'

Spirit Hunt

Everett was still looking puffy eyed, but he had showered and shaved and changed into a fresh white shirt and fresh-pressed cream-colored pants, and after he had sat down with Sissy and T-Yon at their breakfast table, and drunk a large black coffee with molasses and nutmeg, he began to talk with much more confidence.

'I truly believe we can get past this,' he said. 'OK, yes, we've had the worst publicity that you could ever imagine. But nobody's found any dead bodies yet, and, most important, nobody's found any dead bodies here inside the hotel. That would have done for us, period.'

'How about the opening gala?' asked Sissy. 'Is that still going to go ahead?'

Everett tapped the table to show that he was touching wood. 'I'm still waiting for Detective Garrity to give me the final word, but I haven't canceled anything yet, and we're still taking new bookings. In fact, bookings have been really brisk, under the circumstances.'

'That doesn't altogether surprise me. You know how ghoulish some people can be.'

'Oh, come on, Sissy, I don't think they're coming here because of that. They're coming here because we've had such good reviews. We had a terrific report in the *Louisiana Hotel Guide*, just posted online this morning. They said that we had really raised the bar.'

Sissy cut the last of her maple pancakes with her fork. 'You're still amenable to my taking a look around?'

'I guess so. A little reluctantly, I have to admit – but so long as you don't advertise what you're doing to all and sundry. I'll fix you up with an identity badge, you'll need it.' He paused, and then he said, 'I still don't really get what it is you're looking for.'

'T-Yon had a very eerie experience last night.'

Everett reached across the table and squeezed T-Yon's hand. 'Yes, I know. Samuel told me about it, first thing this morning.'

'*That's* the kind of thing I'm looking for.'

'Samuel said that two people came into T-Yon's room while she was asleep. Or at least she thought they did.'

'You sound a little skeptical.'

Everett put down his coffee mug and spread his arms wide, as if he were embracing the world. 'Like I told you, I don't disrespect anybody who believes in the supernatural. I don't disrespect *anybody* for what they believe in. Muslim, Mormon, Seventh Day Adventist. Tea Party. I honestly don't care. But Samuel searched every empty room on the second floor, and there was nobody there who shouldn't have been, and as soon as everybody came down for breakfast, he also checked the rest of the rooms. He didn't find anybody, Sissy, and whatever spirits or spooks *you* believe in, to *me* that means that T-Yon must have imagined those people, whether she was asleep or whether she was awake.' He turned to T-Yon and said, 'Sorry, sis. No offense, really.'

Sissy shrugged in surrender. 'OK, Everett. Fine. But all I can say is, for your own sake, try to keep a very open mind. Whatever you care to call it, there *is* some spook in this hotel, and it's making no secret of the fact that it doesn't like you being here.'

Everett stood up, took hold of Sissy's hand and kissed her wrist. 'Good luck,' he grinned, and winked at her. 'I'm afraid you're *really* going to need it.'

Sissy took her purple loose-weave shoulder bag with her, so that she could carry her DeVane cards, as well as her Alphabet Cards, her witch compass, her gunja beads, her rosary, and a selection of herbs which she had begged from the chef in the kitchen – fresh cilantro, fresh broad-leaf parsley, fresh oregano, filé, black pepper and chili powder. She also took a crucifix and a bottle of holy water from Lourdes, but she didn't tell T-Yon about these. She had no intention of trying to carry out an exorcism, even if she had known how, but they would help her to trace any spirits who might have held strong religious beliefs when they were alive. From experience, Sissy knew that in death, or in the afterlife, religious people were often deeply resentful that their faith hadn't brought them peace. Instead, they were furious that they had left behind them so much unfinished business, so many scores to settle, and that they had lost forever the people they loved. Occasionally they reacted with such hostility to religious artifacts that crosses would glow red hot and holy water would boil in its bottle – but that, of course, was a sure way of knowing that they were still around.

T-Yon wanted to come with her on her spirit-hunt, but Sissy said, 'No, sweetheart. Absolutely not. Not this time, anyhow – not until I have a much clearer idea what we're up against. The way I understand it, you're a potential victim, and I wouldn't take an antelope along with me if I was out hunting for lions. You'd be a distraction and a liability. I'm sorry. Why don't you spend some time helping your brother with this gala opening of his – that's if the police allow him to hold it.'

T-Yon gave Sissy a hug, and said, 'OK.'

Sissy was really beginning to warm to her. Apart from being very pretty, she had a beguiling mixture of innocence and determination that reminded Sissy of what she had been like when she was in her early twenties. She also felt that T-Yon might have some psychic sensitivity of her own, which she should nurture. One day, she would have to pass the DeVane cards on to somebody younger; and if she couldn't do that, she would probably have no choice but to shred them. That would be a criminal shame, but safer. In the wrong hands, the DeVane cards' predictions could be catastrophic.

She took the elevator to the seventh story, and then walked along the corridor until she found the door to the staircase. The door was wedged open and she found two hotel cleaners in bright red housecoats, scrubbing the concrete landing.

'Can I get up on to the roof this way?' she asked.

'Sure you can, ma'am. Right up them stairs. Far as I know the door ain't locked.'

She looked at the wall, which was still patterned with reddish-brown bloodstains, those bloodstains that had looked to Everett like seven or eight squashed moths. To Sissy, they resembled Rorschach prints, those inky splodges that psychiatrists use to see what their patients read into them.

Sissy could see a face like a troll, and another face that was furtively smiling, as if it knew something that she didn't, but wasn't going to tell her. She saw two eyes wide with bewilderment. She could see what looked like a woman with her arms and her legs wide apart and her head covered by a hood. Also, strangely, she could see one stain that could have been an animal – some ugly breed of dog, by the look of it, like a pit bull terrier.

One of the cleaners was spraying the wall with an anti-graffiti solvent and scrubbing it hard with a scrubbing brush, but it was obvious from her grunting that the stains were proving very hard to clean off.

'Having trouble?' Sissy asked her.

The cleaner wiped the perspiration from her forehead with the back of her hand. 'Never known anything so darn hard to get off. It's worser than that marker pen.'

'It's supposed to be blood, isn't it?' said Sissy. 'That shouldn't be so hard.'

'Whatever it is, it ain't choosing to budge, not one bit. I reckon we'll have to paint over it.'

'OK,' said Sissy. 'Good luck.'

Adjusting her bag on her shoulder, she climbed the steps to the door that led to the roof. She pushed open the bar, and the door opened, and she stepped outside.

It was already warm out here, eighty degrees at least, with seventy-percent humidity. The sky was hazy, and only the faintest westerly wind was blowing, just enough to stir the flag on The Red Hotel's flagpole. Sissy walked across the roof to the east-facing parapet, overlooking Third Street. From here, she could see all the way across the city, from the gray art-deco tower of the State Capitol building in the north to the campanile of Louisiana State University to the south. Traffic sparkled on the interstate.

When she turned around, she could see the mud-brown Mississippi, almost a mile wide, gleaming in the morning sun, and Port Allen on the other side, with its riverside promenade.

In spite of the heat, she shivered, in the same way that she had shivered when she first walked across the lobby of The Red Hotel. Maybe it hadn't been the chilly air conditioning after all, because she had the same sensation up here on the roof. There was something icy in the heart of this building, something so cold that it seemed to be draining all the warmth out of everything around it. She could feel it, right through the soles of her spotty purple Keds.

'Vanessa?' she said, out loud. 'Vanessa Slider? It's *you*, isn't it, Vanessa? You've come back, haven't you? Or maybe you never went away.' She waited, and listened, although she didn't seriously expect a reply. All she heard was the sound of traffic and the mournful hooting of an Exxon petroleum tanker as it left its mooring by the intracoastal waterway.

She crossed over to a rusting metal box that covered one of the vents from the hotel's air conditioning. She took her DeVane cards out of her bag and opened them up. She didn't much like the way the clown on the front was looking at her today, not that she ever did. His eyes seemed to be narrower than usual, with a slight squint, as if he were saying: *You be very careful what you ask us for, Sissy Sawyer.*

She held up the picture of the clown in front of her face and said, 'Oh, yes? And why exactly is that, *Monsieur Le Pitre?*'

We cards – we see the future, as it was seen from the past. We know everything.

'Oh, really?'

You know us better than anybody. You know what we can see. We can tell which loves are going to flourish, long before the lovers are aware of each other's existence. We can see murder, years before the killer or the killed are even born.

'So? What are you trying to say to me, *monsieur*?'

I am reminding you that we are not your obedient servants, Sissy Sawyer. We were not devised and drawn simply to back up your hunches, you withered old flower-child. Don't you forget that, ever, or you might get more than you bargained for.

Sissy lowered the picture of the clown and shook her head. 'Shit and a bit,' she said. 'I'm talking to a pack of cards. No, I'm not. I'm talking to myself. I'm even *insulting* myself.'

She knew that the clown wasn't really saying any of that, but his face had been so artfully drawn that he was not only sly, and knowing, and disapproving, but he appeared to be able to change expression. Looking at that face, anybody who was tempted to use the DeVane cards to answer any frivolous questions would think twice about it.

In spite of that, Sissy shuffled the cards and then laid them out in the Cross of Lorraine pattern on top of the ventilation box. Then she took the card which was her own Predictor card, *La Fille Qui Regarde Fixement Les Étoiles*, The Star-Gazer. It showed a beautiful naked girl with wavy red hair that reached all the way down to her bottom. She was reclining on a chaise longue in the middle of a rose garden, even though it was night-time, and the moon was out, and the sky was crowded with stars. She was staring upward with a dreamy look on her face.

The very first time she had looked at this card, Sissy hadn't seen them, because the background was so dark, but, behind the stone balustrade which surrounded the rose garden, it was just possible to make out that six or seven wolves were gathered – wolves with shaggy black fur and poisonous yellow eyes and their dark red tongues hanging out. Sissy had always taken this card to mean that if she took it upon herself to try and predict the future, she did so at her own peril. The stars spoke to her, yes; but the wolves were always waiting.

She turned over the first card. Again, it was *La Châtelaine*, the thin, disapproving woman in gray – or rather, nine identical, thin, disapproving women in gray – each with their bunches of nine keys around their waists.

'So, you are here, Vanessa,' said Sissy, under her breath. 'Now let's see if we can find out where you are exactly, and what you're so angry about.'

She turned over the next card, and it was *L'Asile De Mon Frère*, My Brother's Asylum, which T-Yon had taken to represent The Red Hotel. So far, the cards were giving Sissy the same warnings that they had given T-Yon, only in a different sequence. But Sissy had no illusions about it. The fact that her first card had been *La Châtelaine* had shown her that Vanessa Slider was aware that she was here, and that she probably knew *why*.

The third card surprised her, and it surprised her because she couldn't remember ever having seen it before. She was sure that she knew every single DeVane card intimately, and all of the myriad meanings that their pictures symbolized, from the stampeding black horses which could predict either a catastrophic failure in business or else a huge breakthrough in somebody's career, to the coy lovers hiding naked in a forest, which predicted either a secret affair or else a newly flourishing adventurousness in a long-lasting relationship.

This card was simply called *Le Mur*, The Wall. It showed a woman in a black floor-length robe standing in a corridor in front of a whitewashed wall. She had her left hand pressed flat against it and her right hand held to her heart. A small sepia portrait was hanging on the wall, in the top-left corner.

It showed a handsome man in a felt hat, looking at the woman with a sad expression on his face.

'Now what in the name of heck are *you* trying to tell me?' said Sissy. She couldn't believe that she had never seen this card before. She must have done, but how she could have forgotten it she couldn't imagine. She was tempted to pick up all the cards and count them, just to make sure that she hadn't mysteriously acquired one extra.

'The wall . . .' she whispered. But *which* wall? Was it a real wall or a metaphorical wall, some obstruction that was preventing somebody from getting where they wanted to go? And who was the woman? Was it Vanessa Slider, or some other woman, and why was she pressing her hand against the wall like that?

The man appeared only as a portrait, and Sissy knew what this signified: that he had left the woman, and was now far away. Either that, or he was dead.

The petroleum tanker hooted again as it began to make its way southward down the river. Sissy looked up, and as she did so, a woman appeared.

Sissy couldn't stop herself from letting out an '*ah!*' of sheer surprise. The woman had stepped out from behind the square concrete elevator housing, where she must have been standing ever since Sissy came out on to the roof, but how Sissy had failed to see her when she had crossed from one side of the roof to the other, she couldn't think.

The woman had dark red hair pinned back in a French pleat, and a very white oval face. In fact her face was so white that it looked blurry and unfocused in the morning sunshine, and Sissy found it hard to see exactly what she looked like. She was wearing a pale green button-through dress and pale green shoes to match. She didn't acknowledge Sissy at all, but walked directly to the door which led to the staircase, which Sissy had left half open.

Sissy raised her hand and said, '*Excuse me!*' but the woman ignored her and disappeared down the stairs.

For a moment, Sissy couldn't think what to do. After all, it was none of her business why the woman had come up on to the roof. Maybe she had felt like a cigarette, or had an argument with her partner and needed a break to think about it. Maybe she had just wanted to look at the river and meditate.

Or maybe it was none of those things. Maybe she wasn't a real woman at all. Maybe she was no more than a memory of a woman, an image of somebody who was no longer alive.

Oh, for God's sake! Sissy admonished herself. *Stop letting your damned imagination run away with you! Go ask her! It may be embarrassing but at least you'll know!*

She hurriedly scooped up her DeVane cards and dropped them, loose, into her bag. She could sort them out later. Then she hurried across to the exit door, and began to climb down the concrete stairs as fast as she dared, holding tightly on to the railing as she did so.

When she reached the landing, she found that the two cleaners were still at work. The bloodstains on the wall were fainter, but they still hadn't managed to erase them completely.

'Did a woman just come past you?'

The cleaners frowned at each other and then shook their heads. 'Woman? No. We didn't see no woman. Mind you, I can't say that we was paying too much attention.'

Sissy hesitated for a moment. Then she thought she heard footsteps echoing up the stairwell from the flight below. She leaned over and saw a white hand sliding down the railing – a white hand with a pale green cuff.

'Thanks,' she told the cleaners, and continued to make her way down the stairs. She was frightened that she was going to stumble and fall. Her good friend, Grace, had fallen only last year, and broken her hip, and died from the complications. But she could hear the woman continuing downward, and she was determined to catch up with her. There was something strange about her, even if she *were* real. After all, why was she using the stairs, instead of the elevator? Maybe she didn't want anybody else to see her. That's if anybody else *could* see her.

She leaned over again and glimpsed the hem of the woman's dress as she crossed the sixth story landing. Then she heard her shoes pattering down to the fifth.

'*Excuse me!*' she called out. '*Excuse me, can you wait up a moment, please?*'

Her voice echoed in the stairwell, but even if the woman heard her, she didn't answer, and she didn't stop. Sissy reached the sixth story, and hurried across to the next flight down.

She was only halfway down to five, however, when she thought she heard a door squeal on its hinges, and then bang shut. She stopped, and listened. All she could hear was a soft upward draft, and the muted, barely audible sound of people talking, and doors opening and closing, and vacuum cleaners, and elevators whining up and down.

There was no more pattering of shoes, and when she looked over the railing she could no longer see the woman's hand.

She carried on down to the fifth-story landing as quickly as she could. She went across to the exit door and pulled it open and – sure enough – it made the same squealing noise that she had heard as she was coming down the stairs. She stepped out into the corridor, and as she did so the door closed behind her with a bang – which, even though she was expecting it, made her jump.

She looked to the left, guessing that the woman would be heading for the elevators, but there was no sign of her. When she looked to the right, however, she was just in time to see the woman's pale green dress as she turned the corner and disappeared from sight.

Well, she thought, *unless she has a room here, which she* won't *have, because the fifth story hasn't yet been cleared for occupation by guests, there is absolutely no place for her to go.* The corridor in that direction was a dead end.

With renewed determination, she stalked along the corridor with her bag making a chunking sound with every step. She reached the corner, but the corridor ahead of her was empty. At the far end, there was a window with a view of the Hilton hotel on the opposite side of Lafayette Street, its facade glaring white in the sunshine, but there was no woman to be seen.

Sissy walked halfway along the corridor, then turned around, frowning. Maybe the woman had previously been booked into one of the rooms and still had her key. But what had she been doing on the roof, and why hadn't she answered when Sissy called her? And how was it possible that she had passed those two cleaners without them seeing her?

She took her bag off her shoulder and rummaged inside it until she found her witch compass. She had bought it over twenty years ago, in an antique store in Glastonbury. It was the size and shape of a pocket watch, made of tarnished silver with a hinged lid. Inside, under glass, was a pointer like an ordinary compass, except that there were no markings for NESW.

She opened the lid and held the witch compass out in front of her, in the flat of her hand. Then she slowly walked along the left side of the corridor, all the way to the window. Nothing. The needle didn't even stir. She paused for a moment and then she walked back along the right side. She made sure that she held the witch compass close to each door in turn, in case the woman was inside one of the rooms, and hiding inside the bathroom, or one of the closets, which would make it more difficult for the needle to sense her presence.

She was halfway back to the corner when the needle suddenly swung to the left. It wasn't pointing to any of the doors, but to the middle of a length of totally blank wall.

'What in the name of . . .?' Sissy murmured.

She walked a few steps further, but the needle continued to point to the same spot. She stepped back, and there was no question about it. The witch compass was insistent that there was a spirit here, either alive or passed over, although she couldn't guess how a living being could be right inside a wall.

She rummaged around in her bag again until she dug up her cellphone. She found the number of The Red Hotel on the back of the identity badge that Everett had given her, and tapped it out with her silver-polished fingernail.

'The Red Hotel, good morning, *bon jour* . . . how may I help you?' asked the receptionist.

'Yes, this is Ms Sawyer. I'm visiting the hotel with Mr Savoie's sister.'

'Of course, Ms Sawyer. What can I do for you?'

'I'd like you to put me through to that Detective Garrity, if he's around.'

'Detective Garrity? Oh – he's not here right now. I think

he went to get some breakfast. But his partner is right here in the lobby. Would you care to speak to him?'

'Sure. OK. He'll do.'

While the receptionist went off to bring Detective Mullard to the phone, Sissy kept the witch compass pointing at the wall, just to make sure that the spirit didn't shift its location, or vanish altogether.

At last, Detective Mullard said, 'Mullard here. Hi. Where you at, Ms Sawyer?'

'I'm up on the fifth floor, Detective, between rooms Five-Oh-Nine and Five-Eleven. I think I've found some evidence and I need to take a look inside those two rooms.'

'Evidence such as?' said Detective Mullard. He made no attempt to disguise his lack of interest.

'I'm not sure yet. But I believe it might help us to find out who abducted Ella-mae Grover.'

'Oh yeah? The fact is I'm pretty tied up right now, ma'am.'

'This won't take you long, Detective. And if you don't come take a look now, it may be too late.'

A pause. A sigh. Then, 'OK, ma'am. I'll bring up the keys. But I sincerely hope this isn't going to be a waste of my valuable time.'

'Oh, my dear Detective Mullard. Heaven forbid.'

Vanishing Point

While she waited for Detective Mullard to come up to the fifth floor, Sissy sat on the window sill and tidied up her DeVane cards.

She counted them out as she did so, to make sure that *Le Mur* hadn't mysteriously appeared as an extra card. There were fifty-nine cards, as usual, but she couldn't find *Le Mur*. She searched through her bag again, but there was no trace of it. It had disappeared as inexplicably as it had appeared.

She sat there feeling as if the world were revolving slowly around her. This was extraordinary trickery – like nothing that she had ever encountered before. She was ninety percent convinced that it was Vanessa Slider, or her spirit, if she were dead, and her son, Shem, too. It was frightening enough that they were capable of entering and leaving rooms without leaving any trace of how they had managed to get in or out, but what really worried Sissy was that they could manipulate her DeVane cards to the point where she was reluctant to rely on them any longer. Supposing she acted on the advice of some card that didn't really exist, like *Le Mur*?

Sissy had encountered plenty of hostile spirits before, but most of the time they felt simply cheated and bewildered because they had died. Almost all of the spirits with whom she communicated were gentle and loving – sad that their lives were over, nothing more – missing their loved ones as much as their loved ones missed them.

But this was something else altogether. She could feel that there was *hatred* here, almost tangible hatred.

She heard the elevator chime, and then Detective Mullard appeared around the corner of the corridor in his flappy green suit.

'Ah, Detective. Thank you for coming up.'

'Sure,' he sniffed. 'You said you had evidence?'

'That's right. I do.'

Detective Mullard stood looking at her for a few seconds, and then he said, 'You want to, like, *share* it with me, this evidence?'

'There's somebody in one of these two rooms. A woman. I'm not sure which one, because they appear to be someplace between the two.'

Detective Mullard turned to Room 511 and then to Room 509. 'I see. OK. You saw somebody go inside?'

'No.'

'You *heard* them, then?'

'No.'

'Then, excuse me for asking, how is it can you tell if she's in there?'

Sissy held up her witch compass. 'I used *this*. It's kind of like a metal detector, only for spirits.'

'*Spirits?* You mean like ghosts?'

'Well, souls if you prefer. It can sense the presence of any kind of human spirit, alive or gone beyond. You see how the needle is pointing to the wall? I can move it here, like so. Then I can move it back again, but it's still pointing to the same place.'

'So, OK. How exactly does it do that?'

'Simple. The needle's made out of pure magnetized cobalt. A lot of ordinary compasses have a small amount of cobalt in the needle, although they're mainly steel. But this is *pure* cobalt, and pure cobalt has some remarkable spiritual properties.'

'Really?'

Sissy lifted up the compass even higher, so that Detective Mullard could see it more closely, but he leaned away from it, as if he were afraid it was some kind of practical joke, and it was going to snap at him, or go off with a bang.

Sissy said, 'The word cobalt comes from the German word *kobold*, which means goblin. That was what iron miners in Germany and Bohemia used to call it. Whenever a mine had a large amount of cobalt ore in it, they claimed that they could see and hear spirits. Apparently they could see them running through the tunnels and hear them knocking on the walls.'

'And this . . . needle? This is your evidence?'

'It's worth checking out, Detective. Where's the harm? After all, what evidence have *you* come up with?'

Detective Mullard blew out his cheeks. 'All right, Ms Sawyer. I'll indulge you. But only out of good old Southern courtesy. To be quite frank with you, I think this is horse manure.'

'Let's see, shall we?'

Detective Mullard had brought key cards for both rooms. He opened 509 and they went inside. It was very similar to Sissy's room on the second floor, only larger, with a gilded rococo sofa as well as a chair. Detective Mullard looked inside the bathroom, and then the closets. He even knelt down on the floor, lifted the side of the red embroidered throw, and peered under the bed.

While he was doing this, Sissy was holding her witch

compass close to the wall. Its needle had swung around and
was pointing directly at the wallpaper.

'Nobody here that I can see,' said Detective Mullard,
climbing to his feet. 'Nobody visible, anyhow. Maybe there's
a ghost, but I don't have my ghost glasses with me.'

'The compass is still telling me that there's a spirit here,'
Sissy told him.

Detective Mullard looked down at the compass needle and
shook his head. 'Maybe you need to take it in for a service,'
he said.

'Detective – there's a presence here in this hotel, I can
assure you. How do you explain that rug, all soaked in blood
but not a single spatter anywhere around it? How did Ella-mae
disappear from that washroom without leaving any bloody
footprints? Where did that whistling noise come from?'

'What are you trying to suggest here, Ms Sawyer? Are you
trying to tell me that this hotel is, like, *haunted*? Hey . . .
maybe we should call in Scooby-Doo.'

'Haunted isn't quite the word I'd use myself, Detective. And
you can make a joke of it if you want to, but there *is* something here. You can't see radon gas, can you? But it can still
kill you.'

'OK. I'm sorry. But you want to try being a detective here
in BR and see if you don't end up kind of cynical, especially
when it comes to superstition. We're not like New Orleans,
we don't go in for all of that voodoo crap, pardon my French.
Look – maybe this woman is in the room next door, and that's
why your compass is pointing at the wall. Let's go check.'

Sissy looked at the witch compass. The needle was shivering
slightly, as if the presence which it had detected had started
to edge very gradually toward the left, and further away.

'You go,' she said. 'I'll stay here. It's started to move, and
I don't want to lose contact with it.'

'Whatever you say, Ms Sawyer.'

There was no question about it, the needle was showing
that the presence was inching further toward the window. It
could be that it *was* next door, in Room 511, and the needle
was tracking its progress through the wall. Or it could be that
it was right here in the room with her, but it was invisible.

Maybe Detective Mullard's suggestion hadn't been so ridiculous after all: maybe they did need ghost glasses, if only such
things existed for real.

Sissy heard Detective Mullard open the door to Room 511,
and then the door quietly close itself behind him. After a few
seconds, the needle stopped shivering, and stayed perfectly
still. She waited, and waited. There was no sound from next
door, but neither did Detective Mullard come back. She waved
the witch compass from side to side, but now the needle simply
swung in response to her hand movements. The presence had
gone.

*Lost it, damn it! And who knows where it might have slunk
off to now?*

She opened the door and stepped out into the corridor.
Detective Mullard still hadn't reappeared, so she went to Room
511 and tried the door handle. The door had locked itself, and
so she knocked at it, and called out, 'Detective! Did you find
anything?'

No answer. She knocked again, and said, 'Detective Mullard!
Can you open the door? I think the presence must have taken
a powder!'

Still no answer. She knocked a third time, but now she was
beginning to think that if anybody had taken a powder, it was
Detective Mullard. He had probably looked into Room 511,
seen that there was nobody in there, and decided to leave
without even bothering to tell her. So much for his talk about
'good old Southern courtesy'.

She was starting to walk back along the corridor when one
of the security men came around the corner, jingling his keys.

'Ah!' said Sissy. 'Just the fellow I need!'

'Ma'am?' said the security man. He was African-American,
with braided hair and a pencil moustache.

'I have to get into Room Five-Eleven. I'm sure I left my
bag in there.'

'Ma'am?' he repeated. Sissy could see him looking at her
ID tag, and then at the bag hanging over her shoulder.

'Oh . . .' she flustered. 'My *other* bag.'

'No problem, ma'am,' said the security man. 'In any case,
everything's all clear now, and all of the guests can return

to their rooms. I'm up here doing a double-*double*-check, that's all.'

Sissy followed him back to Room 511. He swiped open the door with his key card and then held it wide so that she could go inside.

She looked quickly around. Detective Mullard certainly wasn't here. He wasn't in the bathroom and he wasn't hiding behind the drapes and he was far too bulky to have squeezed himself under the bed, him in his crumpled green three-piece suit, even if he had any reason to. No, he had obviously taken a quick look, found nothing, and walked off without telling her. Great. She would give him a piece of her mind for doing that.

'No, sorry,' she told the security man. 'I must have left it someplace else. Thank you anyhow.'

'No problem,' the security man repeated, although he was looking at her as if she were a likely candidate for Sunrise Assisted Living.

Sissy walked slowly up and down all of the fifth-floor corridors, waving her witch compass as she went, but the needle didn't even twitch, not once.

She went back and held it close to the wall in between Rooms 509 and 511 one last time, just to make sure, but there was still no response.

When she reached the elevators, she turned around and listened again, and then she said, under her breath, 'Where in the heck are you hiding, Vanessa? Come on, show yourself. Maybe we can work something out.' She waited two or three minutes, and then she pressed the elevator button for up. She would have to return to the seventh story so that she could start her spirit hunt over.

It took her nearly two hours. Floor by floor, she went down through The Red Hotel, using the witch compass to sense for Vanessa Slider and her son, Shem, and scattering some of her herbs and spices on the carpets to see if they had left any footprints, or drag marks, or any evidence at all that they had been there.

On every floor, she could still feel that pervasive coldness, that bitter sense of resentment, as if somebody had maliciously left a waiting-room door wide open so that everybody inside would feel an icy-cold draft. *The trouble is, nobody else seems to feel it but me.*

If Detective Mullard had sensed it even slightly, he wouldn't have been so dismissive, and he wouldn't have walked off like that and left her. And Detective Garrity hadn't shown any awareness of it, either, even though he dealt with evil on a daily basis. As for Everett – he flatly refused to believe that there were any spirits here – or at least he didn't *want* to believe it. Spirits were seriously bad for business.

She had just stepped out of the elevator on the third floor when – off to her left – she saw a dim figure flit across the corridor, from one room to the room directly opposite. The figure looked like a woman, but she was silhouetted by the window at the end of the corridor, so it was difficult to tell if it was the same red-haired woman in the pale green dress that she had seen on the roof. Also, strangely, she appeared to be out of focus, like a figure seen through bright early-morning fog.

Maybe I need some new eyeglasses, thought Sissy. But she went up to the door through which the figure had disappeared and took out her witch compass. She moved it slowly left and right, left and right. The needle trembled once, and then trembled again, as if it had caught the faintest hint of something, but after that it spun aimlessly around. *Darn.* Even if that out-of-focus woman *had* been a spirit, she was gone now.

Sissy started to walk back to the other end of the corridor, but she had only just turned the corner when she thought she heard a woman say, '—*deserved it? What do you care?*'

Sissy froze, with her head cocked to one side, and listened. It was difficult to tell where the voice might have come from. On the one hand it had sounded very close, as if the woman were standing only a few inches behind her, but on the other hand it had sounded muted, as if she had been shouting from a long way away, or through a very thick wall. Maybe it was a TV, with its volume turned right down.

She waited and waited. A whole minute passed, then another. *I must have imagined it*, she thought. But then she heard a young boy's voice. He was shouting, too, but his words were suppressed in the same way that the woman's had been. She tried to make out what they were saying to each other, but it wasn't easy because their voices were not only muted, but they came and went, like voices on a long-wave radio.

'—*hate doing this*—' the young boy shouted. In fact, he was almost screaming. '—*it's horrible!*' He had a strong local accent, and he pronounced it '*hawble*'.

A pause, and then the woman shouted back at him: '*Quit your griping, will you? You think* this *is horrible? At your age I had to do things a whole lot worser'n that*—'

'—*come you never do it, then*—?'

'—*'cause I told* you *to do it, that's why*—'

'—*it's* horrible. *It makes me barf*—'

'—*pick up that goddamned cleaver and get on with it*—'

Sissy shuffled around and around, three or four times, trying to make out where the voices were coming from. It didn't sound as if the woman and the boy were inside any of the rooms. It was more like they were deep inside the walls – very close by, but muffled by brick and plaster and wallpaper.

The woman shouted one thing more, although Sissy couldn't understand what she meant. She thought it was some-thing like '—*stab ornery Anne*—!' but she couldn't make any sense of it.

After that, the third floor became completely hushed – except for the usual hotel noises and the sound of traffic in the streets outside. Sissy waited for another minute or two, and then decided to continue with her spirit-hunt. She made her way back to the elevators, and as she did so she heard a sudden outburst of jazz music from somewhere down below – *Muskrat Ramble* if she guessed it right. Everett must have started rehearsals for his grand opening gala.

She was beginning to flag a little and her ankles were begin-ning to ache, but she hobbled around the rest of the third floor as quickly as she could. Nothing. Not a single shiver from her witch compass. No more foggy women. No more voices.

'You're here someplace, Vanessa,' she repeated, in a chal-lenging whisper, as she waited for the elevator to take her down to the second floor. 'Come on – why won't you show me where?'

Down on the second floor, guests were beginning to arrive, chatting and laughing, and bellhops were showing them to their rooms. As they passed her in the corridor, Sissy took care to make sure that they didn't see what she was doing, a batty silver-haired woman in a multicolored silk kaftan and strings of chunky beads, swooshing her witch compass slowly from side to side like a Geiger counter. But she picked up no more psychic disturbances at all.

She was sure now the spirits were here, somewhere in the building, and as she stood waiting for the elevator to take her back down to the lobby, she tried to think what she ought to say to Everett and T-Yon, and Detective Garrity, too.

No doubt about it – there is a presence in The Red Hotel. In fact I've even seen it. It could be Vanessa Slider. She's my number one suspect, but I don't have any proof of it. All I can tell you for sure is that she means you no good.

What can we do about it? I really don't know.

Whether it is her or not, I have a very bad feeling about this, and I can't even trust my cards to tell me how to keep you from harm.

The elevator doors chimed open, and she saw her own reflection standing inside. She suddenly realized that she looked less like an ageing flower-child, and more like a witch.

Mirror Image

When she stepped out of the elevator, Sissy found that the lobby was already packed. A jazz quartet in Derby hats and candy-striped silk vests were tootling away beside the reception desk, although they were finding it hard to make themselves heard over the chatter and laughter of more than three hundred people crowded around the fountain – local dignitaries and their wives, restaurant and hotel critics, newspaper and TV and radio reporters, as well as the entire LSU Tigers team, along with their managers and their cheerleaders in their purple-and-gold uniforms. The noise was deafening.

She weaved her way across the lobby to Everett's office. Everett was there with T-Yon and Luther and a big-bellied man with a beard who was wearing a white jacket and checkered pants, whom Sissy took to be The Red Hotel's head chef.

Everett was running through the last-minute details of the buffet they were going to be serving after the formal opening speeches.

'We're serving all of our specialties, right? Crawfish and cornbread cake, charbroiled oysters, shrimp Vacherie. How about the cedar-roasted redfish?'

T-Yon had pinned up her hair and was wearing a low-cut tube dress in startling red, with a large red silk flower pinned to the front.

'Well, look at you,' smiled Sissy.

'How did it go?' mouthed T-Yon, very quietly. Everett gave them a sharp glance but continued with his list of buffet dishes. 'Did you find anything?'

'I'm not quite sure what to tell you,' said Sissy. 'I saw a strange woman who seemed to vanish into thin air; and I heard some voices that seemed to be coming from out of the walls.'

'My God. So there *is* something here.'

'My witch compass seems pretty certain of it, and so am I. I can feel it in my bones. But I don't have any evidence that's going to convince your brother. It certainly didn't convince that Detective What's-his-face.'

'Garrity?'

'No, the other one, in that terrible green suit. I was up on the fifth floor and the witch compass was giving me such a strong indication that there was a spirit in one of the rooms there that I called him up to take a look. Which he did – *very* grudgingly, I may add – and then he left me without so much as saying that he didn't believe me.'

T-Yon said, 'I guess it *is* pretty hard for people to believe. I can hardly believe it myself. If I hadn't seen those two people in my room . . .'

'I'm trying to think what to do next,' Sissy told her. 'The trouble is, I don't really know what Vanessa Slider wants – assuming it *is* her – or if she's just causing mischief. You know, like a poltergeist. But I'm very worried that somebody else is going to get hurt, or maybe killed, even.'

'I've been trying to talk to Ev about it,' said T-Yon. 'But he has so much invested in this hotel, so much money, so much hard work.'

'I know. But maybe that's one of the reasons why Mrs Slider is so resentful.'

'You said you saw a woman. Do you think it was *her*? What did she look like?'

Sissy described the red-haired woman in the pale green dress, and how she had escaped down the stairwell to the fifth floor, and then disappeared.

'I can't think where she went. I had a very strong feeling that she *was* Vanessa Slider, or Vanessa Slider's spirit, but then I might have been deluding myself. Or worse than that, this spirit might well have been deluding me. You saw how it made all my cards go blank, when we did that second reading, and then today I swear to God it invented a card that doesn't even exist. That really freaked me out, T-Yon. I don't have anything more powerful than my DeVane cards and if I can't rely on those, I don't know *what* I can do.'

'Maybe we should just wait and see what happens. Everything's going OK at the moment. Maybe she won't do anything terrible. Maybe she *can't* do anything really terrible – like, she's only a spirit, after all.'

'Believe me,' said Sissy, 'spirits *can* do really terrible things, if they want to. I've seen it happen, often enough. If there's anything more dangerous than a jealous spirit, I'm glad I don't know what it is.'

At that moment, Detective Garrity knocked at the door. 'Detective?' said Everett. 'Any news of anything? We're all clear to go, right?'

'Sure but I'm looking for Mullard. You haven't seen him lately?'

'No, Detective, sorry.'

'I saw him a little less than an hour ago,' Sissy volunteered.

'I came across some psychic disturbance on the fifth floor and I invited him to come up and take a look at it. Which he did.'

'Psychic disturbance.' The black turtle eyes didn't blink.

Sissy looked across at Everett who was staring at her with his eyes narrowed as if to tell her, *'Just you be careful what you say, you old hippie. This is no time for scaremongering.'* The head chef just looked puzzled, and obviously didn't understand what she was talking about.

'I have this English measuring device back from the time of witch trials,' Sissy explained. 'People used it to detect if there was any kind of malevolent presence hiding in their house, or in their barn, or their cowshed, or wherever.'

'Malevolent presence.' Detective Garrity enunciated the words as if they were a foreign language.

'That's right, malevolent presence. And between Room Five-Oh-Nine I think it was and Room Five-Eleven, the device was showing positive. So I asked Detective Mullard to come see for himself.'

'OK. So now where is he?'

'I'm sorry, Detective, I have no idea. I don't think he believed what I was telling him, so he left without saying a word, which I thought was rather impolite of him. I didn't even see him go.'

Detective Garrity tugged thoughtfully at his pointed nose. Sissy guessed that he wanted to ask her more about the 'malevolent presence' but it was obvious that Everett was beginning to lose his patience.

'Maybe we can discuss this later,' said Everett. 'Right now, we're up to our ears. The opening gala starts in twenty minutes and we have about eleven thousand details still to sort out.'

'OK,' said Detective Garrity. 'But if you do see Mullard, tell him I need to talk to him urgent, would you.'

'Of course,' Sissy told him. For the first time, however, she began to wonder if Detective Mullard actually *had* walked out on her. After all, she had heard the door to Room 511 close only once, when he first went in there. If he had taken a look inside and then walked out again, she would have heard it close twice.

'Excuse me,' she said to Everett, 'but do you possibly have

a master key I could borrow? I think I need to take another look at those rooms on the fifth floor.'

'Is that really necessary?' asked Everett. 'Why don't you go out there and grab yourself a Sazerac and spend the rest of the day enjoying yourself?'

'Oh, go on, Ev,' said T-Yon. 'I'll go with her.'

Everett's phone buzzed, and he picked it up. 'OK,' he said. 'Go ask Clarice Johnson, she'll let you in. But, please, Sissy – you can see what's happening here. All of these people are here to *laissez les bon temps rouler*. So be discreet, will you? No more talk of malevolent what's-their-names, if you don't mind.'

Sissy made a zipper gesture across her lips, and then said, 'Promise. No more talk of malevolent what's-their-names.'

Clarice was busy working out a new room-cleaning schedule when they knocked at her office door, but she seemed to be pleased to have an excuse for a break.

'This is driving me plumb crazy,' she said, as she took them up to the fifth floor in the service elevator. 'Cancellations one minute, new bookings the next. And each time the guests leave the room we have to clean it all over.'

'Still no news of Ella-mae,' said T-Yon.

'Her momma came to see me,' said Clarice. 'She was in pieces with the worry. I tried to give her some hope, but, between you and me, I believe that poor young girl is gone for good.'

They reached the fifth floor and Clarice led the way to Room 511, her large hips swaying from side to side as she walked.

'Mr Everett says that everything is OK now,' she said, over her shoulder. 'But me, I'm not so sure. I still got this *uneasy* feeling, if you know what I mean.'

Sissy said nothing. She had promised Everett that she wouldn't spread alarm and distress, and she always kept her promises. The only promise she had so far failed to fulfill was the promise that she had made to Frank that if anything ever happened to him, she would find herself another husband.

Clarice took out her master key and opened the door to 511. 'There you go, Miss T-Yon. Do you want me to stick around?'

Sissy said, 'No, thanks, Clarice. This won't take long.'

'Well, you're welcome,' Clarice told them, and went swaying away.

Sissy and T-Yon stepped into the room and looked around. Sissy opened the closet doors, but all she found inside was coat hangers and plastic laundry bags and a small guest safe.

'Check under the bed for me, could you?' she asked T-Yon. 'I'm a little stiff these days, when it comes to bending.'

T-Yon knelt down and lifted up the bedcover. 'No . . . no boogie men under the bed.'

Sissy reached into her bag and took out her witch compass. She laid it in the flat of her hand and slowly circled around. 'I don't know . . .' she said. 'It *feels* like there's something here, but I'm not sure what it is.'

'I don't feel anything,' said T-Yon. 'Maybe that Detective Mullard just gave himself some unauthorized time off. He kept telling me that he was jonesing for a cheeseburger from Downtown Seafood.'

'Well, you could be right,' said Sissy. 'In fact, that does seem more likely, when I come to think of it.' But she was just about to put away her witch compass when the needle abruptly jerked toward the bathroom door.

'Wait up,' she said. Very slowly, she swung the witch compass from side to side, but the needle remained pointing in the same direction, and it was actually *trembling*, like a gun dog that senses a quail.

She approached the bathroom door and opened it. There was nobody inside. Only a gleaming white bath with old-style brass faucets, and a shower, and two handbasins, and a mirror that completely filled the opposite wall. She could see herself peering in through the door, holding the witch compass in the palm of her hand.

T-Yon said, 'What is it, Sissy?' and came up close behind her.

Sissy shook her head. 'The compass . . . it definitely seems to sense something, but . . . I don't know—'

'*My God!*' screamed T-Yon, right in her ear. Her voice so high pitched that it was almost inaudible. '*My God, Sissy! Look! Look in the mirror! Oh my God!*'

Sissy stared at the mirror but she could still see nothing but herself. Behind her, though, T-Yon's eyes were wide and her face was rigid with shock. She clutched Sissy's shoulder and pointed at the mirror but she didn't seem capable of getting any more words out.

'*What?*' said Sissy. 'What is it, T-Yon?'

'Can't you see them?' squeaked T-Yon. 'They're looking at us! They're looking straight at us! They know we're here! Oh my God, can't you see what they're doing?'

'I don't see anybody,' said Sissy. 'Only you and me, nobody else. Who is it, T-Yon?'

T-Yon tugged at the sleeve of Sissy's kaftan. 'We have to get out of here! We have to get out of here now! They're looking at us, Sissy! They know that we're here!'

Sissy grabbed hold of the bathroom door-handle and quickly pulled it shut. She took T-Yon out into the corridor, although she deliberately dropped her bag on to the floor so that the outside door wouldn't close by itself. T-Yon was shaking and she wouldn't release her grip on Sissy's sleeve.

'T-Yon, what did you see in there? I didn't see anything at all in the mirror except our reflections.'

T-Yon took several deep breaths, and then she pressed her hand over her mouth to calm herself down.

'Who were they?' Sissy asked her. 'How many of them were there?'

T-Yon was still trying to regain her composure, and at first she couldn't answer.

'What were they doing? Please, T-Yon, try! You have to tell me!'

At last T-Yon managed to say, 'It was horrible. It was so, so horrible!'

Sissy waited, and then T-Yon said, 'There was a *body*. A man's dead body, lying on a table. It was all cut up and bloody. There was so much blood! It was all the way up the walls, everywhere! And there was this *boy*.'

'Go on,' Sissy coaxed her.

'The boy . . . *he* was all bloody, too. His hands, his clothes. He even had spots of blood on his face. He had . . . he had a really huge knife. He had a really huge knife and he was cutting the body up into pieces. Like, cutting the muscles away from the arms. But he had this *angry* look on his face, as if he hated what he was doing.'

She stopped, and took another deep breath.

'You said *they*,' said Sissy. 'Who else was there, apart from the boy?'

'A woman. A woman in a green dress with buttons all down it. She was standing nearby, watching what the boy was doing, but not so near that she had any blood on her.'

T-Yon turned and looked at the door to Room 511 and saw that Sissy had left her bag on the floor to keep it open.

'What if they come after us?' she said, in a panicky voice. 'What if they come out of the mirror and kill *us*, too?'

'T-Yon, I don't think that they can,' said Sissy, trying to calm her down. 'You saw them but I didn't, and that tells me that they were giving you a personal message – but only you.'

'What do you mean?'

'It's happened to me before. I've read people's fortunes, and when I do they can sometimes hear their loved ones talking to them, even though *I* can't hear anything. Once or twice they've even *seen* them, sitting in the room, but I never have. The message is for them and them alone.'

'Oh, God,' said T-Yon. 'Why don't you just close the door? There's no way I'm ever going back in there.'

'Well, I'm going to take one more look,' said Sissy. 'They might have left some evidence that they were there.'

'Don't be long,' T-Yon begged her. 'Please, that was so horrible. It was like my nightmare. All of his insides were hanging out.'

'I won't be a moment, I promise.' Sissy pushed her way back into Room 511 and walked across to the bathroom door. Before she opened it, however, she pressed her ear to it and listened. She was sure that she could hear voices, although they may have been the voices of guests in the corridor outside as they were being shown to their rooms.

'—*told you I didn't like it*—'

It was a boy's voice, shouting, and it sounded like the same boy that Sissy had heard when she was down on the third floor, although she couldn't be certain.

Then she heard the woman's voice, with that sour, distinctive accent, and she was sure of it.

'—*I don't give a two-cent damn whether you like it or not – you make sure you finish up here and don't you go leaving no mess*—'

Sissy hesitated for a second. Then another second. Then another. Her heart was beating so hard that it hurt. Then she flung open the bathroom door and said, '*Vanessa?*'

But again, there was nobody there. The bathroom was empty, with its clean white towels neatly arranged on the shelves, and its cluster of complimentary toiletries, and its drinking glasses with cardboard covers.

Sissy went right up to the washbasins and peered intently into the mirror. Then she reached up and tapped it with her silver rings. What T-Yon had seen had definitely been intended for her eyes only. Either that, or she had been hallucinating. But while Sissy had told her that the woman that she had seen running downstairs from the roof had been wearing a pale green dress, she hadn't told her that it was button-through, and it would be too much of a coincidence for her to hallucinate a detail like that.

She was about to leave the bathroom when her eye was caught by a bright red triangle of toweling hanging behind the door. She opened the door wider and saw that it was a bathrobe with *The Red Hotel* embroidered on the breast pocket.

Beside it, however, there was an equally bright red handprint, a handprint that was still glistening wet. It was clear, too. She could see the heart line and the head line and the life line – all the lines she usually used for telling fortunes.

She took off her eyeglasses and peered at it closely. It was high up on the door, even higher than the hook from which the bathrobe was hanging, and it was very broad, with splayed-out fingers, so that it had almost certainly been made by a man.

She looked around the bathroom again. She even opened the frosted glass shower door, to see if there were any more handprints in there. But the handprint on the door was the only one, and there were no red spots or smears or squiggles anywhere else, not even on the white-tiled floor.

She closed the bathroom door behind her and went back out into the corridor, where T-Yon was waiting for her, even more agitated than she had been before.

'Did you see them?' asked T-Yon. 'It was like that boy was *butchering* that body, wasn't it? It was like he was cutting him up for meat.'

They could faintly hear jazz music from down in the lobby. This time they were playing the old Louis Armstrong song *Didn't He Ramble*, which Sissy thought was horribly appropriate, considering the words. '*Didn't he ramble . . . didn't he ramble . . . he rambled in and out of town till the butcher cut him down.*'

Sissy said, 'I'm sorry, T-Yon. I still didn't see them. But I do believe that *you* did. And . . . I found a man's handprint in back of the bathroom door. It looks as if it could be blood.'

'Oh, no. Oh, God. This is terrible. What are we going to do now? Ev won't believe what I saw in the mirror, will he? Especially since *you* didn't see it. But what about this handprint? We'll have to tell that detective, won't we?'

'Yes, T-Yon. We will.'

'Oh, no. Poor Ev. He's going to go ape. He's going to think that I'm inventing all of this on purpose, just to spoil his big day.'

'No, he's not. I mean, why on earth should you?'

'Maybe he thinks that I'm jealous. I don't know.'

'Don't be ridiculous. Besides – you didn't invent that handprint. And for now, you don't have to tell him what you saw in the mirror. In fact, don't tell anybody. We need to understand what's happening here first. Who you saw, and why *you* could see them, when I couldn't.'

Sissy rummaged in her bag and produced a pad of Post-it notes. She wrote ROOM NOT CLEANED YET – PLEASE DO NOT ENTER with her mascara pencil, and stuck it on the door of Room 511.

'Who do you think they were?' asked T-Yon. 'Do you really think they were *spirits*?'

'I'm not sure. Kind of. But there's a whole lot more to it than that. I'm not even sure that I'm capable of finding out what. Even if I can, I'm even less sure that I'm capable of doing anything about it.'

'Sissy—'

'I'm sorry, T-Yon. I'm a fortune-teller, a clairvoyant, and I suppose you could say that I'm something of a medium, too. But I'm not an exorcist. Even if I can find out for sure who a spirit is, and what she wants, I don't necessarily have the power to make her go away. Especially when that spirit is making a point of showing me how goddamned ineffectual I am.'

'You can't say that.'

'Are you kidding me? She made a fool of me when she ran downstairs from the roof and then totally disappeared. She's made a fool of me again, by showing *you* what she's doing, but not me. She knows why I'm here, I'm sure of it, and she's mocking me.'

T-Yon said, '*I* believe in you. I really do. The way you understood my nightmares . . . I can't thank you enough for that.'

Sissy laid a hand on her arm and said, 'I appreciate that, T-Yon. I'll do my best. But I don't want you to have any illusions.'

'Illusions? I think I've had enough of those already.'

'You know what I think? I think a couple of stiff Sazeracs would do us both good.'

Blood Gala

B y the time they returned to the first floor, the opening gala was almost ready to begin. The Ralph Dickerson Ensemble was furiously playing *Muskrat Ramble* and the guests were noisily making their way into the Showboat Saloon and taking their places. A stage had been set up at the far end of the saloon, with a red-velvet awning, and all along the right-hand side of the room, red-jacketed waiters and waitresses were setting up a lavish buffet table, heaping it with fruit and salads and hams and cold shrimp and oysters. The hot food would be brought in later, after the speeches, but the blue spirit-lamps were already lit, ready for the Cajun chicken legs and the cedar-roasted redfish and the soft-shelled crabs.

Sissy looked around for Detective Garrity but she couldn't see him at first. She sat at the bar with T-Yon and ordered them both a Sazerac – a cocktail of cognac, rye whiskey, absinthe and Peychaud's Bitters. T-Yon was still so shaky that she could barely pick up her glass. Sissy squeezed her hand tightly to try and reassure her that everything was going to be all right.

'We'll find a way, T-Yon, I promise you. I don't know how, sweetheart, but we will.'

The jazz ensemble played a fanfare, and the assembled guests all applauded as Everett and Luther came into the saloon, accompanied by Mayor Dolan, who was wearing one of his trademark flappy white suits, and his daughter, Lolana, who was wearing a short, tight, sparkly silver dress. They were followed by six or seven other dignitaries from the Baton Rouge Area Convention and Visitors' Bureau and the Baton Rouge Sports Foundation.

They mounted the stage and took their seats. When the clapping and whistling had subsided, Everett went up to the microphone and said, 'Welcome, everybody, to The Red Hotel!'

There was more applause, and then he announced, 'This is a great day for Baton Rouge and a momentous day for me. This hotel has a wonderful location, so close to the mighty Mississippi, and so close to all the amenities of the city center, and it has been crying out for so long to have its pride and its reputation restored. What my fellow investors and I have tried to recreate in The Red Hotel is the true spirit of the Red Stick – the hospitality, the warmth, the fun, the flamboyance.

'Our aim is to provide our guests with supreme comfort in every room, as well as every modern facility they could wish for. On top of that, our restaurant will be serving the finest Cajun and Creole food in the parish, as well as top-class nightly entertainment.

'Most of all, we want our guests to feel that they're being

pampered – pampered in the old-fashioned, turn-of-the-century style – from the moment they walk in through the front door until the moment they bid us *au revoir*.'

When he had finished speaking, he caught sight of Sissy and T-Yon at the bar, and frantically beckoned them to come up to the front. But T-Yon shook her head.

'I *can't*,' she told Sissy. 'I would have to tell him what I saw in that mirror, and I don't want to upset him, not now.'

Mayor Dolan got to his feet and started to speak in soaring rhetoric about the 'irrepressible spirit and boundless warm-heartedness of the City of Baton Rouge.'

'BR is the epicenter of tolerance and mutual respect and good-neighborliness, where *all* are welcome, regardless of who they are or where in the world they come from.'

They were still listening to Mayor Dolan when Detective Garrity came into the saloon. He perched himself on a bar stool next to them and said, 'No sign of Mullard, then.'

'No, Detective,' said Sissy. 'But I've been looking for you.'

'Oh, yeah.' He lifted his finger to the barman and said, 'Give me a club soda, would you, with a twist.'

Sissy said, 'T-Yon and me, we went back up to Room Five-Eleven which is where I last saw Detective Mullard.'

'Oh, yeah.' Detective Garrity's eyes were roaming restlessly around the room.

'I found a handprint in back of the bathroom door, quite high up. I may be wrong, but it looks like it could be blood.'

Detective Garrity stared at her narrowly. 'A handprint.'

'That's right. A man's hand, by the size of it.'

'This is the same room where you said you'd located some kind of psychic disturbance?'

Sissy nodded.

'And there's only one single handprint? Any other blood spatter?'

'That's all there is, Detective. And I made sure that I didn't touch it, or anything else for that matter.'

'OK,' said Detective Garrity. 'Mr Savoie gave me the use of a master key, so why don't you show me.' He drank his club soda in two large gulps and then climbed off his bar stool. 'I wish to hell I knew where Mullard was hiding himself.

I've been calling him for damn near on twenty minutes now and still no answer.'

'T-Yon?' asked Sissy. 'Are you going to stay here, sweetheart? You don't want to come back up there, do you?'

T-Yon mouthed, 'No, no way,' and then she said, 'I'll wait for Ev to finish.'

Sissy could understand why she wanted to stay here. The crowd was loud and happy, and everything was real. No sourfaced women in pale green dresses, no hacked-up bodies and no blood-spattered boys. 'I'll see you a little later, in that case,' she told her, and reassuringly touched her shoulder.

Sissy and Detective Garrity went up in the elevator to the fifth floor. Detective Garrity dry-washed his face with his hands and then he said, 'So . . . tell me something about yourself, whyn't you.'

Sissy shrugged. 'Not much to tell, Detective. I live in Allen's Corners, Connecticut, with my dog and my memories. My late husband, Frank, was a Master Sergeant in the State Police.'

'But you claim you have this, uh –' and here Detective Garrity pointed to his forehead and twirled his finger – 'psychic sensitivity.'

'That's right. Yes, I do. I guess it's something that you're born with, like a talent for playing the piano, or athletics, or any other kind of a talent. You don't choose to have it, and a whole lot of people are born with it but never choose to use it, on account of it's such a great responsibility, telling people's futures, and letting them know how their gone-beyonders are getting along. And it can be scary at times, believe me. Not every ghost is as friendly as Casper.'

Detective Garrity stood back while Sissy stepped out of the elevator. 'I hope you don't take exception when I tell you that I find this all pretty hard to swallow. My old man was a physics teacher at Magnet High. He didn't believe in nothing that couldn't be proven in the science laboratory.'

'Did he believe in God?'

'Oh, yes, ma'am. He believed in God.'

'Well, then,' said Sissy, as they reached the door of Room 511. '*Quod erat demonstrandum.*'

*   *   *

Detective Garrity pointed to the Post-it note that Sissy had stuck to the door.

'Good thinking,' he said. 'I could use more people like you.'

He dug into the pocket of his narrow-tailored coat and produced two latex gloves, which he snapped on to his fingers. 'I have only the one pair of these, so please don't touch anything, OK.'

'I'll try not to.'

Detective Garrity walked into the center of the bedroom and looked around. 'No obvious sign that anybody's been here. Nothing's disturbed, so far as I can see.'

Sissy was wondering if she ought to produce her witch compass and show Detective Garrity how it worked, but she decided against it. Just for now, a single bloody handprint was enough of a puzzle for him to deal with, without challenging his fundamental disbelief in spirits.

'So where did you say this handprint was? In the bathroom?'

Detective Garrity approached the bathroom door and was already grasping the handle when the whole room was shaken by a deep, reverberating, grinding noise. It started up suddenly, and it was so loud and caused so much vibration that the bedside clock began to rattle and slowly creep sideways across the nightstand, and the complimentary bottles of body lotion and eau de toilette that stood on the dressing table started frantically clinking together, as if they were panicking. Even the glass in the windows began to buzz.

'What in God's name is *that*?' shouted Detective Garrity, and that was the first time that Sissy had ever heard him use any emphasis in his voice at all. He twisted around and looked up at the ceiling, and then at each of the walls in turn, and then back up at the ceiling again. The noise was so overwhelming that it was impossible to tell where it was coming from.

To Sissy, it sounded like a concrete mixer and a giant meat mincer, both grinding away together, one of them churning wet cement and the other one liquefying muscle and connective tissue, one of them punctuated by the ping and clatter of shingle and the other by the spasmodic crackling of bones.

'*I think it's a warning!*' she shouted back at Detective Garrity.

'*A warning? What the hell of? Feels more like a goddamn earthquake.*'

'*That presence I've been telling you about. She's trying to show us how angry she is.*'

'*What does she have to be angry about? Christ on a bicycle I can't hear myself think.*'

The grinding went on and on, and grew louder with every passing minute. The bedside clock at last dropped on to the floor, and all the bottles of toiletries fell over. Even the floorboards beneath their feet were vibrating. Sissy had to hold on to the carved wooden bedposts to stop herself from losing her balance.

'*What can we do?*' Detective Garrity yelled at her. '*Is there anything that* you *can do?*'

Sissy wasn't at all sure if there was, but she clung tightly on to the bedpost with both hands and shouted out, '*Vanessa! Vanessa Slider! Stop! I promise we'll go! All of us! I promise we'll go and leave you alone! You and your boy, both!*'

The grinding continued. The clattering and pinging and crackling had subsided, but this had been replaced by a thick, repetitive *shhluggg, shhluggg, shhluggg.*

Suddenly, it stopped, and the room was silent again. Detective Garrity looked around, listening, and then he turned to Sissy and said, 'Did you do that?'

'I'm sure I don't know. Maybe.'

'You shouted out "Vanessa Slider".'

'That's right.'

'Vanessa Slider is the woman who used to own this hotel, back in the eighties, when it was the Hotel Rouge.'

'I know. She was jailed, wasn't she, for attempted murder? I think the presence we've been feeling in The Red Hotel is her. In fact, I've been pretty sure of it, even before we came here.'

'Vanessa Slider. You mean that? I would say that Vanessa Slider must be long dead.'

'That doesn't make any difference, Detective. What we're talking about here is Vanessa Slider's influence. She may be a gone-beyonder, but her vengefulness is still with us. She's trying to scare the new owners off. All of these disturbances, I believe they're all down to her. The bloody mat, Ella-mae's disappearance, that grinding noise we just heard.'

'You really believe that.'

'Yes, Detective, I do, and it happens a whole lot more than you think. There was Amityville.'

'*Amityville* was a movie, ma'am. With James Brolin in it if I remember rightly.'

'Of course, and because of that the true story was blown way out of all proportion. But what *really* happened at Amityville was a classic example of what we have here. I've come across it before. An old friend of mine bought a house in New Canaan and she could hear a woman screaming in the attic almost every single night. I spent the night there once, and heard the woman myself.'

'Stop,' said Detective Garrity. 'You're not going to convince me. I don't believe in any of this stuff, not for a second. That noise we just heard, there's a straightforward technical explanation for it. There has to be. A pocket of air in the water pipes, something like that.'

'I'm not going to disagree with you, Detective,' Sissy told him. 'In fact I would be very much happier if that's all it was.'

Detective Garrity listened for a moment longer. From the Showboat Saloon they could faintly hear the jazz quartet playing *Alexander's Ragtime Band*.

'*Come on and hear, come on and hear, it's the best band in the land . . .*'

For some reason that she couldn't have explained to anybody, Sissy had always found that song supremely irritating. She looked round at Detective Garrity but all he said was, 'Hear that? It don't sound to me like *they* heard any of that noise.'

'Maybe it was only audible *here*, in this room,' Sissy suggested. 'Maybe it was meant for us, and us alone.'

Detective Garrity frowned at her, but he didn't say anything. He went back to the bathroom door and cautiously opened it.

'Top left-hand side, next to the bathrobe,' said Sissy.

Detective Garrity stepped into the bathroom but before he

could take a look behind the door, he said, in the quietest of voices, '*Jesus.*'

'What is it?' asked Sissy. 'Have you found something else?'

He came back out of the bathroom and his face was gray. Without saying a word he took out his cell and started to jab at the keypad.

'*What?* What is it?' Sissy repeated. She tried to look over his shoulder into the bathroom but he stepped to one side to block her view. When she leaned the other way, to look over his other shoulder, he leaned the other way, too.

'Mike?' he said, into his cell. 'It's Garrity.' He was out of breath, as if he had been running. 'I'm up in Room Five-Eleven. That's it, Five-Eleven. Listen, Mike – we got ourselves a thirty-C up here by the look of it. A thirty-C, man, like no other thirty-C you ever saw. No. You'll understand what I mean when you come up and see it for yourself, OK. Just send me some backup and a forensic team. And for Christ's sake don't say a word to Mr Savoie down there, or any of his staff, and don't say a word to any of the guests, either. Just for now, let them carry on like they are. Is Hizzoner still there? Get him and his daughter off the premises now. But don't let anybody else leave the building. No. Nobody. Not even the veeps. If they want to know why, tell them that we have some minor and probably unfounded concerns about security but to keep it to themselves.'

He cut the connection and then he started to punch out another number.

'A thirty-C?' asked Sissy. 'What's a thirty-C when it's at home?'

Detective Garrity took a breath, paused, and then said, 'Homicide by cutting. Only in this case it's a considerable understatement.'

'You mean there's a dead body in there?'

'You don't want to look, ma'am. I promise you.'

'But it's important that I do. Who is it?'

'Right now, ma'am, I don't have any idea.'

'Is it a man or a woman?'

'Ma'am, please. I have enough on my plate. And damn it, I still can't raise Mullard.'

'Detective, I know how skeptical you are about my psychic facility, but this is really, *really* important.'

Detective Garrity stared at her and took another deep breath, as if he were about to shout at her. But then – in what was little more than a whisper, he said – 'I don't *know* if it's a man or a woman. The truth is, I simply can't tell. That's what I meant when I told my sergeant that it's a thirty-C like he never saw before.'

He raised both eyebrows – as if to say, 'Satisfied?' – and then he went back to punching out numbers on his cell.

Sissy stayed where she was, in the center of the room. She closed her eyes for a moment and tried to sense if Vanessa Slider were anywhere near. She could feel that uncomfortable *chilliness*, yes, but she had felt it everywhere inside The Red Hotel since the moment she had first stepped into the lobby. When she opened her eyes again, Detective Garrity was talking to his captain at the second precinct, and pacing around the bedroom as he did so.

She sidled her way nearer to the bathroom door. She knew that what she was going to see would be horrible, but she had to find out what Vanessa Slider was doing, and why, and what she was capable of.

'Yes, Captain, we've searched the whole goddamned building roof to basement twice over,' Detective Garrity was saying. 'I don't know where the hell the perp could be hiding, but we can't risk any more fatalities. We'll have to evacuate everybody. Then we'll have to tear the place apart all over again.'

He paced right over to the closet, and was standing with his back toward her, so Sissy took three quick tiptoes to the bathroom door and opened it.

She had expected a body, and she had expected blood. She had seen dead people before, in the mortuary, almost turquoise some of them. But sitting in the bathtub was a headless figure that was nothing but a glistening red tangle of muscle and bone and stringy connective tissue, with a pale pile of intestines in its lap. Its neck was nothing more than a corrugated pipe, and there was no sign of what might have happened to its head.

Sissy closed the door quietly behind her. Her stomach began to clench and unclench, and she could feel bile rising in her throat. It took several deep breaths to stop herself from retching. When she turned around she found Detective Garrity staring at her.

'I thought I specifically told you not to look.'

Sissy nodded. She took out her handkerchief and pressed it against her mouth, and after a few moments the bile subsided.

'I'm afraid I'll have to ask you to leave now, Ms Sawyer,' said Detective Garrity. 'I appreciate your good intentions and all, but this entire hotel is a crime scene now.'

'My *God*, Detective. Whoever that body is, that isn't just murder, is it?'

Detective Garrity was silent for a moment, although he didn't take his eyes off her. At first Sissy didn't think he was going to answer her, but now that she had seen the body for herself, there was no point in him not telling her what he thought, and she could tell that he was just as shaken as she was.

At length he said, 'Let me tell you this, ma'am. I've seen cadavers cut up for the purposes of easy disposal – you know, packing them in suitcases or flushing them down drains – but I can't say that I've seen anything quite like this before. Looks to me like that cadaver's been cut up like an animal carcass.'

'As in *butchered*?' said Sissy.

This time, Detective Garrity said nothing. They stood side by side for two or three minutes, neither of them speaking, trying to come to terms with the grisly horror that they had witnessed in the bath.

They heard somebody laughing hilariously in the corridor outside; and from downstairs, they could still faintly hear the wheedling clarinet strains of *Alexander's Ragtime Band*.

After a while, Sissy said, 'You're going to evacuate *everybody*?'

'Of course. We'll have to. Discreetly, of course. We don't want a panic.'

Sissy said, 'OK, then. I'll go now, Detective. But I'll stay here in Baton Rouge and I'll make sure you know how to get in touch with me.'

'Kind of you to offer, ma'am, but I doubt if that will be necessary.'

'You're going to need me, Detective, you mark my words.'

'You mean, if it really *is* the ghost of Vanessa Slider who's been doing all of this.'

Sissy slung her bag over her shoulder. 'You can be as skeptical as you like. But don't say I didn't warn you. I promise you that I won't hold it against you when you decide that you can't solve this case without me. Because I honestly don't believe that you can.'

The House Within

'That's it, we're finished,' said Everett. 'We're finished and we haven't even started.'

The last of the gala guests were being ushered through the hotel lobby and interviewed by more than twenty uniformed police officers. The music had been silenced, the conversation was muted, and all they could hear was the shuffling of shoes on the marble floor. So far, nobody had been told exactly why The Red Hotel was being evacuated, only that the management had received a 'low-level security alert.'

The media had gathered outside and Detective Garrity had promised them a statement within the hour. A team of five criminalists had already arrived in their white Tyvek suits and gone rustling up in the elevator to room 511, like the crew of a space shuttle that was going nowhere.

T-Yon was sitting next to Everett, holding his hand to comfort him. Luther was perched on the edge of Everett's desk, looking glum. Sissy wandered around for a while, and then went through to the Showboat Saloon, which was almost completely deserted now, except for the kitchen staff taking away the remains of the buffet, and the jazz ensemble packing away their instruments. Paper streamers and party poppers littered the carpet.

She sat down at a table in the corner and took out her

DeVane Cards. She badly needed guidance and reassurance, and some kind of explanation for the horror that she had witnessed in Room 511.

She dealt out the cards as she always did, in a Cross of Lorraine, but this time she used a different card to represent herself. Instead of The Star-Gazer, she chose *La Menteuse*, The Liar. This card showed a sly, deceitful-looking old woman with a pointed nose and a strange turban-like hat, dealing out playing cards to three innocently laughing men.

What the men couldn't see was that all the cards that the woman was holding in her hand were the same, the ace of spades. Sissy thought that by using this card as her Predictor, she might be able to outwit Vanessa Slider, and prevent her from tampering with her pack.

The first card she turned up, again, was *La Châtelaine*, so it was clear that Vanessa Slider's influence was still overwhelming. Then again, she turned up *La Cuisine De Nuit*, the Night Kitchen, with the pale girl frying her own intestines. So it looked as if T-Yon was still in danger.

The third card, however, made Sissy frown in puzzlement. She had often turned up the same card before, when she had been reading people's fortunes back at home in Allen's Corners. It was *Un Maison, Deux Maisons* – One House, Two Houses. It showed a grand French country house, with a pillared portico, and red rambling roses growing around its facade. A man and his wife were standing proudly together on the front steps. He was wearing a green frock coat and white breeches and buckled shoes, while she was wearing an extravagant pink dress decorated with ribbons, and a tall powdered wig.

Inside the open front doors, however, appeared the front porch of another house, as if one house were built inside the other. The same man was standing on the steps of this house, although he was wearing only an open shirt and black breeches, and his feet were bare. There was a woman standing next to him, but it was a different woman, and she was naked apart from a pearl necklace and a pair of pink slippers.

In the orchards that surrounded this house within a house, children of various ages were playing with hoops and hobby horses, and small dogs were running around.

Usually, when this card came up, it told Sissy that a husband was having an affair, and might even be leading a double life with a mistress and children of which his wife was completely unaware. Once, it had even revealed that a friend's husband was bigamous. He had been living with one wife in New Milford for eleven years, although three years ago he had married a second wife, ten years younger, forty miles away in Darien.

But this time, One House, Two Houses had to have a different meaning altogether. She wasn't asking the cards about anybody's marital relationship. She wanted to know more about the mutilated body in the bathroom, and what kind of danger *she* might be facing.

One House, Two Houses? One house inside another? What did that mean, in the context of Vanessa Slider and The Red Hotel?

She was still frowning at the card when Luther walked in. One crumpled shirt-tail was hanging out of his baggy red pants and he looked exhausted.

'Oh, *that's* where you at,' he said. He pulled up a chair and sat down next to her. 'We should all be vacating the premises in a half hour or so, just as soon as we've finished tidying everything up. I was wondering if you'd like to come stay with me and Shatoya for a day or two. I was going to introduce you to Shatoya earlier on, but I didn't get the chance. Ms T-Yon's going to be staying with Mister Everett but he only has the one spare room.'

'Well, that's very generous of you,' said Sissy. 'So long as it's not going to put you out. I could always find another hotel. There's the Hilton right next door.'

'Shatoya give me such a hard time if I let you do that,' said Luther. 'Pervided you don't mind my Aunt Epiphany. She lives with us permanent. She's kind of individual in her ways but she's good for babysitting and she cooks up the best smothered pork chops you ever tasted.'

'Didn't you say your Aunt Epiphany was a voodoo queen?'

'That's correct, Ms Sissy, but we don't encourage her to practice it too much around the house. We let her have her dolls, but we don't want our kids growing up thinking that the way to get your revenge on somebody is to go sticking pins in no effigy.'

He looked down at the cards that Sissy had laid out. 'What those telling you? Good news, I hope. We could sure do with some.'

Sissy was just about to tell him about the house within a house when a pretty black waitress in a short red skirt came up to them. 'If you're hungry, Mr Broody, we have a whole stack of burgers left over.'

'Sure, why not?' said Luther. 'I was so busy organizing that gala I never got the time to eat nothing. How about you, Ms Sissy? Think you could go for a burger?'

Sissy shook her head. 'I'm not hungry at the moment, thanks. But an iced tea would be very welcome.'

'Great. Cheeseburger charred, with one large Diet Coke and a ice tea for the lady here.'

When the waitress had gone, Sissy held up *Un Maison, Deux Maisons* so that Luther could focus on it clearly. 'You see this card, Luther? This card is telling me that something highly unusual is happening here in this hotel.'

'*Unusual?* Shoot. You are seriously not joking.'

'How can I put it? It's like there's not just one reality, but *two*, and one reality overlaps the other.'

'Say *what*?'

'Well, look – the picture on this card here shows us one house hidden inside another house. So these people have an outside life which all the world can see quite openly, but behind the front door, they have another life, which is secret, and which nobody else gets to see.'

'OK . . .' said Luther, dubiously.

'Most of the time, this card indicates that a woman's husband is having an adulterous affair. But not here, and not now.'

Luther pulled a face, almost as if he were in pain. 'I'm not too sure what you driving at, Ms Sissy.'

Sissy laid the card back on the table. 'You may think I'm just a nutty old woman, Luther, but I'm sure that this is the answer. Or *part* of the answer, anyhow. That rug that was soaked in blood, what room did Ella-mae find it in?'

'Suite Seven-Oh-Three.'

'OK. She found it in Suite Seven-Oh-Three. But what I'm saying is that – originally – it didn't come from *that* Suite Seven-Oh-Three.'

'Ms Sissy,' said Luther, trying to be patient. 'We only have one Suite Seven-Oh-Three.'

Sissy lifted her finger. 'You *think* you do, Luther, but it's the same as this card. A house within a house. Inside Suite Seven-Oh-Three is another Suite Seven-Oh-Three. Not existing in the same dimension, maybe. But there, all the same. And somebody has the ability to move between one Suite Seven-Oh-Three and the other Suite Seven-Oh-Three, which is why there were no footprints and no fingerprints and no blood spattered all over the place.'

Luther looked at Sissy for almost half a minute before he said anything. Then he traced a pattern on the tabletop with his fingertip, as if he were trying to draw an explanatory diagram.

'You trying to tell me there's *two* Suite Seven-Oh-Threes?'

'For all I know there may be even more.'

'Well, let's just stick with two of them for now. But one of them exists in another dimension?'

'Exactly. But when I'm talking about another dimension, I don't mean like some science-fiction story, with Martians in it. You know, *The Creature from the Tenth Dimension.* I simply mean another dimension like time, or space. They could be slightly out of sync. *Infinitesimally* out of sync, which does happen. Some psychics call it phasing. Phasing accounts for the appearance of what we call ghosts, and why it's possible for us to talk to gone-beyonders.'

'Gone-beyonders? Who are they?'

'Dead people, to you.'

Luther thought for another long while. Then he said, 'I don't know what to say to you, Ms Sissy. Do you *really* believe we got two Suite Seven-Oh-Threes? I don't mean to cause you no offense but you beginning to sound even wackier than my Aunt Epiphany.'

'No, Luther, I don't believe you have two Suite Seven-Oh-Threes. I believe you have much more than that. I believe you have two entire hotels.'

She picked up the One House, Two Houses card again. 'This is what this card is telling me. You have two hotels, almost identical except for one fraction of a fraction's difference, either in time or in location, which is why one can exist inside the other.'

Luther looked around the Showboat Saloon. Then he looked back at Sissy. 'So you think we're sitting inside a saloon, inside a saloon?'

'I don't know,' Sissy admitted. 'Like I said, there may be many more. There may be an infinite number. It could be like looking into one of those three-piece dressing-table mirrors, and seeing your reflections going off left and right, hundreds of them. Where do they end? Do they end at all? And how do you know which one of them is the real you?'

'You messing with my head, Ms Sissy. Are you going to explain all of this to Mr Everett? How about the poh-lice? Think they'll understand it any better than I do?'

'Not just yet, Luther,' said Sissy. She nodded toward her DeVane cards. 'I need to finish this reading first. It could tell me a whole lot more.'

At that moment, the waitress came back with Luther's cheeseburger and Coke and Sissy's iced tea.

'You don't mind if I dig in, do you?' asked Luther. 'I'm so hungry I could eat two of these. Well – from what you say, maybe I'm going to. One burger inside of another burger.'

He opened his cheeseburger and smothered it with tomato relish before picking it up in both hands and starting to eat. 'Mmm-mmhh!' he said, with his mouth full. 'You don't know what you missing here, Ms Sissy! This is *good*!'

Sissy smiled, but all she could think about was that bloody, headless body sitting in the bath in Room 511, and she seriously wondered if she would ever be able to eat meat ever again.

She continued to turn over her DeVane cards. The rest of them told much the same enigmatic story as her previous reading. Somewhere, a whistling shadow was patiently waiting for T-Yon. Somewhere, an unknown woman was pressing her hand against a whitewashed wall, while the portrait of a man looked mournfully down at her. Pastry cooks were baking pies with human fingers protruding from their crusts, and leaving them to cool on their kitchen window sill. Down by the water's edge, Everett was frantically waving a red banner for help, while brown pelicans flocked all around him.

Sissy had never known the cards to be so urgent, and so alarmist, and yet so confused. She felt almost as if they were panicking.

'You should have ordered one of these,' said Luther, holding up his cheeseburger, of which he had already devoured more than half. 'Our grill chef, Jimmy, he's the best in town. We stole him from Louie's on West State Street.'

Sissy gave him a quick-dissolving smile. 'Maybe some other time.'

She was just about to turn over the last card but as soon as she touched it she knew that she didn't need to. She could feel instinctively that it was the Night Kitchen. In spite of that, and even though the cards were so unsettled, she felt a small amount of satisfaction that she had probably learned more from this reading than Vanessa Slider had wanted her to.

Vanessa Slider had run down the stairs from the roof in her pale green dress, but where had she vanished then? To Sissy, the logical answer was that she had disappeared from one Red Hotel and reappeared in another.

As she was gathering up her cards, she heard Detective Garrity call out, 'Ah, Ms Sawyer, ma'am. You're still here, then.' He came across the saloon, closely followed by a sallow young detective with shiny black hair and a raspberry-colored coat.

'Hallo, Detective,' said Sissy. 'I'm just waiting for Mr Savoie to finish up and then I'll be leaving. Mr Broody here has kindly offered me a roof over my head.'

'Afraid I have some bad news,' said Detective Garrity.

'You've identified the body?'

He nodded. 'The CSIs found a billfold and a signet ring in the bottom of the bathtub, underneath the cadaver. They both belonged to Kevin Mullard.'

'Oh, no, I'm so sorry. Oh, that's terrible.'

Detective Garrity was trying hard not to sound too emotional. 'That's only a preliminary ID, of course. But I can't see how there's any doubt. Kevin – you know – Kevin was a truly great guy. Rough at the edges, if you know what I mean. Terrible taste in suits. But you could always count on him, day or night. God knows what the hell they did to him.'

Luther was still chewing the last of his hamburger. Suddenly he frowned, and stopped chewing, and chased something around the inside of his mouth with his tongue. He reached up with finger and thumb and carefully spat it out.

'Gristle?' asked Sissy.

Luther picked up his napkin and wiped it and then he held it up. It was a green plastic button.

Vanished

Sissy went back to Everett's office. Everett was standing around talking to Charlie Bowdre and two other maintenance men, while Bella was tidying up his desk for him.

'You all ready to go?' asked Everett.

'Yes,' said Sissy. 'My bag's at reception. I'm waiting on Luther, that's all. He's not feeling too good.'

'Oh, yeah? What's the problem?'

'I think you'd better ask him yourself.'

She didn't know for sure that Luther had been eating what he had suspected he was eating, and she didn't want to upset Everett more than was necessary. The CSIs had asked Luther to stick his finger down his throat and vomit into a bowl so that they could analyze his stomach contents. Just thinking about it made Sissy feel nauseous.

She looked around. 'Where's T-Yon? I wanted to make sure that she was OK.'

'She'll be here directly. She forgot her make-up, that's all, and she went back up to her room to get it.'

Sissy sat down in the corner. Detective Garrity came into the office and took Everett aside, speaking to him quietly and intently. It was obvious from the look on Everett's face that

Detective Garrity was telling him what Luther had found in his cheeseburger.

When he had gone, Everett turned to Sissy and said, 'You knew about this?'

'Yes,' Sissy admitted.

'You're a fortune teller. Tell me this. Can things get any frigging worse than they are already? Personally, I don't see how they can.'

Sissy was tempted to try and explain her idea about the hotel within a hotel. The more she thought about it, the more it made sense. It was a known phenomenon, phasing, scientifically measurable, and it had been the only plausible explanation for countless so-called 'hauntings.' True, she had never come across it on such a massive scale before. Usually, it was little more than singing in an empty room; or the reflection of a dead husband, seen through a window; or the smell of baking when the stove was cold, and the wife who had once bustled around the kitchen was lying in the cemetery.

But Sissy thought: *it's possible, if Vanessa Slider is vengeful enough. Who knows what people can do when they feel bitterly wronged?*

Luther appeared, gray-faced, his eyes red-rimmed, as if he had been dusted with ash.

'How are you feeling now?' she asked him.

He wiped his mouth with the back of his hand. 'That's three times I swilled out my mouth with Listerine but I can still taste it. *Yecchh!* One of those CSI women promised to call me as soon as she's analyzed it, but I'm not too sure I want to find out, to tell you the God's honest truth.'

'I expect you want to go home,' said Sissy. 'I was hoping to have a quick word with T-Yon, but I have her cell number. I can call her later.'

'Thanks, Ms Sissy. Appreciate it. You're a lady.'

T-Yon stepped out of the elevator when it reached the second floor and walked quickly along to Room 209. Police officers and security guards were still searching the upper floors, but now that everybody else had been evacuated The Red Hotel was unnaturally quiet. Occasionally she heard a shout or an echo, or the whine of an elevator, but the only other sound was her wedge-heeled sandals on the thick gold carpet.

She reached Room 209 and opened the door. She went directly to the bathroom where she had left her make-up. She wouldn't have bothered but it was a nearly new bottle of Diorskin Nude foundation which had cost her forty-six dollars.

She dropped the bottle into her gray leather purse, and checked her hair in the bathroom mirror, flicking her fringe with her fingertips. She thought that her eyes looked swollen, which was hardly surprising after last night's interrupted sleep and the grisly scenario she had witnessed in the mirror of Room 511.

She went back into the bedroom and stopped dead.

The two figures who had materialized at the end of her bed last night were standing between her and the door. One was about as tall as she was, while the other was much shorter, like a child, but both of them were draped in black sheets, so it was impossible to tell who they were or what they looked like.

'What?' she said. Her voice came out much higher than she had intended, and it was tight with fright.

The two figures said nothing, but simply stood there, side by side. T-Yon could hear them breathing under their sheets, and the smaller one sounded as if it were suffering from a cold.

'*What do you want?*' T-Yon screamed at them. '*Get out of my way!*'

She raised her purse over her head and took two steps toward them, but without hesitation the taller one lifted both of its black-sheeted arms and pushed her, hard. She stumbled backward over the large wooden linen chest at the foot of the bed and fell heavily on to the floor, hitting her shoulder against the dressing table.

She tried to climb back up on to her feet, but the figure came up to her and pushed her again, and then again.

'Get away from me!' she shouted. 'What do you want?'

The taller figure reached out an arm from underneath the folds of its sheets, took hold of the sheet that covered its head, and dragged it to one side. As it pulled the sheet clear, it revealed itself to be a man. He looked about thirty-five, very pallid, as if he never went outside in the sunlight. He had sparse, spiky hair, drooping eyes, and a bulbous nose with a cleft in the end of it. His lips were crusted with scabs, and his front teeth were missing. A razor-wire tattoo encircled his neck, and his hands were crawling with tattoos, too.

T-Yon thought that he looked like an ex-convict. Whatever he was, he wasn't a ghost, but in some ways he was even more frightening than a ghost, because T-Yon suspected that he had come here for the sole purpose of doing her harm. He stood staring down at her, shifting a large wad of gray gum from one side of his mouth to the other. The smaller figure remained under its sheet. T-Yon could hear its phlegm cackling in the back of its nostrils.

'What do you want?' T-Yon repeated. 'The cops know where I am. If I don't go back downstairs in a couple of minutes, they'll come up here looking for me.'

'I ain't concerned about that, bo,' the man replied. His voice was high and reedy for a man of his bulk, with a strong local accent. 'By the time the cops come looking for you, you'll be someplace where nobody on God's good earth will be able to find you.'

'Just let me out of here,' said T-Yon. Then she screamed out, '*Help! Somebody help me! I'm in here! Help me!*'

The man gave a wheezy laugh, and the smaller figure giggled, too, underneath its sheet, and then gave a thick, viscous sniff.

'You shouldn't waste your breath, bo,' the man told her. 'There ain't nobody on this floor excepting you and me and little peeshwank here. Now, let's get going, shall we? We don't want to keep the *pauvre defante mom* waiting, now do we?'

'Get out of here! Get away from me! *Somebody help me! Anybody!*'

T-Yon seized the edge of the dressing table and managed to pull herself on to her feet. She feinted left, and then right, and then made a rush toward the door. She had hardly taken two steps, however, when the smaller figure wrapped its sheeted arms around her legs, just above the knees, and clung on tight. She staggered, and tried to wade forward, but the man hooked his left arm around her neck and wrenched her head sideways.

'There ain't no future in trying to run off,' he told her. His breath stank of garlic and that sweet, dark brown odor of decaying teeth, which not even his chewing gum had been able to mask. 'Ain't nobody can hear you – and like I say, you'll be long gone before anybody starts asking theirselves what's become of you.'

'You're choking me!' gasped T-Yon.

'Oh, I won't choke you, bo. Not before the *pauvre defante* gets to talk to you.'

T-Yon tried to scream again, but she managed only a muffled blurt before the man clamped his hand over her mouth.

'Let's get the fuck out of here, peeshwank,' he said. The smaller figure opened the door and held it open while he frogmarched T-Yon out into the corridor.

T-Yon was hyperventilating now. She twisted from side to side and kicked her legs up into the air, but the man was much too strong for her. He held her so close and so tight that his stubble rasped against the side of her cheek and she could smell not only the blasts of fetid breath that came out of his mouth but his body odor, too.

The man half pushed her and half swung her along the corridor. As they passed the last bedroom door she felt a rising flood of terror, because there was nothing ahead of them now but the window at the far end. She could see the Hilton Hotel on the opposite side of Lafayette and she could hear the noise of traffic two stories below.

Still the man kept humping and heaving her along, and she was helpless to stop him. *Dear God*, she thought. *He's going to throw me out.*

Strutting beside them, its black sheets rustling, the smaller figure started singing in its catarrhal voice:

'*Jolie blonde, regardez donc quoi t'as fait!*
Tu m'as quitté pour t'en aller,
Pour t'en aller avec un autre, oui, que moi,
Quel espoir et quelle avenir, mais, moi, je vais à voir!'

T-Yon was blinded by the afternoon sunlight shining in through the window and she squeezed her eyes tight shut.

Bitter Feelings

Luther said, glumly, 'How about you, Ms Sissy? You reckon we'll get over all of this? The way it looks to me now, it wouldn't surprise me if we have to close our doors for good.'

'Oh, you'll get over it somehow,' said Sissy, looking out of the window of his Jeep as they drove southward through the subdivisions of East Baton Rouge.

'Is that what your cards tell you?'

'Right now my cards can't see beyond any of this mayhem. I just *feel* that you'll get over it, that's all – feel it in my water. But I don't think it's going to be easy, and it could be highly dangerous.'

'Why, thank you, Ms Sissy,' said Luther. 'You sure know how to cheer a body up, not.' He licked his lips, and swallowed, and grimaced. 'Sheesh, I can still taste that goddamn cheeseburger. I think I'm going to be tasting that goddamn cheeseburger for the rest of my life.'

They were passing a cemetery, clustered with hundreds of marble headstones, all of them shining orange in the light from the sinking sun.

'See that?' said Luther. 'That's the Sweet Olive Cemetery. That's where my uncle is interred, Aunt Epiphany's late husband, Elijah. She comes up here just about every Sunday afternoon to talk to him. According to her, he still has plenty to say, even though he's passed over. Sometimes she says that she can't get a word in edgewise.'

'There's a lot of gone-beyonders like that,' said Sissy. 'A few of them don't even realize that they've passed away. Most of them do, sure, but they still haven't finished speaking their mind, and they don't see why a minor inconvenience like being dead should shut them up.'

They turned into Drehr Avenue, and continued south. This was a quiet, shady street, lined on either side with live oaks and southern magnolia. Set back behind the trees Sissy could see grand family houses, some with sweeping driveways and pillared porticos. Eventually, however, they reached a more modest house, a 1920s Colonial Revival painted primrose yellow and surrounded by a picket fence. Luther parked his Jeep in front of the garage and opened the passenger door so that Sissy could climb down.

Although the sun was so low, it was still fiercely hot and humid, and the chirruping of insects made it sound as if they were surrounded by thousands of sewing machines. There was a strong fragrance of gardenias in the air.

'Pretty house,' said Sissy.

'Couldn't afford it if I wanted to buy it now,' said Luther. 'Four hundred thousand and upward, some of these properties. But we ain't thinking of moving. Not till they take *us* up to the Sweet Olive Cemetery, anyhow, to join Uncle Elijah, and I hope that won't be anytime soon. Never could stand the fellow, to tell you the truth.'

Luther lifted Sissy's suitcase out of the back of the Jeep and followed her up the steps on to the porch. 'Shatoya!' he called out.

Almost at once the screen door opened with a loud squeak and a smiling woman came bustling out, wiping her hands on her frilly pink apron. She was big-bosomed and wide-hipped, and she had a broad, well-boned face, with an immaculate Michelle Obama-style bob that was held in place by plenty of shiny hairspray. She wore huge hoop earrings and a necklace of chunky blue crystal beads.

'Ms Sissy, this is my wife Shatoya. Shatoya, this is Ms Sissy Sawyer.'

'I saw you at the gala,' smiled Shatoya. 'Welcome to our home, Ms Sissy. I only wish we could have invited you here under happier circumstances.'

'Well, me too,' said Sissy. 'Has Luther told you the latest?'

She nodded, and stopped smiling. 'Do the police have any idea who did it yet?'

'Not so far,' said Luther. 'If they do, they ain't telling us. They still don't know what happened to that chambermaid yet, Ella-mae.'

Shatoya opened the screen door wider and said, 'Come on in, Ms Sissy. You'll have to excuse the chaos. I only came home myself not more than twenty minutes ago.'

'Thank you,' said Sissy. 'And, please, Shatoya – just call me Sissy.'

Inside, the Broody home was middle-class comfortable, furnished with oversized armchairs upholstered in gold brocade and feathery pampas grass in big copper pots and glass figurines of unicorns over the fireplace. One wall was taken up with an arrangement of framed family photographs, with the Broody children triumphantly holding up sports trophies and high school diplomas. In the opposite corner stood a bookshelf filled with a thirty-volume *Americana Encyclopedia,* as well as books on hotel management and African-American history. On top of this bookshelf, however, sat a scruffy, tufty-haired doll. It looked out of place, but Sissy immediately recognized it for what it was. It had criss-cross red stitches for eyes, and it was wearing what looked like a white kimono with gray twine wrapped around its waist. A *wanga* doll, commonly used in voodoo rituals, and, in this particular costume, specifically dressed for the removal of curses.

'You'd like a drink?' asked Shatoya.

'A glass of white wine if you have it. If you don't, a soda would be fine. Anything cold. I haven't gotten used to this heat yet.'

'Oh, we have *plenty* of wine,' said a hoarse female voice. 'Nobody else drinks in this house except for me.'

A startlingly thin woman in a silky black dress came into the living room from the kitchen. She was very dark-skinned, much darker than Shatoya, and her hair was gray and close-cropped. Her bone structure was just as striking, though. She had high cheekbones and slanting, Egyptian-looking eyes. She was wearing even more jewelry than Shatoya, too: a heavy silver necklet and six or seven clanking silver bangles on each skinny wrist. On her right shoulder she had a tattoo of a serpent swallowing its own tail.

She came over to Sissy with her hand held out in greeting. She seemed to *undulate* rather than walk, as if she were performing some kind of ritual dance.

'This is my Aunt Epiphany,' said Luther. 'Epiphany, this is Ms Sissy Sawyer I was telling you about.'

'*Ohhhh*,' said Aunt Epiphany, drawing her lips back over her teeth in a wide, feral smile. 'You the *visionary*.'

'I don't know about visionary,' said Sissy. 'I can tell fortunes, yes, and some of the time those fortunes come true, but it doesn't go a whole lot further than that.'

But Aunt Epiphany leaned toward her and pressed one fingertip to her right nostril and sharply sniffed. 'You got the vision all right. I can smell the *gunja* on you. That's why they axe you down to BR, isn't it? Something ain't right at that Red Hotel, and nobody can work out what it is, because it's not of this world.'

'Oh, hush up, Epiphany,' said Luther. He turned to Sissy and said, 'Aunt Epiphany thinks that everything that goes wrong in this life is caused by *loa*.'

'You mean voodoo spirits?' Sissy asked her.

Aunt Epiphany vigorously nodded her head. 'I say to Luther – when he tell me about that cleaning girl going missing like that, in such a mysterious way with no footprint – I say let me talk to Papa Legba. He will communicate with the *loa* for me, and explain where that girl disappear to.'

'Well, I have some ideas of my own about that,' said Sissy, but then she saw Shatoya frowning at Luther as if to say – *please, not* more *superstitious mumbo-jumbo*. So she took hold of Aunt Epiphany's bony hand and squeezed it. It was surprisingly cold, as if she had been holding a glass full of iced tea. 'Why don't we just sit down and enjoy a drink? It's been such a stressful day for all of us, hasn't it, especially Luther. Maybe we can talk about The Red Hotel later.'

Aunt Epiphany looked at her with narrowed eyes, and gave her hand a squeeze in return, as if to confirm that they were sisters in the supernatural.

They sat in the kitchen for supper – spicy chicken legs with collard greens and sweet potatoes. Sissy wasn't feeling at all hungry because she still couldn't get the gory image of Detective Mullard's butchered body out of her mind, but she managed to eat a little.

Luther poured himself a large glass of cloudy lemonade. 'Do you know when they first developed this subdivision, people thought that none of the plots would ever sell, because they were so far out of town? More than two and a half miles. But they did sell. This particular plot went for four hundred dollars, and that was a whole lot of money in nineteen twenty-five. You could buy a new Model T Ford in those days for less than three hundred.'

It was obvious that he was trying to keep the topic of conversation away from The Red Hotel, but Sissy could tell that they all had it in the back of their minds, like a semi-transparent ghost standing in the corner of the kitchen.

'You sure you've had enough, Sissy?' asked Shatoya. 'You haven't eaten enough to keep a gnatcatcher alive.'

'It's delicious,' Sissy told her. 'In fact I insist that you give me the recipe. But, like I say, it's been a very stressful day.'

At that moment, Luther's cell jangled. He said, 'Excuse me,' and got up from the table. He went into the living room and Sissy could hear him saying, 'What?' and 'what?' and 'when?' and 'how long ago was that?'

After a minute he came back into the kitchen and said, 'That was Mr Everett. Seems like his sister, T-Yon, has gone missing. He asked me if I'd bring Ms Sissy here back to the hotel.'

'Gone missing?'

'She went back up to her room on the second floor because she'd forgotten something, and that was the last time anybody saw her. Mr Everett says they've searched all over but there ain't no trace nowhere.'

'In that case, the sooner we get back there the better,' said Sissy. She dropped her napkin on to the table, pushed back her chair and stood up. 'I'm sorry, Shatoya. That was a truly lovely supper.'

Aunt Epiphany said, 'You need me to come?'

'No, you stay here, Epiphany,' said Luther. 'This whole thing is weird enough without you and Papa Legba.'

'Don't you go denigrating Papa Legba,' Aunt Epiphany retorted. 'Papa Legba has saved my skin many, many times when I was going through difficult days; and many more of my friends besides.'

Sissy said, 'I'll talk to you later, Epiphany. Right now I think I know what's happening at The Red Hotel, and it doesn't have anything to do with voodoo.'

'*Everything* has something to do with voodoo,' said Aunt Epiphany. 'Voodoo is life and death, happiness and sadness, wealth and poverty, hatred and love. Voodoo is all about setting wrong things right.'

'Well, we'll see,' said Sissy. 'Meanwhile we need to get back to Convention Street, just as quick as we can.'

She went to the bathroom before she left. There was even a *wanga* doll in here, too, sitting on top of the toilet cistern. This one was wearing the yellow and green robe of a success *wanga*, which was supposed to bring its owner happiness and wealth.

Sissy tidied her flyaway hair in the mirror. Maybe it was just the soft lighting in the bathroom, but she was surprised how young she looked, as if the challenge of The Red Hotel had brought her a freshness that she had been gradually losing in her lengthening widowhood in Allen's Corners. She realized that she had only smoked three cigarettes all day, and two of those she had lit and then crushed out almost immediately.

As they drove back to The Red Hotel, Luther said, 'Mr Everett sounds real desperate, I can tell you. I can't say I blame him, after what happened to Ella-mae and that detective.'

Sissy said nothing. It was a measure of how worried Everett must be, if he was asking *her* to help him look for T-Yon. People resorted to the supernatural only when they had lost their faith in everything else, and sometimes that included God.

Luther pulled in behind two white squad cars that were parked in front of The Red Hotel's main entrance, which was floodlit now that it was dark. They climbed out into the sticky evening heat and found Everett waiting for them outside. Six or seven uniformed police were gathered on the sidewalk, as well as two TV crews and a knot of local reporters. The reporters called out, '*Mr Savoie! Mr Savoie!*' but Everett showed them the flat of his hand to make it clear that he wasn't going to answer any questions. He ushered Sissy through the revolving door, with Luther following close behind.

Detective Garrity was waiting for them by the fountain in the lobby, drinking a plastic cup of coffee with a lid on. His skinny necktie was loose and there were dark circles under his eyes.

He wiped his mouth with his fingers and said, 'It wasn't my idea, Ms Sawyer, bringing you back here. But Mr Savoie believes you might have some kind of intuition where his sister has disappeared to.'

'Yes, I do think I might,' said Sissy.

She sounded so confident that Detective Garrity was taken aback. 'Oh, really. Do you want to *share* this intuition?'

'Not just yet. First of all I need to go up to T-Yon's room, and see if I can pick up any resonance.'

'Resonance?'

'Everybody leaves some resonance behind them, especially when they're stressed. It's the same as a scent that a police tracker dog can follow. In fact many people think that tracker dogs can sense a person's resonance as *well* as their smell.'

Detective Garrity shook his head and turned to his young partner in the raspberry-colored coat. 'Can you believe this lady? She knows more about detecting than I do. Even our dogs are psychic and I never knew it.'

'Right,' said Sissy. 'The sooner I get started the clearer any resonance is going to be.'

'Detective Thibodeaux here will go up with you.'

'I'll come too,' said Everett.

'No,' said Sissy. 'I have to go up on my own. If there *is* anything there, or anybody there, they won't come out unless it's just me. And *you*, Everett, I think you need to have some-body with you at all times. I really mean that, day and night.'

Detective Garrity tugged at his nose and looked distinctly unhappy. 'I'm supposed to be responsible for this crime scene, Ms Sawyer, and if I allow you to go upstairs and something untoward should happen to you—'

'I don't think it will, Detective, and even if it does it won't be your fault. It would reflect very much worse on you if you *didn't* allow me to go up there and we never saw T-Yon again.'

She stopped short of saying '*or found her butchered in a bathtub.*' Everett was probably having mental images of that already.

Detective Garrity said, 'OK. But I'll post some officers on the staircase, right outside the door on the second-story landing, and I want you to take a radio up with you. If anything spooks you in any way at all, you call for assistance.'

'Very well,' said Sissy. 'Is there any special code I should use?'

'You could say "one-oh-eight" which means "officer needs assistance". On the other hand you could simply yell "help". That would do it.'

Detective Martin went off to find Sissy a radio. Everett said, 'You *will* be able to find her, won't you?'

'I hope so, Everett. She's a lovely girl, your sister, and . . . well, she and I were beginning to form quite a bond. Not quite mother and daughter, but almost.'

'Everything I said before about all of this psychic stuff – you know, not believing in spirits or anything – I didn't cause you any offense, did I?'

Sissy laid her hand on Everett's arm. 'Everett – if I took umbrage every time somebody told me that they didn't believe in spirits, I'd be sulking twenty-four seven.'

Detective Martin came back and helped Sissy to fasten the radio to the collar of her kaftan. She tested it. 'Psychic Sissy to Dour Detective, come back?'

'This is a police radio, Ms Sawyer,' said Detective Garrity. 'Not a CB.'

'So long as it works, and you come running if I need you.'

Detective Garrity and Detective Thibodeaux escorted Sissy up in the elevator to the second floor.

'I don't know why the hell I'm going along with this,' said Detective Garrity.

Sissy gave him a quick, tight smile. 'You're going along with this, Detective, because just like me you know there's nothing else left for us to try.'

'*Ma mère* saw a ghost once,' put in Detective Thibodeaux. 'It was the pet cat she used to have when she was a kid.'

'Oh, sure,' said Detective Garrity.

'You'd be surprised,' Sissy told him. 'Dogs and cats have been known to come back, in spirit form. Even canaries.'

The elevator doors opened and Sissy stepped out. Detective Garrity said, 'Don't forget, Ms Sawyer. If anything goes wrong – if anything doesn't look right or sound right – you call for help.'

'I will.' The elevator doors closed and Sissy started to walk along the corridor to Room 209. Before she reached it, however, she stopped and sorted through her bag to find her witch compass. She opened it up and held it out in front of her. For the first few yards its needle rotated aimlessly, but as she came closer to Room 209 it suddenly swung around, and began to point directly ahead of her.

By the time she reached the door the needle was quivering excitedly. Sissy took out the key card that Everett had given her and slid it into the lock. The door opened and she stepped inside. She was tempted to call out, 'Hallo! Is there anybody in there?' but she knew that there was no point. All of the guests had been evacuated, and if there *were* anybody here, even if they were human, they wouldn't call back.

She walked into the middle of the room and looked around. The needle of the witch compass began spinning now, very fast, which told Sissy that T-Yon had been here not too long ago, but that she had been interrupted, or disturbed. The spinning came from fear, and uncertainty, and the appearance of something unexpected.

She stopped, and listened. Very faintly, she could hear a childish voice singing. It was somewhere out in the corridor, by the sound of it. She stepped back out of the room and stood in the middle of the corridor, straining her ears. The voice was high and strangulated and singing in French.

'*Jolie blonde, regardez donc quoi t'as fait!*
Tu m'as quitté pour t'en aller . . .'

She wasn't a fan of Cajun music, and she knew almost nothing about it, but she had heard *Jolie Blonde* before. She walked at a slow, measured pace along the corridor, clasping her witch compass tightly in her fist. She didn't need to look at it. She could hear its needle spinning around and around, faster and faster.

The singing continued. As she approached the window at the far end of the corridor, it grew louder, but then it gradually began to fade, until it sounded so faint and far away that she could barely hear it.

She stopped. She had passed the last doorway in the corridor. The singing had died away completely, and now the only noise was the soft, moth-like whirring of her witch compass.

Something was here. Something very powerful, and very close. Sissy could feel a cold, crawling sensation on the back of her neck, which gradually spread across her shoulders and down her spine.

Something was right behind her.

She turned around. Her heart was knocking against her ribcage in slow, congested thumps.

Not more than ten feet in front of her the woman in the pale green dress was standing by the wall. Her face was dead white, thin and oval, with eyes that looked more like smudges of shadow than eyes. Her hair was a dark, rusty red, and loosely tied back with a pale green ribbon.

She stood with her hands clasped together in front of her, in a pose that was simple and modest but very self-possessed. The witch compass kept on whirring and whirring, and Sissy knew that it was the proximity of this woman who was causing it to spin so fast.

'Who are you?' Sissy asked her. She had a catch in her throat so she repeated herself. 'Who are you? What are you doing here?'

'You're asking *me* that?' the woman replied. Her voice was extraordinary, thick with static, as if she were talking on a crackly old Zenith radio.

'I'm looking for a young girl,' said Sissy, trying to sound undaunted. 'She came up here but she's disappeared. I need to know where she is. I don't want her to come to any harm.'

'You're asking *me* who I am? You're asking *me* what I'm doing here?'

'I just want to know where this girl is. I'm very anxious that she doesn't get hurt.'

'What are *you* doing here? This is no business of yours. Go home. I know what you are. Go away.'

'Have you seen her? Blonde, very pretty. She came up here to collect something from Room Two-Oh-Nine but now she's missing.'

The woman was silent for a few moments. She appeared to be slightly out of focus, which Sissy at first thought was her fault, because she had mistakenly put on her old spectacles. When she squinched up her eyes, however, she realized that the woman *was* out of focus. Her outline was blurred, and she appeared to twitch now and again, like a home movie with broken sprockets.

'Of all people . . .' the woman said. 'Of *all* people – these two should never have taken over my memories. This brother and this sister, they took *everything*. My life. My world. *Everything*. Now they want my memories too?'

'I'm sorry,' said Sissy. 'I don't understand what you're talking about. I just want to know where this girl is. Her name is Lilian Savoie, they call her T-Yon. Have you seen her?'

'I want *both* of them,' said the woman, in her crackly voice. 'I want both of them together. They took everything.'

'Do you have her hidden?'

'What business is it of yours? Go home. I know what you are. Go away.'

'She's my friend and I don't want her hurt. Do you have her hidden someplace?'

'I want both of them. Both of them together. They took *everything*. My life. My dream. The love of my life. *Everything*.'

'Please!' said Sissy. 'Please tell me where she is! Please! Or if you have her hidden someplace, for whatever reason, please let her go!'

The woman didn't answer. She stood by the wall for almost half a minute, staring at Sissy with those smudgy eyes. Then, without any hesitation, she turned to her left, crossed the corridor in three steps and walked straight into the wall, and vanished.

The witch compass gradually stopped whirring, and now the corridor was totally silent. Sissy stood staring at the wall in shock. Her DeVane cards had clearly shown her that one

Red Hotel was existing inside another, only a heartbeat apart, and she had already accepted that this was the only logical explanation for what had been happening here. But seeing the evidence of it with her own eyes was still stunning. The woman in the pale green dress had simply *gone*, as if there had been a doorway there, instead of a solid wall.

Past Sins

Sissy clicked the switch on the side of her radio and said, 'Detective Garrity? It's Sissy Sawyer. Yes. I'm all done up here now. You can tell your officers to stand down.'

'*Ten-four, Ms Sawyer. I hear you.*'

She walked quickly back to the elevators, glancing behind her two or three times to make sure that the red-haired woman in the pale green dress wasn't following her. The elevator car seemed to take whole minutes to arrive. When it did she immediately stepped inside and jabbed at the buttons for the lobby and the doors to close. In the mirrors that surrounded her on three sides, she didn't think that she looked shocked, but she was still trembling from what she had witnessed.

When the doors slid open, Everett was standing right outside, waiting for her.

'Well?' he said. 'Any sign of her?'

'I think we'd better go back to your office,' said Sissy. 'And I think I need a drink.'

'But where is she? Is she OK?'

'Let me put it like this: she hasn't left the hotel. And so far as I can tell, she hasn't been harmed in any way.'

'I don't get it,' said Everett, looking back toward the elevator as the doors slid shut. 'If she hasn't left the hotel, why didn't she come back down with you?'

Detectives Garrity and Thibodeaux joined them. Detective Garrity said, 'You didn't manage to find her, then.'

'No, I didn't. Not exactly. But I believe I know what's happened to her.'

She led the way across to Everett's office and sat down in a chair beside his desk. Luther came in, too, and said, 'Everything OK, Ms Sissy?'

Sissy held out her hands and said, 'Not exactly. See? I'm still shaking.'

Everett opened the bottom drawer of his desk and took out his bottle of Heaven Hill whiskey and a glass. He poured Sissy a large measure and passed it over. She swallowed a little, coughed, and then reached into her bag for her DeVane cards.

'I read my cards earlier and I explained to Luther what I thought they were telling me. Now, I'm quite aware how skeptical you all are about cards and fortune-telling and the spirit world. But as far as I can make out, this is the only explanation that makes any sense.'

She shuffled the cards until she found *Un Maison, Deux Maisons*, and held it up so that everybody could see it.

Detective Garrity leaned forward so that he could peer at it more closely, but then he leaned back and shrugged and said, 'I see one house kind of jammed inside of another house. Is that right? If so, I don't get it.'

'Well, let me explain it to you,' said Sissy. As simply as she could, she told him about phasing, and how two buildings could coexist in the same space because essentially they were the same building, only at different times. Then she told them about the woman she had seen on the second floor, and how she had disappeared into the wall.

'What I'm saying is that T-Yon is still here, in The Red Hotel, but not *this* Red Hotel. It's my guess that she's been abducted and now she's in *another* Red Hotel . . . the Red Hotel that this red-haired woman seems to be in charge of.'

'Another Red Hotel. But not another Red Hotel someplace else. Another Red Hotel right here.'

'That's it exactly. The same thing happened to your partner, Detective Mullard, and to Ella-mae, the maid. And that also explains how that bedside rug got bloody, and all those bloodstains appeared on the staircase, but there was no trace of how they got there. Whoever killed Detective Mullard, and whoever took Ella-mae, and whoever left that rug and those bloodstains, they came through the wall, from one Red Hotel to the other.'

'And you seriously expect us to believe this? What do you think, Mr Savoie? Can you believe that some woman took your sister through a solid wall?'

'It's not necessary for you to *believe* it,' said Sissy. 'All you have to do is *act* on it.'

'Ms Sawyer, ma'am, how do you expect me to justify to my superiors my deployment of officers to enter some hotel that don't exist no more?'

'Before you do that, I think it's essential that we do some research. I'm totally convinced now that the woman I saw was Vanessa Slider. The cards have been telling me that again and again, right from the very beginning. If it *is* her, or her spirit, then we need to understand why she's feeling so vengeful. She said over and over that Everett and T-Yon had stolen her memories.'

'I don't know what she could mean by that,' said Everett. 'Before Stanley and I invested in The Red Hotel, I'd never even *heard* of Vanessa Slider.'

Luther said, 'We still have all of those old papers and photographs and blueprints in the storeroom, Mr Everett. You know, the ones that the hotel's attorneys handed over after all of the deeds was transferred.'

'I don't know what use they could be.'

'You never know,' said Sissy. 'They might give us some clues. And I'll tell you what else we should do. We should look up Vanessa Slider on the Internet, and in newspaper files, and go through the court records about her trial. We don't even know for sure if she's dead or still alive, although judging from that presence I saw up on the second floor, I would say indisputably dead.'

Detective Garrity said, 'You had a conversation with her and you're saying that she's dead.'

'Indisputably.'

'Well, for want of any other leads I'll have Detective Thibodeaux here pull the City Court files of Vanessa Slider's trial, and also check the public records directory to see if she's still alive and kicking or not.'

'Thank you, Detective. I appreciate it.'

'How are you feeling, Sissy?' Everett asked her. 'Care for another shot of whiskey?'

'No, I'll pass on that,' said Sissy. 'Let's start looking through those old papers, shall we? I don't think we have very much time to lose.'

'You said that this woman wanted to get ahold of both of us. Maybe she won't do anything to hurt T-Yon until she does.'

'I'm hoping and praying, Everett. A little hope and a little prayer never did anybody any harm.'

Bella went across to the storeroom in back of the staff quarters to find the papers and the photographs for them. Five minutes later she carried them into Everett's office and stacked them on his desk – three large cardboard box-files, covered in mottled gray paper, with handwritten labels that said *Hotel Rouge 1979 – 1988*. They smelled strongly of mildew.

Everett untied the stringy black ribbon that fastened the first box and opened it up. It was filled with old newspaper cuttings from the *Baton Rouge Advocate* and faxes that had turned orange with age and faded Polaroid and black-and-white photographs.

Detective Garrity came back into the room, holding up his notebook. 'I've just been talking on the phone to a retired captain of detectives from the East Baton Rouge Sheriff's Office, guy called John Deliverer.'

He crossed his fingers tightly together and said, 'Captain Deliverer says he knew both of the Sliders like *this*, back in the day. Sliders by name, sliders by nature, that's what he told me. Two people you could never get a grip on.'

Everett lifted seven or eight large photographs out of the box and shuffled through them. They were all taken from different viewpoints, but every one of them showed a stocky, round-faced man with a small moustache and slicked-back hair, wearing a white tuxedo. He had his arm around a skinny girl in a lacy white dress and a tilted white bonnet with a lacy bow. Several other men in tuxedos were standing around in the background, as well as women in dresses with layers of flared petticoats and stiletto-heeled shoes.

He turned the photograph over and read out the caption that was penciled on the back. '*Gerard and Vanessa, Wedding Day, Saturday 7/17/65*'.

He passed it over to Sissy and said, 'Is that her? Is that the woman you saw upstairs?'

Sissy tilted her spectacles on to the end of her nose. 'She's a lot younger . . . but yes. Yes, that *was* Vanessa Slider. No question about it.'

'So this retired captain of detectives knew them pretty good?' asked Everett.

Detective Garrity nodded. 'He didn't admit as much, but it sounded to me like Gerard Slider had him on his payroll, him and quite a few more deputies from the East Baton Rouge Sheriff's Office. Apparently Gerard Slider was all tied up with the people who ran the Baton Rouge casinos, on the waterfront. In nineteen eighty-five, though, he pulled off some really tricky betting scam and made himself a shitload of money, excusing my French. He and his wife Vanessa invested it all in buying this hotel.

'It was called the Hotel Rouge in those days, and it had a pretty racy reputation. Gambling, good-time girls. Gerard Slider apparently was that kind of a guy. *Laissez les bon temps rouler* and nothing barred, and he was paying off the cops big time to turn a blind eye. Not that John Deliverer admitted to taking anything.'

Detective Garrity checked his notebook. 'In April of nineteen eighty-nine, Gerard died. He couldn't have been that old, maybe no more than forty-one or forty-two. Vanessa took over the running of the Hotel Rouge, and, even though John Deliverer said she was a sourpuss, she ran it just the same way that her husband had, with poker and roulette and plenty of girls to keep those lonely businessmen happy.

'Then, in September of nineteen ninety-one, she got caught trying to strangle one of those girls, for some reason that she would never explain, even to the city court. She was given a seven-year sentence for attempted murder and sent to the slammer. She had a son, Shem, who had helped her in her attempt to strangle this girl, and he was sent to a juvenile facility.'

'So the sixty-four-thousand-dollar question is, is Vanessa Slider still alive?'

It was then that Detective Thibodeaux came into the office, almost as if he had been prompted in a play. 'That I can answer you conclusively,' he said. 'Vanessa Jane Slider died on August twelfth, nineteen ninety-eight, at Baton Rouge General Medical Center. Cause of death: cervical cancer.'

'So we're talking about a ghost,' said Everett. 'Or a spirit, or a presence, or a *soul*.'

'Maybe we're not,' put in Detective Garrity. 'Maybe we're talking about somebody who's masquerading as Vanessa Slider. Maybe there's some member of her family who bears a grudge against you and your sister because you've taken over this hotel, when they believe that it's rightfully theirs.'

'You should write crime novels, Detective,' said Sissy.

'And you should write ghost stories.'

Sissy untied the ribbon that fastened the second box. Inside she found blueprints of the Hotel Rouge, dated March, 1986, one blueprint for each floor. They were covered with scribbles and comments such as *'call LaSalle!!'* and *'extend this bath-room??'* and *'new window here??'*

'Tell me,' she asked Everett, 'when you and your partner remodeled this hotel, did you make any structural changes? Like, did you block off doorways, or knock two rooms together, or brick up windows?'

'Oh, sure. We did a whole lot of alterations like that. We created larger suites on every floor, especially on the fifth and the sixth and the seventh, but some of the existing suites we divided into double rooms and twins. The plan was to give us plenty of luxury accommodation, but more rooms in total.'

'Do you have any plans of what you did?'

'A schematic? Absolutely. It's all on the hotel's database.'

'Do you think you could print one off for me? I want to compare what you did with these old blueprints.'

'Of course. But how do you think that's going to help?'

'I don't know for sure. Not yet. Let me take a look at it first.'

Detective Garrity said, 'Meantime, Ms Sawyer, although I personally can't believe that Ms Savoie is still anywheres here

inside this hotel, I'm going to initiate one more search. I'll
have them take the dogs again, too.'

'She's here, Detective. I'm sure of that. The dogs may even
pick up her scent. But I doubt you'll find her.'

'If I do, you can tell me my fortune for free.'

'I'll do that anyhow, and gladly. But – you know – be careful
what you wish for.'

Once Bella had printed out all the schematics, Everett and
Luther took them through the Showboat Saloon to the Smoking
Parlor and spread them all out on the pool table. There were
more than forty sheets of them in all, with details of every
alteration that Everett and Stanley Tierney had made to the
Hotel Rouge since they had bought it.

'You can light up in here if you like, Sissy,' said Everett.
'Louisiana State Legislature have been trying for years to pass
a total smoking ban, but you can still smoke in casinos and
bars and dedicated hotel rooms.'

Sissy took out her crumpled pack of Marlboro and shook
one out. She flicked her Zippo alight, but then she hesitated,
and snapped it shut, and tucked the cigarette back. She was
so tired and trembly that she thought that smoking would only
make her feel nauseous. It was already 11.25 p.m. and she
was usually in bed by now, with a last glass of Zinfandel,
finishing off her crossword.

'Do you have the plan for the second floor there?' she asked.
Luther leafed through the schematics until he found it for her,
and handed it across the pool table. She folded it over, and
laid it next to the blueprint of the second floor from 1986.
With her fingertip she carefully traced her path from Room
209 toward the window at the end of the corridor, where she
had encountered Vanessa Slider.

'*There*,' she said, pointing to the blueprint. 'I thought so.
When Vanessa Slider owned the Hotel Rouge, there was a
doorway right there, which led to a service corridor and a linen
closet. That was how she appeared to walk through a solid
wall. In *her* hotel, you can still do that.

She examined the blueprint more closely. 'And look – this
service corridor connects directly with the main staircase, so

once you've gone through that door, you have access to every other floor in the entire hotel. For my money, Everett, that's how T-Yon disappeared.'

'But how did *she* go through the wall? T-Yon isn't a spirit, or a presence, or whatever you call it.'

'She didn't need to be. Now that the two Red Hotels are in phase, anybody can cross from one to the other and back again, no matter if they're still alive or a gone-beyonder. I can do it. You can do it. The only thing you need to know is exactly *where* you can do it. And now you do.'

Everett said, 'In that case, what the hell are we waiting for? Let's go find her.'

'Everett, wait up. I really, strongly advise you not to.'

'What? Why?'

'It was what Vanessa Slider said to me. "*I want both of them. I want both of them together.*"'

'So what? She's only a fricking ghost. What can she do?'

'I hope you're not serious. She managed to kill Detective Mullard, didn't she, and cut him up like a cattle carcass? She probably killed Ella-mae, too, and cut her up, too, judging by all of that blood. And who knows where that blood on the rug came from. Besides . . .'

Everett looked at Sissy sharply. 'Besides, *what*? Is there something you haven't told me?'

'I promised T-Yon that I wouldn't, but under the circumstances—'

'Is this something about her nightmares? She kept promising that she would tell me all about them, but then she kept finding excuses why she couldn't.'

Sissy said, 'She was very embarrassed about them, that's why. Come over here, and I'll tell you.'

She took Everett across to the bookcase, out of earshot of Luther and Bella. In a quiet voice, trying not to be too graphic, she described T-Yon's nightmare about having sex with him, and how their stomachs were slit open and their intestines were tangled together.

When she had finished, Everett puffed out his cheeks and said, 'Jesus H. Christ. Some goddamned nightmare. No wonder she didn't want to tell me about it. But what does it mean?

Does it mean anything at all? Maybe she's been suffering from stress, that's all.'

'I think it means that the spirit of Vanessa Slider is trying very hard to get you two together so that she can take her revenge on both of you at once. For some reason that's important to her. In Vanessa's mind, it seems like you two have ruined her life.'

'But how? Like I said before, I never even *heard* of Vanessa Slider before Stanley and I bought The Red Hotel.'

Sissy said, 'Everett – I won't go into everything that the DeVane cards have been telling me. Some of it is very horrible and a whole lot of it I don't yet understand myself. But the cards have never given me warnings like this before. It's almost like they're screaming *watch out!*'

'So how are we going to get T-Yon back?'

'I'll go. I'll try to go through the wall and talk to Vanessa Slider and see if I can't find out *why* she's feeling so vengeful. Maybe there's a way of negotiating some kind of settlement between us.'

'For Christ's sake, Sissy, that's crazy. For one thing, how are you going to go through a solid wall? For another thing, that detective got chopped into hamburger meat and it could be that Ella-mae did too and who knows that the same thing won't happen to you? Even if it's possible, which I don't believe it is, I can't let you do it.'

'How else can we get T-Yon back, Everett? The police won't help us. Detective Garrity doesn't even believe that she's still here. I'll try to go through the wall but I won't go alone. I'll take somebody big and strong, like Luther, if he'll agree to come with me. Besides, I don't think Vanessa Slider will hurt me. She doesn't bear me any ill will personally. She just wants me to go away and mind my own business.'

'I still think I should come. T-Yon's my sister, Sissy. It's my hotel. If I hadn't bought it, this never would have happened.'

'You don't know that, Everett. But I honestly believe that if you come too, you'll be putting T-Yon in even greater danger. And yourself, too.'

They went back over to the pool table, still strewn with blueprints and schematics. Luther could tell that they had been talking about him, and he said, '*What?*'

The Door to Yesterday

Detective Garrity was deeply unamused, and his voice was dry-throated and even less expressionless than it usually was.

'I'll tell you, we've just finished another search, and I can categorically guarantee to you that Ms Savoie is not in this hotel, and neither is this Slider woman nor anybody else. The tracker dogs traced Ms Savoie's scent halfway along the second-floor corridor but then they lost it. According to the dog handlers, that means she went halfway along the corridor and then turned around and retraced her steps.'

'So where did she go from there?' Sissy asked him. 'Why didn't she come back down to the lobby? Mr Savoie was waiting for her, she knew that. He was going to take her back home.'

'I can't tell you what went on inside Ms Savoie's mind, Ms Sawyer. All I know for sure is that she is not on the premises. Period.'

'How about you accompany me up to the second floor, Detective, to see if *I* can get through the wall? You can always stand there and say "I told you so, you batty old psychic" if I can't do it.'

Detective Garrity closed his eyes for a moment, as if he were looking inside himself for any remaining reserves of patience. 'Ms Sawyer, ma'am, I have been up and down to every single floor in this hotel all day, again and again. I have initiated three full searches, two with bloodhounds. Right now I have to go back and report to my captain so that he can make a statement to the media. After that I am going to go home and get myself something to eat and two or three hours' sleep. I suggest you do the same.'

With that, he walked away across the lobby.

Sissy looked at Luther and said, 'I thought, from what he said earlier, that maybe he *half* believed me.'

'He's a cop,' said Luther. 'Cops only believe what they can persuade a public prosecutor to believe. Don't matter if it's true or not.'

'How about you, Luther? Do you believe me?'

'Me? I always keep an open mind, Ms Sissy. If we try to walk through that wall and all we succeed in doing is flattening our faces, then I *won't* believe you. But if we *do* go through it, then what can I say? The Lord works in all kinds of miraculous ways that we can't understand, but just because we can't understand them, that don't mean they ain't true. I can't understand nuclear physics, but that don't mean it don't work.'

'You're a good man, Luther,' said Sissy, laying her hand on his arm. 'A good man and a clever one, too.'

The two of them took the elevator to the second floor. As they went up, Luther smiled and shook his head and said, 'There's one thing I can't believe. I can't believe I'm even thinking of doing this. If Shatoya could see me now.'

'If your Aunt Epiphany could see you now, I think she'd be proud of you.'

They walked along the corridor until they reached the place where Sissy had seen Vanessa Slider. Sissy had brought the 1986 blueprint with her, tucked in her bag, so that she could precisely pinpoint the place where there had once been a doorway.

'OK . . .' she said. 'This should be it. The wallpaper and the skirting board don't look any different from the rest of the corridor, do they? I mean, you couldn't tell that there used to be a door here.'

'Oh, when they remodeled, they stripped this place right back to the bare brick. They replastered, they replaced all of the moldings. All of the doors is original, but they burned them right down to the bare wood and repainted them.'

Sissy looked up and down the corridor. Through the window at the end, she could see the twinkling lights of Lafayette Street. She couldn't pretend to herself that she wasn't frightened. She almost found herself wishing that the wall would prove to be solid, and impenetrable, even though she had seen Vanessa Slider walk through it with her own eyes.

'Are you ready for this?' she asked Luther.

'Ready as I'll ever be, I guess. There's only one question I'm axing myself, and that's what happens if we go through but we can't get back. I don't want to spend the rest of my days in nineteen eighty-six. I been there, when I was eleven years old, and I hated every minute of it.'

'Vanessa Slider came through to this side, and *she* managed to go back. There's no reason why we shouldn't be able to do the same.'

'This is sheer craziness, isn't it?' said Luther. 'Here we are discussing something downright impossible. I mean – *look.*'

With that, without waiting for Sissy, he took three steps across the corridor, swinging his arms with an exaggerated swagger.

Even Sissy expected him to collide with the wall with a thud, and she let out a high-pitched '*ha!*' of amusement. But he vanished through the patterned wallpaper as if it were mist, and he was gone.

My good God, thought Sissy. *My good God you actually can walk through it. Oh my God he's disappeared.*

Her heart was beating like a panicky canary in a cage, but she knew that she had to follow him. Who knows what Vanessa Slider would do to him if he appeared without warning and without explanation in the Hotel Rouge, the way that Detective Mullard must have done? Now that Sissy came to think of it, Vanessa Slider and her son, Shem, had probably killed Detective Mullard out of self-preservation, especially if he had told them that he was a cop.

She squeezed her eyes tight shut, held her arms out in front of her, and walked toward the wall.

It was the most extraordinary sensation that she had ever felt in her life. It was like walking through a sharp blast of icy-cold wind, thick with fine, abrasive granules of sand. There was a sound like *sshhhhhhhh!* and then she was through.

She opened her eyes. She was standing in a dingy corridor lit only by a single naked light bulb. The walls were papered

with maroon-and-gold stripes, but the paper was very faded
and peeling with damp in places. The carpet was green and
worn through to the string. The first thing that struck her was
the *smell*. Stale cigar smoke, mingled with mildew, and bleach,
and burned cooking fat.

Luther was standing halfway along the corridor, peering
into a closet. He turned around as she appeared and said,
'There you are, Ms Sissy! Welcome to the Hotel Rouge!'

'My God,' said Sissy. 'We actually came through! Even I
didn't believe that we could really do it for real.'

'You and me both. It's like a dream, ain't it? And not like
the one that Martin Luther King had, neither.'

'What's in the closet?' Sissy asked him.

'Laundry, mostly. Sheets, pillowslips. No Ms T-Yon.'

'Well, we'd better see if we can find her.'

'How exactly we going to do that? We can't search the
whole damn hotel. We don't have no keys, for a start, so that
we can access the rooms.'

'We call her. We walk up and down the corridors, one after
the other, and we shout out, *T-Yon! Are you there, T-Yon?
Teeeeee-Yon!*'

'Holy shit, Ms Sissy! That Vanessa Slider's going to hear
you, if you screech like that! Fact she probably heard you
loud and clear already!'

Sissy hefted her shoulder bag. 'That's the idea, Luther. If
there's one person who knows where T-Yon is, it's her.'

She led the way along to the end of the service corridor.
Luther cautiously pushed open the door to the main staircase,
and it gave a soft, squeaky groan. Compared to the same
staircase in The Red Hotel it was airless and humid and badly
lit and it reeked of dried urine. They could hear echoing voices
from below them, and the sound of radio music, and a constant
grinding noise, like the grinding that Sissy and Detective
Garrity had heard in Room 511.

'Sounds like a kid, as well as a woman,' said Luther. 'That
Vanessa Slider ain't on her own here and that's for sure. Not
unless she's some kind of ventriloquist.'

They negotiated the landing, which was cluttered with
stacking metal chairs and empty cardboard boxes and brooms

and a broken vacuum cleaner, and opened the door which led
to the main second-floor corridor.

It was hard to believe that this was the same corridor along
which they had walked after they had stepped out of the
elevator. The walls were papered in the same maroon-and-gold
stripes as the service corridor, and the floors were carpeted in
the same grass green, disfigured with stains and black spots
of discarded chewing gum and threadbare in places.

Luther looked around as he padded along the corridor and
shook his head in disbelief. 'Can't believe how she could have
allowed the place get so run down.'

'I know. Especially when she said that Everett and T-Yon
had taken her dream. If I ever had dreams like this I'd be
afraid to go to sleep.'

She lifted her bag from her shoulder and took out her witch
compass. Even if shouting out T-Yon's name brought no
response, there was at least a chance that the cobalt needle
would sense where she was.

'*T-Yon!*' she called out. '*Are you here, T-Yon? Teeee-yon!
It's Sissy! Can you hear me, T-Yon?*'

Luther said, 'Are you *kidding* me, Ms Sissy? The way you
screaming, they going to hear you way over in the Sweet
Olive Cemetery. My Uncle Elijah going to be rolling over in
his casket, saying "who's that disturbing my well-deserved
rest?"'

They reached the corner at the end of the corridor, and they
had just turned around it when they both stumbled to an abrupt
stop, and retreated. Halfway along the corridor, the door to
one of the rooms was wedged open, and a man in a black
T-shirt and jeans was backing out of it.

'Do you think he saw us?' hissed Sissy, as they pressed
themselves close to the wall.

Luther peeked around the corner again. 'I don't think so.
Couldn't have heard us, either, or even if he did he's not paying
us any mind.'

Sissy peeked around the corner, too. The man was carefully
maneuvering a wheelchair out of the door and into the corridor.
Lolling in the seat was a girl with her head completely covered
by a green hand-towel. One skinny-wristed arm rested in her

lap while the other hung down by the wheel. She was wearing a very short black dress and only one sandal.

'Is that T-Yon?' breathed Luther.

'I don't know. I can't see her face at all. I don't know what she was wearing, either.'

The man started to push the wheelchair along the corridor toward them. As he did so, a small figure emerged from the room behind him – a figure no taller than a child of six or seven, or maybe a dwarf. It was completely covered by a black sheet and so it was impossible for them to tell.

From the way that T-Yon had described the two black-sheeted figures that had appeared in her room, however, Sissy guessed that it was the smaller one of those two.

The man pushing the wheelchair passed close by, but, instead of turning the corner, in which case he would have caught sight of them immediately, he kept on going straight ahead, in the direction of the service elevator. Sissy caught only a glimpse of him, but he had a blocky head, with acne-pitted skin, and a protuberant, clown-like nose.

He wore a sleeveless black T-shirt, and his upper arms were so grotesquely overdeveloped that they looked as if they had been turned inside out, all muscles and sinews. His forearms and his chest were a writhing mass of tattoos, and he had a tattooed necklace that looked like razor wire.

Sissy tried to see if the girl in the wheelchair was wearing the same kind of bracelets as T-Yon, but the diminutive figure in the black sheets came dancing up alongside the wheelchair and obstructed her view. Underneath its sheets the figure was walking with a repetitive one-two-three *skip*, and it was singing *Jolie Blonde*, in the same strangled voice that Sissy had heard before.

'*Jolie blonde, regardez donc quoi t'as fait!*

Tu m'as quitté pour t'en aller avec un autre . . . oui, que moi!'

Sissy and Luther waited until they heard the door to the service elevator open and then close, and then the distinctive whine as it began to move.

'*Quick!*' urged Sissy, and Luther went waddling off as fast as he could along the corridor. He came back panting, with one of his shirt tails untucked, but with a thumbs-up gesture. 'They stopped at the first basement level. That's where the kitchens used to be, before the hotel was all changed around.'

'I couldn't tell if that was T-Yon he was pushing in that wheelchair or not,' said Sissy. 'Whoever it was, we need to get down to the kitchens right now.'

Luther frowned at her. 'You're not saying what I think you're saying?'

'I don't actually know what I'm saying. But let's get down there.'

'I'll say something for you, Ms Sissy. You one feisty woman.'

'You think so? Very nice of you to say so, but to tell you the God's honest truth I'm scared shitless.'

Body Count

The service elevator was dirty and battered inside, with dented metal panels on the walls, and it smelled as bad as the rest of the Hotel Rouge, with the added stench of long-dead fish.

As it creaked and clanked its way down to the basement, Sissy and Luther heard the sound of grinding grow progressively louder, punctuated by an occasional screech. The radio music grew louder too: Larry Gatlin singing *I've Done Enough Dyin' Today*, which Sissy coincidentally used to play after Frank died, and which always used to reduce her to tears. She looked up at Luther and gave him a puckered little smile.

The elevator stopped at the basement with a bang and a shudder. Luther pushed open the door and they stepped out into a shadowy corridor with grimy gray cinder-block walls. The grinding was so relentless that Sissy was sure that whoever was working in the kitchen couldn't have heard the elevator arrive. Apart from that, that high strangled voice was singing along with the radio.

'And how will we live now? You tell me

With parts of our hearts torn away . . .'

Sissy and Luther made their way along the corridor until they reached the open doorway to the kitchen. Sissy hesitated for a moment and then she quickly looked in.

The kitchen was at least forty feet long and thirty feet wide, with two long metal-topped counters running almost the whole length of it. Four stoves were set into the counters at intervals, and on one of them three large aluminum pots were furiously boiling. Hanging from the ceiling above the counters were dozens more aluminum pots, as well as skillets and colanders and ladles and whisks.

On the left-hand side, with his back to Sissy, his arms folded, stood the tattooed man. Close beside him, almost touching him, was the small figure draped in its black sheet, swaying from side to side in time to the music from the radio and singing along.

'Just existin' makes dyin' look easy
But I've done enough dyin' today.'

They were both watching as a lanky young African-American in a bloodstained chef's apron was picking up large red pieces of raw meat from a metal table and pushing them into the feeder pan of a meat grinder. The table was heaped up with meat – Sissy guessed nearly a hundred pounds of it – but even though the grinder was so old and so noisy he was getting through it very fast. A large aluminum tray underneath the grinder was already piled up with coarsely-ground meat, like a wriggling mass of scarlet worms, and more were dropping down to join them all the time.

The kitchen was lit by fluorescent lights, one of which kept flickering, which gave the whole scene the appearance of a silent movie, even though the grinding was so loud.

Sissy drew back a little. Luther said, 'Any sign of T-Yon in there?'

'She might be. But I can't see the whole kitchen from here. I can't see that girl in the wheelchair, either.'

'Maybe we should just walk straight on in.'

'I think you're probably right. We can't stay out here all night.'

'Risk it?' said Luther, raising his right hand.

'Risk it,' said Sissy, and gave him a high five.

The two of them entered the kitchen. At first, neither the tattooed man nor the figure in the black sheet nor the young chef noticed them. Sissy looked to the left, to the part of the kitchen which she had been unable to see when she was standing outside in the corridor. She didn't know what she had been expecting to see there, but she was so shocked that she couldn't speak, and she could only reach out and pull at Luther's sleeve.

'Lord have *mercy*,' said Luther.

Five hospital gurneys were lined up along the left-hand wall of the kitchen, and on each gurney lay a female body, three white girls and two black. Three of them had been decapitated, although their heads were still lying between their shoulders. Not only that, these three had all been disemboweled and the flesh scraped away from their bones, so that they were held together with little more than tendons and strings of fat and connective tissue. They looked more like smashed musical instruments than human beings.

Sissy looked at the grinder, aghast, and then at Luther.

Luther was slowly shaking his head from side to side and mouthing, 'This ain't right. This ain't right at all. If the Lord God find out about this . . . He going to be so full of wrath, He going to bring this whole place down on top of us.'

Sissy turned back to the bodies. One of the two women who had not yet been butchered appeared to be staring at her. It was a pretty black girl with cornrow braids. Her lips were parted as if she were just about to say something, as if she recognized that Sissy could speak to the dead, and was desperate to tell her what she knew.

But it was then that the tattooed man turned around and saw them standing there, and came right over.

'*What the fuck?*' he shouted, over the noise of the meat grinder and the country and western music on the radio.

Sissy pointed stiffly to the bodies on the gurneys. '*What have you done?*' she screamed at him. '*What in God's name have you done?*'

'*None of your fucking business! How the fuck did you get in here, anyways?*'

'*Where's T-Yon?*' screamed Sissy. '*What have you done with her? She's not one of these bodies, is she?*'

'*I told you! None of your fucking business!*'

At that instant, the meat grinder groaned into silence, and the radio was switched off, too. Apart from the persistent rattling of saucepan lids on the stove, the kitchen was deathly silent.

Out of the shadows behind the gurneys, or maybe out of nowhere at all, stepped Vanessa Slider. Sissy knew that Vanessa Slider was dead, and that this was nothing more than a presence, but she still *appeared* to be real.

'So, you old fool, you followed me,' she said, in that voice that was thick with white noise.

'Of course I did. You still have T-Yon and I need to take T-Yon back where she belongs.'

'You should have brought her brother. Then I could have settled the score, couldn't I, once and for all.'

'What *score*?' Sissy demanded. 'What kind of a grudge could you possibly have against Everett and T-Yon? They never even knew who you were until Everett bought The Red Hotel.'

'They took away everything, that family. They took away my happiness. They stole away my dreams.'

'Well, that's what you told me before. But you didn't explain *how*. If they didn't even know you, how could they have taken away your happiness? You lost the Hotel Rouge in nineteen ninety-one, didn't you, when you were sent to prison? Everett was only thirteen years old in nineteen ninety-one, and T-Yon was no more than six.'

'You don't understand anything, do you?' said Vanessa Slider. Her eyes were even darker and blurrier than the last time Sissy had seen her. 'It wasn't the hotel they took. I *hated* this hotel. I hated everything about it.'

'Vanessa, listen to me,' said Sissy, as firmly as she could, although she was having to make a conscious effort not to look at the bone-and-gristle bodies on the gurneys. 'You have to let me take T-Yon back with me. You can't keep her here. Whatever misfortune happened to you, T-Yon couldn't have had anything to do with it.'

'Oh, she surely did, you mark my words, and she stays here,' said Vanessa Slider. 'You bring Everett back with you, and then we'll see.'

'T-Yon told me about her nightmares. I know what you want to do to them. Look at what you've done to these people here.'

'*Bring Everett back with you*,' Vanessa Slider spat back at her.

'And what if I say that I won't?'

'Then Shem here will have to do what Shem's always been good at.'

Sissy turned to look at the tattooed man. In return he gave her a contemptuous lip-curling snarl, like a pantomime character.

'So this is young Shem,' said Sissy. 'Well, I declare. Hasn't he grown? But who's the little fellow in the sheet?'

'Don't you try to mock me, you witch,' said Vanessa Slider.

'Don't you understand?' Sissy retorted. 'I'm not mocking you, I'm afraid of you! I'm *very* afraid. I'm afraid of Shem here, too, and what you're doing here, and I don't know what I can do to stop you. I can't let you keep T-Yon, and I can't bring Everett here, either.'

Vanessa Slider came closer. She had no smell, no fragrance at all, but she was so strongly charged with static that Sissy felt the hairs on the back of her neck prickling up.

'Let me tell you this, witch. Whatever the worst possible thing is that you can possibly imagine, I can do worse. Now you go back for me, if you please, and bring me T-Yon's brother.'

'No,' said Sissy.

Vanessa Slider turned to Shem and gave him a one-shouldered shrug. Shem went across to one of the kitchen counters and picked up a ten-inch knife. He came back, grinning, and waving it around in circles, around and around, so that it softly whistled.

'If you knew a *half* of what I can do to you with this knife before you die, *vieille*, you would be down on your bended knees right now and promising my maw everything she axe you for. I been cutting and trimming and boning since I was knee high to a high knee, and believe me, I can slice your liver like a fan dancer's fan, right in front of your eyes.'

'I can vouch for that,' said Vanessa Slider. 'And of course, Shem is still in the land of the living. Maybe *I* can't hurt you any, but my Shem can.'

Sissy looked up at Luther. Luther's eyes were darting from side to side as if he were trying to think of a way to escape. She could see that he was just as frightened as she was.

'I need to understand,' she insisted, even though she couldn't stop her voice from wavering. 'I can't just go get Everett without you telling me *why*, because that's the first thing that he's going to ask me. *He* knows all about T-Yon's nightmares, too, and he won't be willing to follow me back here if he thinks you're going to cut him up the same as these poor people. Who are they, anyhow? Why have you done *this* to them?'

Vanessa Slider looked back at the bodies on the gurneys. 'Whores. Hookers. *Bonne à riennes.*'

Sissy recalled what she had heard Vanessa Slider saying in the corridor. It had sounded like '—*stab ornery Anne*—' but in fact it was '—*cette bonne à rienne*—' meaning 'that good for nothing slut.'

'What do you have against hookers?' she asked. 'My God, Vanessa, you've killed them and butchered them and now you're grinding them up like hamburger.'

'It was a hooker killed my Gerard,' said Vanessa. 'It was a filthy diseased hooker who killed my Gerard and killed my dream. I loved that man beyond any love you can think of. He was my life. I hated this hotel but I put up with it because it was Gerard's dream, and he was my dream. But a filthy diseased hooker, she killed him, and that's why all these girls have to pay the price for what they took away from me.'

'I still don't see why you're blaming Everett and T-Yon.'

'I don't care a damn if you understand why or not! You go back through that wall and you bring me that Everett Savoie, and you go do it right now!'

'*No,*' said Sissy, lifting up her chin in defiance.

Shem stepped closer to her, until she could smell his sweet brown body odor. He lifted the knife in front of his face, holding it horizontally in both hands so that all she could see were his eyes looking over the top of the blade. She had met many cruel people in her life, although most of them had been unfeeling and inconsiderate rather than intentionally sadistic. But she had never seen cruelty to compare with the cruelty she saw in the eyes of Shem Slider. This was a man who had been brought up ever since he was a small boy to hurt people in the most pitiless way possible.

The voice of the boy that she had heard in the corridor had probably been him, when he was much younger, protesting because his mother made him cut people up, regardless of whether they were alive or half-alive or dead.

'There is nothing that you can do to me that will make me bring Everett here,' said Sissy, but even as she said it she felt warm urine running down inside her kaftan. She had never been afraid of death, especially since Frank had gone, but she was terrified of being hurt.

'Nothing?' said Shem. 'You want to bet?' He grasped the knife in his right hand and lifted it up to his shoulder as if he were going to stab her in the face with it. She let out a mewling sound and raised her hands to shield herself, but even as she did so Shem twisted himself around and plunged the knife right up to the handle into Luther's belly. Sissy even heard the *pop*! as his abdominal wall was punctured.

Luther gave a loud shout of shock, and stared down at his stomach in horror, just as Shem was pulling the knife out. His shirt was solid red, so that the blood didn't show, but Sissy could see that it was wet, and the wetness was spreading.

'No!' she shouted, and tried to snatch at Shem's arm, but Shem pushed her roughly away and stabbed Luther again.

Luther stared at him, his eyes bulging, and Shem stared back at him, their faces so close that the tips of their noses were almost touching.

'Whachew done?' gasped Luther. 'Whachew done to me, boy?'

'Learned you a lesson, with any luck,' said Shem, grinning at him. The few teeth that he had left were all broken and brown.

'*No! Don't! Please!*' begged Sissy, but Shem pushed her away again, and this time she lost her balance. She hit the cinder-block wall and fell sideways on to the floor, jarring her hip. She could do nothing but look at Luther helplessly as Shem slowly pulled the knife upward, from the bulge of Luther's belly that hung over his belt, all the way up to his breastbone.

Luther whispered, '*Dear Lord. Dear Lord forgive me.*'

'Oh, He's going to forgive you, cousin, no trouble at all,' Shem grinned at him, triumphantly. 'I don't think He's going to forgive *me*, though. But who gives a shit?'

He stepped back, and when he did, Luther's intestines fell out of his slit-open shirt in a heavy wet avalanche, and dropped on to the floor. Luther seemed to make a half-hearted grab to save them, but then he pitched forward and Sissy heard his skull knocking on the concrete.

Shem came over and offered Sissy his hand, to help her up. She stared up at him in fear and outrage and crossed her arms tightly across her chest. She couldn't speak. All she could do was sniff repeatedly, because she could scarcely breathe.

'You see?' said Vanessa Slider. 'I'm a woman of my word.'

Sissy managed to climb back awkwardly on to her feet. She stared at Vanessa Slider for a long time, still sniffing, but after a while she managed to say, 'I don't know *what* you are, Vanessa, but you're not a woman. Not of any description.'

'Oh, you're blaming *me* now, are you? It was you who refused to go get Everett. You had your choice, and look what it led to. You were *warned*, you old witch.'

Sissy looked around the kitchen in desperation. The young African-American chef was standing by the meat grinder with a bored look on his face, as if he couldn't wait to get back to his work. The small figure had stopped singing, but under its sheet it kept doing a little soft-shoe shuffle. Shem wiped his knife on a tattered gray rag and tossed it back on to the metal counter with a clang.

Luther was not quite dead, even though he looked as if he were lying on top of a mass of shiny beige water snakes, which was his guts. His left foot kept shuddering and he was breathing in short bubbly bursts. Sissy was about to go over to him and give him a blessing, because she couldn't think what else to do for him. But when she took a step forward, Shem blocked her way and said, 'Unh-hunh. Let the poor guy pass in peace.' He looked her up and down and furrowed his brow, and then he looked down at the floor. 'Have you *pissed* yourself, maw-maw? I do believe you have. How disrespectful is that?'

Despite herself, Sissy's eyes filled with tears. In the whole of her life, nobody had ever made her feel as hopeless as this.

Vanessa Slider hissed, 'Go get Everett. I want Everett. You can tell him whatever you like, so far as *why* is concerned. It don't really matter. Just go get him.'

'So that you can murder him, just like you've murdered Luther? Him and T-Yon together?'

'That's for us to know and for you to find out.'

Luther let out one last groan and then shuddered and lay still. Sissy closed her eyes for a few seconds and commended his soul to peace and contentment in the world beyond, which was all she could do. Then she wiped her eyes with the sleeve of her kaftan and said, 'Very well. I'll go get him.'

Without another word, Vanessa Slider turned around and walked back past the gurneys where the corpses were lying – or *glided*, almost, as if she were on wheels. She melted into the shadows and vanished. For the first time Sissy noticed that the folded wheelchair was resting against the wall.

Shem said, 'You're doing the right thing, let me tell you. The *pauvre defante mom* never took no for an answer, never. How about me and the peeshwank keep you company on your way back upstairs?'

'You stay away from me, you monster,' Sissy spat at him. 'The only time I ever want to see you again is in prison, waiting to be given a lethal injection.'

Shem grinned and winked. 'You know what I love, maw-maw? I love a woman with a fine sense of humor.'

Cry for Help

S he hobbled as fast as she could along the green-carpeted service corridor and pushed her way back through the wall, her elbows held up in front of her face. As she passed through the plaster, she felt the same sharp, gritty blast as she had when she and Luther had entered it.

To her relief, Everett was standing in the corridor. He was talking on his cell to someone but when Sissy appeared he did an exaggerated double take, and said, '*Jesus! Sissy!*'

Losing her balance, Sissy reached out for him and stumbled into his arms. She looked up at him, her chest rising and falling with effort. 'Everett, that was awful! That was just too awful!'

'You came clean out of that wall,' said Everett, in disbelief. 'You actually came out of that wall. If I hadn't seen it with my own eyes—'

'The Hotel Rouge is still here, Everett. The only thing that separates it from *this* hotel is a split second in time.'

'I'm sorry, Sissy, I really am. I thought you were cracked. I didn't like to say anything, but I thought that you and Luther were going to come straight back down and say that you couldn't do it. It was only after you were gone so long that I came up here to see where you were.'

He stared at the wall and said, 'Where *is* Luther? Is he with you? Did you find T-Yon? Is she OK? Where's T-Yon?'

'I'm sorry, Everett. I'm so sorry. Luther's dead. Vanessa Slider's son, Shem, he stabbed him and killed him.'

'*What?* How is that possible?'

'I'm sorry, Everett, but it's true. We went through the wall and followed Shem down to the kitchen. Vanessa was there too. She wanted me to come back here and fetch you. I said no, I wouldn't, because I was afraid of what she would do to you and T-Yon. And Shem just stabbed Luther, just like that, and then he stabbed him again and it was awful.'

'Oh, God. What about T-Yon? Is T-Yon OK?'

Sissy shook her head. 'I didn't see her, but I think she's all right for now. Vanessa wants to get you both together for some reason, and I don't think she's going to hurt T-Yon until she does.'

Everett said, 'You're shaking like a goddamn leaf, Sissy. Here, look, let's get you into this room so that you can sit down.'

He took out his key card and opened up the nearest room. He helped Sissy inside and guided her over to the couch. She sat down, still trembling, and she was so choked up and distressed that she could hardly speak sense.

'Here,' said Everett. He opened the minibar and took out a miniature bottle of Jack Daniel's. He poured it into a glass for her and stood over her while she drank it, his hand on her shoulder. 'Better?' he asked her, and she nodded.

'I'm going to have to change, too. I was so frightened I wet myself.'

'You can have one of the maids' dresses for now. I'll have somebody bring you one up. How about another drink?'

'No, thanks. No. I have to keep a clear head. I need to work out what we're going to do next.'

'It looks like there's only one choice,' said Everett. 'I can't leave T-Yon there, can I? I'll *have* to go after her.'

'You can't, Everett. I'm sure she wants to kill you both. She wants to cut you both open just like in T-Yon's nightmare. She wants revenge on the two of you together, although I have no idea why. I asked her but she wouldn't tell me. All she kept saying was that you and T-Yon had destroyed her dream.'

Everett went over to the dressing table and pulled out two tissues, so that she could wipe her eyes.

'There's something else,' she said. 'It's truly terrible.'

'Go on.'

Sissy blew her nose again and tried to compose herself. 'Vanessa Slider has *bodies* down there too – in the kitchen. Bodies all butchered like Detective Mullard. Five of them at least.'

'Jesus. Did she tell you who they were?'

'She said they were hookers, and that she had killed them because a hooker had killed her husband Gerard. Given him AIDS or syphilis or something, by the sound of it. Some "filthy diseased hooker", that's what she kept saying.'

Everett stood up straight. 'My God. Maybe this is all beginning to make sense.'

'What do you mean?'

'After you and Luther had gone, I carried on looking through the photographs and the news cuttings from the old Hotel Rouge. I found a picture. Let me go get it and show it to you.'

'No – no. Don't leave me here, please. I'll come with you.

I don't want to be here on my own if that Shem comes back through the wall.'

Everett took her hand and helped her up and the two of them went back along the corridor to the elevators. Everett said, 'Maybe we should tell the cops about this. They have people trained to deal with hostage situations, don't they? And that's what this is, after all – a hostage situation. If *I* don't go after T-Yon, I don't see what else we can do.'

'The cops? First of all we would have to convince them that it's possible to walk through walls.'

'But it is possible. You've done it. I've *seen* you do it. And you can physically *show* them, can't you? They would have to believe you if they saw it for themselves.'

'Yes, but then there's the problem of Vanessa Slider. Shem may still be flesh and blood, but Vanessa is only a supernatural resonance – a ghost, if you like, a spirit. A very *strong* spirit, I grant you. She's brought back an entire hotel, out of the past. But how can we persuade the police to open hostage negotiations with a woman who's been dead for over a decade?'

Just as they were crossing the lobby, one of the night-shift girls came out of the staff quarters with a maid's red dress folded over her arm. She gave it to Everett and Everett gave it to Sissy. 'Not exactly your style, Sissy, but I guess it'll do for now.'

They returned to his office and Sissy went through to his bathroom and washed herself and changed. She deliberately didn't look at herself in the mirror. She was afraid that she would either appear pale and ghastly or else she would look as if nothing had happened to her at all, and she didn't know which would be worse.

When she came out of the bathroom Everett was standing by his desk, holding a large color photograph. 'Take a look at this,' he told her, and passed it over.

Sissy put on her spectacles. The picture was captioned *Mardi Gras Festival, Hotel Rouge, 1986*. It had been taken in front of the hotel bar, and showed a crowd of people in fancy dress, with masks and feathers and balloons, all raising champagne glasses. In the center of the group, Sissy recognized Vanessa

Slider, with her husband, Gerard, standing beside her in a white tuxedo.

There were ten or more girls in the picture, some black, some white, most of them attractive, and all of them wearing very skimpy costumes. One of them was standing even closer to Gerard Slider than Vanessa, but he had his arm hooked tightly around her waist, and from the way that she had her head tilted away from him she looked as if she were trying to twist herself free. She had a sparkly sequin crown on top of her head, and a sparkly sequin bra, and a sequin G-string. She was staring straight into the camera, unsmiling, unlike all of the other girls, but Gerard was looking sideways at her, and the expression on his face was both lustful and possessive.

'Remind you of anyone, that girl next to Gerard Slider?' asked Everett.

Sissy lifted her spectacles a little so that she could focus on the girl more sharply. She was blonde, with high cheekbones, a short straight nose and full, pouting lips. She had very large breasts and very long legs. The camera flash had made everybody's eyes red, so it was impossible to tell what color her eyes were, but her face was so distinctive that Sissy could guess.

'She's the spit of T-Yon. If this caption didn't say nineteen eighty-six, I'd have said that she *was* T-Yon.'

'That's right,' said Everett. 'I couldn't credit it myself, when I saw it. But I don't think there's any doubt about it. That girl there – that's our mom.'

'You thought she went out cleaning every night.'

'You can say it, Sissy. She's long dead now. She told us she was out cleaning but all the time she was a hooker.'

Sissy looked at the other girls in the photograph. She thought she recognized one of them, a tall black girl standing behind the bar. She had beaded cornrows, and she bore a very strong resemblance to the girl whose severed head had been staring at her from one of the gurneys.

'What did your mom die of?' asked Sissy. 'Did anybody ever tell you? She died very young, didn't she?'

'Pneumonia, that's what they told us.'

'Pneumonia. That figures. It's a very common cause of death in people suffering from AIDS.'

Sissy passed the photograph back. 'This could be Vanessa Slider's motive for wanting her revenge on you and T-Yon. If your mom had AIDS, she could have given it to Gerard Slider, and that could have been what killed him.

'Even if she couldn't manage to take personal revenge on your mom, it certainly seems like she took her revenge on every other hooker she could lay her hands on. Do you know what they were doing, down in that kitchen? They were cutting the flesh from those women's bodies and grinding it up like hamburger.'

Everett sat down, staring at the photograph of his mother as if he never wanted to take his eyes off it again.

'Mom,' he said, and touched her image with his fingertips.

Sissy said, 'You see that girl with the cornrows, behind the bar? I think I saw her body down there. So I don't think that Vanessa Slider is killing hookers now . . . what I saw was the hookers that she killed in the past. The past and the present, they're happening side by side.'

'To think we never knew what she was doing to take care of us, me and T-Yon.'

'You're not angry with her, are you?'

Everett had tears in his eyes. 'How could I be angry? She was the best mom we could have wished for. She looked after us the only way she knew how, and it cost her her life.'

Sissy said, 'I'm going to need some help to rescue T-Yon.'

'What kind of help?'

'Can you drive me back to Luther's house? I need to tell his wife Shatoya what's happened to him. I also need to talk to Luther's Aunt Epiphany.'

'Aunt Epiphany the voodoo queen?'

'That's the one.'

'You think *she* can help you?'

'I don't know, Everett. But right now I'm willing to try anything. Even voodoo.'

It was ten after two in the morning when they arrived at the Broody house on Drehr Avenue, and all of the windows were dark. Sissy and Everett climbed the steps to the porch and

Sissy rang the door chimes. They stood waiting in the darkness with the endless rasping of insects all around them.

Sissy had to ring twice more before the hall light was switched on, and the front door was opened. Shatoya was standing in front of them in a yellow candlewick robe, her hair all tied up in bows, blinking at them.

'Sissy! I thought Luther had forgotten his key again!'

'I'm so sorry to wake you,' said Sissy.

'And Mr Everett!'

'Hallo, Shatoya.'

Shatoya looked out across the driveway. 'Where's Luther? Didn't Luther come back with you?'

'I think we'd better go inside,' said Sissy. 'Something terrible has happened.'

She had to lie. She didn't tell Shatoya about them going through the wall to the Hotel Rouge, in search of T-Yon. She didn't tell her about Vanessa Slider, either, or the kitchen, or the bodies that they had seen there.

She explained instead that Luther had been stabbed by an unknown assailant in the hotel kitchen and that paramedics had pronounced him dead at the scene. His body had been taken to the morgue and she would be allowed to see him tomorrow sometime.

'Why haven't the police come to tell me?' asked Shatoya. She was gray with shock. 'Don't they have *any* idea who stabbed him? And why? Luther never hurt a fly!'

'The police should be round to see you later,' said Everett. Sissy could tell that he was just as uncomfortable as she was, not telling Shatoya the truth, but they both knew that she wouldn't be able to understand it or accept it. It was hard enough believing it themselves.

On their way there, Sissy had said to Everett, 'Remember, the most important thing is for us to save T-Yon – and to keep *you* alive, too. The truth can come later.'

They were still talking when they heard a cough. Aunt Epiphany was rustling down the stairs in a long black satin robe, with a silver satin scarf tied around her head.

'It's two thirty in the morning,' she said. 'What's going on here?' She lifted her head and sniffed and said, 'Something *mauvais*, by the feel of it.

She came across the living room, trailing a strong waft of musky perfume behind her, and sat down next to Shatoya. She put one arm around her and said, 'What? Has something happened to Luther?'

Shatoya managed to choke out, 'He's dead, Epiphany. Somebody stabbed him.'

'Oh my Lord! No! Who did it? Where? At the hotel?'

Tears rolled down Shatoya's cheeks and all she could do was nod. Aunt Epiphany held her tight and shushed her and then said, 'O seven powers who are so close to our divine Savior, with great humility I ask you to grant this poor woman peace in her hour of grief.'

Sissy waited for a while as Epiphany rocked Shatoya in her arms. Then she said, 'Epiphany . . . why don't you and me go into the kitchen and make Shatoya some tea. She doesn't want to hear all of this again.'

Aunt Epiphany said, 'Would you like some tea, Shatoya? I make you some of my kava kava.'

Shatoya nodded again, and Aunt Epiphany followed Sissy into the kitchen. She filled the kettle and switched it on, and then turned to Sissy and said, 'What really happen? You want to speak to me alone for a special reason, yes?'

'Yes, I do,' said Sissy. 'I think I could use your help. Quite frankly, I don't know who else to turn to.'

As briefly as she could, she explained how she and Luther had gone through the wall and down to the kitchen in the Hotel Rouge. Aunt Epiphany listened impassively, except for one raised eyebrow, perfectly plucked. She spooned kava kava powder into a large green teapot and listened while Sissy told her about the bodies on the gurneys, and how Luther had been stabbed by Shem, and about the photograph that Everett had found, with his mother standing next to Gerard Slider.

When Sissy had finished, she said, 'I told you I should have come with you when this girl first went missing. What you and Luther did, you were both very brave. But to be brave is not enough when you are fighting against a spirit so vengeful.'

Sissy said, 'You're right. I've come across all kinds of gone-beyonders, and some of them have been bitter beyond belief, but I've never known one as bloodthirsty as this.'

Aunt Epiphany stirred the teapot around and around, and then she said, 'I believe I know a way to rescue this girl. But it is voodoo. If you are prepared to have faith in voodoo, in Papa Legba and the *loa*, then maybe we have a chance.'

'I don't have much alternative, do I? At least you believe me, and at least you understand what we're up against.'

'I must dress and gather some things together,' said Aunt Epiphany. 'The sooner we do this, the better. Give this tea to Shatoya. Kava kava is like a sedative. It calms the nerves and makes a person feel numb. That is what Shatoya needs right now, to feel numb. There will be plenty of time for grief in the days to come.'

She went back into the living room and gave Shatoya a kiss. 'I'm going out now, Shatoya. Sissy and me, we have an important errand to run. Don't worry. We won't leave you alone here. I will call Francine from across the street and tell her what has happened. Maybe you can go over and stay with her until we come back.'

'But it's not even three in the morning,' said Shatoya, in bewilderment. 'Where are you going at this time of night?'

Aunt Epiphany kissed her again. 'When we return I promise I will tell you everything. But please don't be axing me now.'

'Sissy?' said Shatoya.

'Don't worry,' Sissy told her. 'It's something that Luther would have wanted us to do. I promise you, it's all going to work out fine.'

She set down the blue ceramic mug of kava kava tea on the coffee table, and then she sat beside Shatoya and held her very close. Over Shatoya's shoulder she could see Everett biting his lip. He looked about as confident as she was, which was only a few degrees south of terrified.

Back to the Wall

S issy went up to her bedroom to change into a cream cotton turtleneck sweater and a pair of jeans. When she came back downstairs, Aunt Epiphany was waiting for her, wearing a long black dress with all of her silver necklaces and silver bangles, and a curious three-pointed hat almost like a pirate's, with a multicolored scarf knotted around it.

She was holding a saggy bag of wrinkled maroon leather, with ribbons and beads and plastic skulls and little wooden dolls tied on strings from the handles.

'Where's Shatoya?' asked Sissy.

'Gone across the street already, to her neighbor's,' said Aunt Epiphany. 'They're good people. They'll take care of her.'

It was still dark as they drove back toward downtown Baton Rouge, and the streets were almost deserted. Everett said, 'Care to tell me what you ladies have in mind?'

'Not one hundred percent sure yet,' said Aunt Epiphany. 'But from what Sissy tell me, this is not a fight we can fight without some serious help.'

'I'm not sure I know what you mean. What kind of help?'

'This is one mean spirit we facing here, right? Mean and powerful, the way that some spirits can be. It is their anger makes them so strong, and because they on the other side, they can bend the rules of nature in a way that you and me cannot even think about. Look how this woman has bring back her old hotel from days gone by, right inside today's hotel, with only a single heartbeat separating one from the other. How you going to fight a woman who can do that?'

'I have no idea.'

'Well, *we* cannot do it on our own, without help, because we nothing more than flesh and blood, and we do not have the power. So we need some people who *do* have the power.'

'Like who? I still don't get it.'

'We need to call on some dead people, that is who. We need

to call on some spirits. And we need to call on some spirits who have good reason to want to help us. I don't know how many hookers this Vanessa Slider killed. Sissy said she seen five at least. But there could be more, and every one of those hookers is going to bear this spirit-woman grave ill will, wouldn't you agree?'

Everett glanced at Sissy, sitting next to him. 'I'm way out of my depth here. I think I understand the logic, but it's only logic if you believe in things like dead people coming to life, and I'm not at all sure that I do.'

Sissy pulled a face. 'If it's any consolation, I'm not at all sure that *I* believe in it, either. But it's like religion, isn't it? It's like God. Sometimes you just have to take things on faith.'

They arrived outside The Red Hotel and parked. The night porter came across the sidewalk and opened the door for them. 'Everything OK, Mr Savoie? How about you, ladies? Want some help getting down?'

'Everything's fine, thanks, Martin.'

'I've been trying to contact Mr Broody, sir. I didn't see him leave tonight and he doesn't answer his cell.'

'That's OK, Martin. When I see him I'll tell him you want to talk to him.'

They walked across the empty, echoing lobby. Apart from their footsteps, the only sound was the clatter of the fountain.

'What do you want to do?' Everett asked them. 'Is there anything that either of you need? I feel pretty helpless, to tell you the truth.'

'Oh, we are going to need you all right,' said Aunt Epiphany. 'The plan is this: we go through the wall, all three of us, and down to the kitchen, and when we meets this Vanessa Slider we show her that we fetched Everett here with us, just like she demand.

'Then, we wait until she bring out T-Yon, and that is when I call on our friends.'

'You mean, like, these dead people?'

'You catching on quick, Everett. That is exactly what I mean. These dead people. And when they come to help us, these dead people, that is when you grab hold of your sister's hand and you drag her out of that place just as fast as you humanly can. Back through the wall, and away.'

'OK,' said Everett, although he sounded more than a little dubious about it. 'But what about you and Sissy?'

'You never mind about me and Sissy. You and your sister, you are both young. You have all of your life in front of you. Me and Sissy, we have reached that time in our lives when the sun is going down. We will take our chances, and more than likely we will be fine. But you just make sure you get yourself and your sister out of there, and as far away from this hotel as you can.'

Everett said, 'Sissy? I can't ask you to risk your life, just for me and T-Yon.'

Sissy gave him a smile. 'I'm not doing it because you're asking me, Everett. I'm doing it because it's the right thing to do.'

'But from what you said about that Shem—'

'Shem? He scares the crap out of me. But if you never face up to the people who scare you, you might just as well lie down in your casket and close the lid and wait for the day you die.'

'I have a gun in my office,' said Everett. 'I'll go get it.'

'No,' Aunt Epiphany told him. 'If you go down there with any kind of a weapon, this spirit-woman will know at once. This is a spirit matter. You cannot solve spirit matters with bullets.'

Before they went up to the second floor, Everett took them through to the bar so that Aunt Epiphany could mix up some of the powders that she was carrying in her bag. She had three small glass jars of them, one gray powder, one dull red like paprika, and one white. She poured them in roughly equal amounts into another glass jar and shook them up.

'It has to be fresh, this mixture,' she explained. 'One is ashes; one is dry blood; the other is bone from the cemetery. I call it walking powder. The houngans, the priests, they call it *baka*. *Ba* for the superior soul, which rises to heaven when you die. *Ka* for the inferior soul, which stays in the cemetery with the body.'

She also took out a necklace of bones and gunja beads, and a head on a stick.

The head was about the size of a man's fist. It was fashioned out of black leather, roughly stitched together, with wild gray woolen hair and bulging amber eyes made of glass. Its mouth gaped open to reveal varnished wooden teeth and a rough gray suede tongue.

'This is an effigy of Adjassou-Linguetor, who is one of the most bad-tempered of all spirits. He never tolerate injustice, of any kind. He will support us with his holy rage.'

'I still think I ought to take my thirty-eight,' said Everett.

Aunt Epiphany shook her head emphatically, so that her necklace jangled. 'When we go down there, we must appear at first to have agreed completely to this spirit-woman's wishes. Otherwise she may not produce your sister, and everything will be lost. If she cannot kill you together, she will kill your sister anyhow, believe me.'

'OK, you're the boss,' said Everett. 'But if things go wrong, I swear to God I'm going to come back here and fetch that gun and take those people out, whether they're flesh and blood or spirits or whatever the hell they are.'

Aunt Epiphany didn't reply to that. She finished mixing her walking powder and gathering together all the beads and amulets she needed, and then she said, 'Very well. Now we are ready to go. May the seven powers protect us.'

They went across to the elevators and Everett pressed the button.

Aunt Epiphany looked around and said, 'When you remodel this hotel, did you seal off any other doorways?'

'At least two or three on every level. We blocked off all of the old service corridors.'

'It is probably possible to step through any one of those doorways to the old hotel. But at least you know for certain where this portal is, and that it possible for us to pass through it in both directions. I have known people before who have gone through to the spirit world to visit their dead relatives and never found a way to return. The last thing I want is for you to be trapped in the old hotel when you and your sister make your escape.'

'You and me both.'

They walked along the second-floor corridor until they reached the place in the wall where they would step through.

'Remember,' said Aunt Epiphany, 'you have acceded to the spirit-woman's demands. You are humble. You do not show aggression. You beg for her to be merciful. Do not say anything to anger her. Meanwhile, take no notice of what I do. Do not look at me or pay me any attention. When your sister is brought out, do not seize her immediately. Wait for me to give you the word.'

Sissy and Everett glanced at each other. Sissy was silently praying that this wasn't all madness, and that Aunt Epiphany's voodoo magic would really work. She could tell by the look on Everett's face that he was thinking exactly the same. Maybe they ought to forget this altogether and tell the police where T-Yon was. Even if the police couldn't walk through the wall, they could always break through it with jackhammers.

If they did that, however, Sissy suspected that they wouldn't find the Hotel Rouge on the other side, from twenty years ago. It would be today's Red Hotel, and T-Yon would be lost forever, God alone knew where.

'You are ready?' asked Aunt Epiphany.

Sissy and Everett both nodded.

'Then may the Savior take care of us,' she said, and without any hesitation she stepped straight into the wall, and vanished.

'She's gone,' said Everett. 'I saw it happen and I still can't believe it. What if *you* can go through but I can't – what then?'

'You can, I promise you,' Sissy told him. 'It doesn't matter if you believe it or not. You go first, see for yourself.'

Everett walked right up to the wall but then he stopped.

'Go,' Sissy urged him.

He lifted both hands up in front of his face and squeezed his eyes tight shut. He took a step forward, and then another, and the wall swallowed him up as if it were made of nothing more substantial than thick fog.

Sissy immediately followed him, and almost bumped into him as she emerged in the service corridor on the other side. He was standing there with his hands still raised, but now his eyes were open.

'That was *incredible*,' he said. He turned around and looked back at the wall as if he still couldn't accept that he had passed right through it. 'Imagine what it would be like if you could do that all the time – if you could walk through any wall you wanted to.'

'Unfortunately, you would never know what was on the other side,' said Sissy. 'We're inside Vanessa Slider's memory now, and that's bad enough. Places only come into phase because somebody has died without getting everything they thought they deserved. Love, or appreciation. But mostly revenge. You'd be surprised how many of the dead still have a burning need to get their own back.'

Aunt Epiphany was holding up the black leather head of Adjassou-Linguetor as if it were a torch and she was about to enter a dark tunnel. 'You know the way to the kitchen, Sissy. Please to guide us there.'

Sissy led them along the green-carpeted service corridor until they reached the door to the main staircase. As soon as she eased the door open, she heard music. It was faint but distinctive – some quick-tempo jazz number, with a warbling clarinet and a strutting banjo. When she opened the door wider, she could hear voices, too – people laughing and shouting and singing.

'Place is packed, by the sound of it,' said Everett.

'You know what I think?' said Sissy. 'I think that Vanessa is so confident that I'm bringing you here and that she's soon going to get her revenge, she's celebrating. She's recalling some night when she had a really good time.'

Everett listened for a while and then he shook his head. 'This is scarier than silence. She thinks she's going to cut us both open so she's throwing a party?'

'That just goes to show you how vengeful she is. God knows how much venom she must have in her spirit to be able to recreate all of this. They talk about the power of love, don't they? But that's nothing compared to the power of hatred.'

They crossed the rubbish-cluttered landing and opened the door to the second-floor corridor. Out here, the jazz music was even louder, and as they walked along to the elevators, they could hear a couple arguing in one of the bedrooms.

Sissy said, 'We went down in the service elevator the last time, Luther and me. But I think it may be safer if we use the guest elevators. Also, I'd like to see what kind of a shindig Vanessa Slider has dreamed up.'

As they reached the elevators, four people appeared around the corner – three young men in tuxedos and a young blonde woman in a shiny silver evening dress. They were all smoking and laughing and talking about some movie that one of them had been to see.

'He's always coming out with some really cynical line or other. Like, "Bury the dead . . . they stink up the joint." What a character!'

None of them acknowledged Sissy or Everett or Aunt Epiphany. When the elevator arrived and the doors opened, they walked straight in, right in front of them, and stood in the middle of the car so that the three of them were forced to press themselves against the doors. They carried on smoking, too, blowing smoke directly into their faces.

'Do you know something?' said Aunt Epiphany, leaning toward Sissy and half-covering her mouth with her hand. 'I do not think these people are aware that we are here. I do not think they can even *see* us.' She said this very quietly, just in case they *were* aware, and they *could* see them, and were simply being ill-mannered.

When they reached the lobby, however, the four young people brushed their way past them without a word, and it was obvious that Aunt Epiphany was right. To the people in Vanessa Slider's Hotel Rouge, Sissy and Everett and Aunt Epiphany were invisible.

The lobby was crowded, just as it had been for The Red Hotel's gala opening, and the noise was overwhelming. Most of the men were wearing tuxedos of varying colors – whites and blues and maroons – and the women's evening dresses all had deep décolletages and boxy shoulders.

'Jesus,' said Everett. 'It's just like an episode of *Dynasty*.'

'Not surprising,' said Sissy. 'Vanessa Slider's heyday was in the mid nineteen eighties.' She pressed the button, and the elevator doors closed again, and the crowd disappeared from sight.

'I think I'm a little scared,' said Everett, as the elevator sank down to the basement. 'In fact I think I'm crapping myself.'

'If you do everything exactly like I say, you will be fine,' Aunt Epiphany reassured him. 'This spirit-woman is very strong, but we have even stronger spirits on our side. Not only that, we have righteousness.'

'If you say so,' said Everett. 'I still wish I'd brought my thirty-eight.'

The elevator doors opened again, and they found themselves in the gray cinder-block corridor outside the kitchen, about fifty feet farther along than the service elevator. This time, there was no grinding noise, but from out of the kitchen came a deafening cacophony of rattling saucepans and clattering skillets, with the chef and his assistants shouting at each other to make themselves heard. 'Where's that blackened redfish for table twenty?' 'Did you finish off that hot sauce yet?' 'Fried oysters, chef!' 'What the fuck do you call that? That's not a gumbo, it's a swamp!' 'Go easy on the shrimp, will you?' 'Four burgers for table five!'

Aunt Epiphany held up the black leather head of Adjassou-Linguetor with its bulging eyes and said to Sissy and Everett, 'You two go in first. Hand in hand, Everett, as if Sissy is leading you. And remember. You are meek. You are submissive.'

Sissy and Everett held hands and entered the kitchen. It was ferociously hot in there, and so smoky that they could barely see to the end of the counters. The head chef was a hugely fat man with a black beard and fiery cheeks. He was waddling up and down, peering over the shoulders of his four assistants, occasionally dipping his finger into the stews and sauces they were cooking and constantly yelling into their ears. Now and again he cuffed one of them across the back of the head.

On top of the stoves, large cast-iron pots of chowder and shellfish stew and jambalaya were being stirred by a spotty young redhead with her hair tied back, while dozens of hamburger patties were being flipped on a hotplate by the same lanky African-American who had been grinding raw meat when Sissy and Luther had first come down to the kitchen.

It was the hamburgers that were causing most of the smoke, and they had a sweet, cloying smell to them, like no hamburgers that Sissy had ever smelled before. It reminded her of the time that a riding stables in Marble Dale had caught fire, and three palominos had been trapped inside. It was just like the sweet, cloying smell of burning straw and cremated pony.

Sissy wondered if they were going to be invisible to these people, too, but as she and Everett ventured further into the kitchen, the head chef caught sight of them, and immediately slapped one of his assistants on the shoulder. Sissy realized then that the revelers they had seen in the elevator and in the lobby were only the background to Vanessa Slider's recreated Hotel Rouge, like extras in a movie, whereas the head chef and his assistants in the kitchen were her witnesses, and her accomplices.

The head chef bent over and said something in his assistant's ear. His assistant nodded, twice, and then hurriedly wove his way to the far end of the kitchen, wiping his hands on his apron as he went. In the left-hand corner there was a large white enamel door, half ajar. Sissy couldn't see what was behind it, because there was too much smoke. But the assistant banged on it with his fist, and after a few moments Shem Slider stepped out of it, wearing a gory butcher's apron and red rubber gloves.

He slammed the metal door behind him and walked through the smoke toward them. He was wearing white rubber boots, also spattered with blood, which made a wobbling sound as he walked. He was grinning widely, so that they could see his broken, mahogany-colored teeth.

'Well, well, who'd have thunk it?' he said, as he approached. '*La pauvre defante mom*, she's going to be delighted. And me too, I'm delighted. This is going to tie up all of the loose ends real neat, so to speak. Justice at long last!'

He turned toward the wall and called out, 'Momma! Come on out, Momma! Your dream is finally come true!'

There was a long pause during which nothing happened but Shem didn't call out again. He must have known that his mother had heard him. He stood patiently in front of Sissy and Everett in his bloodstained apron, his muscular forearms entwined together like the roots of a swamp cypress, still grinning. Sissy clutched Everett's hand tightly and hoped that Aunt Epiphany knew what she was doing. She hadn't appeared yet, and Sissy couldn't even begin to think what her plan could be. How do you fend off a sadistic brute like Shem Slider with a bottle of colored powder and a black leather head on the end of a stick?

Another cloud of hamburger smoke drifted between them. Sissy tried not to breathe it in. She saw that all of the gurneys were gone, and she made an educated guess that behind that white enamel door there was a cold store, and what was left of the five bodies that had been lying on the gurneys had been wheeled in there, to prevent them from rotting too quickly.

After more than a minute, she heard a sharp shushing sound, the same as the noise she had heard when she passed through the wall upstairs. Vanessa Slider materialized out of the shadows, wearing a pale green evening gown of crumpled satin. The gown was scooped low, but she was flat-chested, and she had hardly any cleavage at all, only a bony freckled ribcage. Everett gripped Sissy's hand even tighter, and she knew that he had seen what she had seen: resting on Vanessa's ribcage was T-Yon's silver pendant of a woman's face, sleeping. Now that Sissy had seen a photograph of T-Yon's and Everett's mother, she recognized the woman for who she was, and she realized that she probably wasn't sleeping, but dead. It was a miniature death mask, which T-Yon had worn to remember her mother, and which Vanessa Slider was now wearing as a trophy.

Vanessa Slider couldn't help smiling as she came out of the shadows. Before she came any nearer, however, she turned and called, 'Come on, *bebette!*' and from the gloom behind her emerged the small figure covered with a black sheet, snuffling and skipping.

She came up close to Sissy, leaning forward a little as if she were finding it difficult to focus. Her eye sockets were filled with nothing but blurry darkness, as if an artist had sketched her eyes in thick black charcoal and then smudged them with his thumb. Her face was deathly pale, even paler than the last time.

'So you decided to see sense,' she said, in that soft, crackly voice of hers.

Sissy said nothing, although she could think of plenty of things she would have liked to have said. *Be meek. Be submissive.* That's what Aunt Epiphany had warned her.

Vanessa Slider smiled again, and looked up at Everett. 'There always comes a time when our sins catch up with us, even if we have to wait for a generation or two. "For the sins of your fathers you, even if you ain't yourself guilty, must suffer." But that goes for mothers, too.'

'My mother did nothing except kill herself to look after her children,' said Everett.

'Oh, she didn't just kill *herself*, young Everett. She killed my Gerard. And who knows how many other men? I'm not trying to tell you that my Gerard wasn't to blame for going with her, nor that any of those other men were pure in heart. But she killed *me*, too. She killed my dreams. When my Gerard passed away, that was the end of my life. I was still breathing and walking around and my heart was still beating but I was as dead as he was.'

Sissy said, 'But you and your son . . . you've been killing all these other girls, too.'

'Aha, but that's retribution! That's what sinners get for sinning, and what else can they expect? We end their sinful lives and we cut up their sinful bodies and we feed them to the men who they've been sinning with. It's the perfect circle of justice. Nobody never misses them, these girls. Nobody never asks where they are or what happened to them. Maybe once or twice a man might say, "Where's that Cherie? I really used to like her." And that's when you're tempted to say, "You and your greedy friends, you came to our restaurant a couple of weeks ago and between you, you ate most of her, and you even told me how delicious she tasted, if only you'd known . . ."'

'My God,' said Sissy. 'What kind of justice is that?'

'It's justice for good lives taken away, before they've had the chance to be lived.'

The small figure in the black sheet let out a strange, goat-like *baaaaah*! Vanessa Slider laid her hand on top of its head and said, 'Yes, *bebette*, you too.'

Sissy said, as firmly as she could manage, 'Is T-Yon here? Can we see that she's safe?'

The banging and clashing of saucepans and spoons and skillets rose to a crescendo, as if the head chef and his assistants were deliberately trying to drown Sissy out. It was surrealistic, like the kitchen scene in *Alice Through The Looking-Glass*. The smoke that was rolling across the kitchen from the hamburger grill was becoming denser and increasingly pungent, and Sissy had to cup her hand over her nose and her mouth to stop herself from coughing. Her eyes were watering and her tears made Vanessa Slider's face appeared to jerk and twitch.

'Oh, for sure your precious T-Yon is safe for now, not hurt at all. Bring her out, Shem! We may not be forgiving, but we're civilized.'

Shem went back to the white enamel door, opened it up and disappeared inside. A few seconds later he came back out again, and this time he was pulling T-Yon behind him, by the wrist.

'For Christ's sake,' said Everett. 'You call this *civilized*? What the hell have you done to her?'

Shem dragged T-Yon closer, but stayed just far enough away so that Everett wouldn't be able to reach out and snatch her. T-Yon looked shocked, as if she couldn't understand where she was or what was happening to her. Her face was white and her eyes were swollen and her blonde hair was all messed up. She was bundled up in a grubby brown blanket, which she was clutching with her free right hand. Her feet were bare and her teeth were chattering uncontrollably.

'There, not a mark on her,' grinned Shem. 'Just like *la pauvre defante mom* told you. You want to see for yourself?'

With that, he wrenched the blanket out of T-Yon's grip and swung it wide open, to reveal that, underneath it, T-Yon was completely naked. She wasn't cut or bruised, but she was covered in scores of grubby black fingermarks, especially her breasts and her thighs.

Everett tried to wrench himself forward, but Sissy gripped his hand as tightly as she could.

'*Don't*,' she whispered, and then coughed. '*Humble, remember. Submissive.*'

Everett was breathing hard. 'Shit, Sissy. I'm going to kill him. I swear it.'

T-Yon dragged the blanket back around her to cover herself up, while Shem gave Everett a self-satisfied wink. He must have heard what Everett had said about killing him but he plainly didn't care. 'Real tasty girl, your sister. Yum-yum-yum! Enough to satisfy any man's appetite, wouldn't you say?'

Everett was so wired up with anger that Sissy didn't know how long she was going to be able to hold him back. But Vanessa Slider said, 'Well, here we are at last. Now that we have you two together, you can make amends, can't you?'

'Amends?'

'Exactly. What your mother did to me, so that she could rear you two sweet little children, that left me gutted. So that's what we're going to do to you.'

Sissy glanced worriedly behind her. There was still no sign of Aunt Epiphany in the kitchen doorway. Where the hell was she, and what was she doing? If she didn't show herself soon, all three of them would be slaughtered like animals and their flesh scraped from their bones and jumbled up together and pushed into the grinder along with all the other poor girls they had killed.

Shem went across to the nearest counter, pulled open the drawer underneath it and took out a heavy stainless-steel cleaver. He came back, smacking the flat of the blade against the palm of his hand.

'See the size of this chopper? Looks real hefty, huh? But it's real surprising how del–i–cate you can be with it, once you know how. The Japanese sushi chefs, they use them, and they can slice a filet of beef so thin you can read your horoscope through it. And do you know what your horoscopes say today? They say, you three assholes thought you were going to get the better of the Sliders, but when it came down to it you don't have the guts. Leastways, you won't in a minute or two!'

He let out a raucous burst of laughter, and the figure in the black sheet jiggled and giggled. Sissy looked at Vanessa Slider and even though she wasn't laughing she was repeatedly running the tip of her tongue backward and forward between her lips, as if she could taste her revenge already.

It was then, though, that Sissy felt something brush against her shoulder. She turned, and saw the faintest outline of a woman, walking down to the far end of the kitchen, and she could only see that because of the smoke. It was Aunt Epiphany, but she was almost totally transparent, like polished glass. She was holding up the equally transparent head of Adjassou-Linguetor in front of her and spinning it in a figure of eight pattern, as if she were winding an endless length of yarn.

Sissy had read that voodoo queens and houngans could walk through a room without anybody seeing them – not because they were really invisible, but because they had the power to distract everybody's attention. They were like magicians, who could vanish from one side of a stage and reappear on the other.

Nobody else saw Aunt Epiphany – not Everett, not Shem, nor the head chef, nor any of his assistants. Not even Vanessa Slider.

But Sissy saw Aunt Epiphany's glassy outline open the white enamel door that led to the cold store and disappear inside, and even though she couldn't guess what she intended to do in there, she began to feel that the balance of power was about to change dramatically, from Vanessa Slider's revenge to Aunt Epiphany's righteousness.

'Everett,' she said. 'Hold on.'

Walking Powder

Vanessa Slider circled around them, her pale green satin dress rustling on the floor. She came up close to Everett and prodded him with one sharp fingernail under the chin, as if he were a slave in a slave market, and she was considering buying him.

'You're a very handsome young fellow, Everett. Just like your sister is so pretty. A pity my two children never had the chance to grow up the same way you two did. Look at poor Shem. All those years in the juvenile detention center, and then the orphanage, and foster parents who beat him, and then prison. Plays havoc with a boy's good looks, that kind of an upbringing, as well as the state of his mind.'

Sissy felt like saying, 'How about a mother who recruited him to murder prostitutes and then cut them up like cattle?' but she kept her mouth tightly shut. She kept glancing down to the white enamel door at the end of the kitchen to see if there was any sign of Aunt Epiphany, but so far the door had remained closed. The clamor of pots and pans continued unabated, and it was so deafening that even Sissy found it hard to believe that it all came from Vanessa Slider's memory. It had really happened, but it had happened over twenty years ago, and now it existed only in the absolute refusal of Vanessa Slider's spirit to forgive and forget.

Vanessa Slider took a step back and said, 'What I want you to do now, Everett, is to take off all of your clothes.'

Everett said, '*What?* You want me to do *what?*'

'You heard me. I want you to take off all your clothes. I want to see you bare naked, the same way that your sister is. You're the son of a whore, why should that worry you?'

'There's no fucking way,' Everett retorted. 'If you think we're going to be acting out that nightmare you kept giving to T-Yon, you are sorely mistaken.'

'*Shem,*' said Vanessa Slider, without even turning around to look at him. Shem twisted T-Yon's left arm high up between her shoulder blades and held the cleaver horizontally against her throat.

'If anybody is sorely mistaken, Everett, it's you. You don't think that Shem would hesitate to cut your sister's head clean off, if I told him to? Shem does everything I tell him to, don't you, Shem?'

'Yes, Momma. You bet.'

Again, Sissy was tempted to argue with her – to tell her that upstairs on the third floor she had heard the voice of a very young Shem protesting that he hated to cut up their victims. But she guessed that their relationship had changed since Shem had gone through juvenile detention, and years of abuse, and prison. And since his mother had died, of course, and become nothing more than a bitter, vengeful, domineering shadow of what she once was.

'You're insane,' Everett told her. 'I don't care whether you're dead or not. The dead are supposed to rest easy, and leave the living to their own affairs.'

'Oh, believe me, I *will* rest easy, once you and your sister have paid the price. I'll be resting easy like Sunday morning.'

Shem made a suggestive grunting noise as if to warn Everett that he was deadly serious, and he lifted the cleaver right up under T-Yon's chin so that she had to tilt her head back.

Everett started to unbutton his shirt, and Vanessa Slider beamed and smacked her hands together. 'You see? Nothing like a little friendly persuasion, is there?'

There was nothing that Sissy could do, except turn her head away as Everett stripped right down to his black Calvin Klein shorts. The head chef and the assistants in the kitchen were turning around and laughing and the girls were nudging each other and banging their skillets even more loudly by way of showing their appreciation.

'Come on, Everett,' said Vanessa Slider. 'Shorts too. Can't make love with your shorts on, can you?'

'You witch,' breathed Everett. But he stepped out of his shorts and dropped them on top of his shirt and his pants and his scarlet Red Hotel socks.

Vanessa Slider came up to him and smoothed the flat of her hand across his chest. He couldn't stop himself from shivering, but he flared his nostrils and held his breath and managed to control his anger.

'I never imagined this day would ever come,' she said. 'All those years of grief. All those years of pain. But here it is at last. Soon I can close my eyes, and sleep forever, like I was supposed to.'

She slid her hand down Everett's side, and down between his legs. She didn't take her eyes away from his eyes, but she cupped his testicles in the palm of her hand, and lifted them a little, feeling their weight. Then she pressed the ball of her thumb against the purple head of his penis, and rotated it around and around, so that her long green-polished thumbnail ran underneath his foreskin.

'You see? Aroused already. This is what your dear sainted mother did to my Gerard, and she killed him. She might just as well have cut him open.'

She kept on rotating her thumb for a while, and in spite of his obvious disgust, Everett's penis began to rise. Vanessa Slider rubbed it up and down a few times, and then said, 'Shem . . . why don't you take off young T-Yon's blanket and fetch her over here. You can spread the blanket on the floor. Give them something to lay on.'

Shem pushed T-Yon roughly forward, until she was standing right next to his mother, and then he dragged the blanket away from her. She stood there, still shivering, still dazed, her hands crossed over her breasts.

'There now,' said Vanessa Slider, stepping back. 'Why don't you take T-Yon in your arms, Everett, and show her just what a loving brother you can be?'

Everett hesitated, but Shem gave another grunt and loose-wristedly swung the cleaver from side to side as if to warn him that he had better do what his mother wanted him to do, or else the disemboweling would come sooner rather than later.

Sissy said, 'Go on, Everett. Hold her. Everything's going to be all right, I promise you.'

Everett took T-Yon in his arms and the two of them clung to each other, shaking with fear and helplessness – two abandoned orphans rather than lovers.

'Now touch her,' said Vanessa Slider. 'Slip your finger in and see if she's ready for you.'

Everett turned his head and gave her a look of such hatred that Sissy could almost imagine his eyes flaring red, like a demon's. But the banging and clashing of kitchen utensils grew louder still, and it seemed to take on a rhythm, urging Everett and T-Yon to get down on the blanket and start copulating.

Everett kissed T-Yon and whispered something in her ear that Sissy couldn't hear. The two of them awkwardly knelt down on the blanket, and then lay side by side, and all the time the saucepans and skillets went clatter-*crash*! clatter-*crash*! clatter-*crash*!

T-Yon reached across for Everett. She said something, but the noise was so loud that Sissy couldn't hear what it was. It looked like *I love you.*

Clatter-*crash*! clatter-*crash*! clatter-*crash*! went the saucepans and skillets, like a locomotive gradually gathering momentum.

Sissy looked away. She knew what a sacrifice that T-Yon and Everett were both making to give themselves a chance of survival, but she didn't want to demean herself by watching them.

Clatter-*crash*! clatter-*crash*! clatter-*crash*!

And then – abruptly – the clattering and crashing stopped. A deathly quiet fell across the kitchen, and all Sissy could hear was the bubbling of chowder and the surreptitious rattling of saucepan lids.

She turned around. The head chef and his assistants were staring down the kitchen to the white enamel door of the cold store, their mouths open in disbelief. One of the girls started to weep – high, panicky yelps of sheer terror.

The door had been flung open wide, and out of it stepped Aunt Epiphany, holding up her black leather head in one hand and a thick cluster of multicolored beads in the other. She had a triumphant look on her face, her thinly plucked eyebrows raised in arches, her eyes glittering, and her lips drawn back across her big white teeth as if she were ready to take a bite out of anybody who dared to challenge her.

But it was the figures who were following her who had stunned the kitchen staff into silence. There were nine or ten of them at least, stumbling a little as they approached, as if they were drunk, and occasionally jostling each other. But this was hardly surprising because they were nothing much more than bones and bloody ribbons of raw flesh, held together only with tendons. Three of them still had their faces intact, but the rest of them had exposed cheekbones and jawbones, and grinning teeth, and triangular holes where their noses had been.

Their eyeballs bulged out of their sockets in a fixed, glassy stare because they had no eyelids or eyebrows to give their faces any expression. But what was even more frightening than their grisly appearance was their silence. Their feet shuffled on the green-tiled floor, but they made no other sound at all. They weren't even breathing.

'You stay back, whoever you are!' shouted Vanessa Slider. 'You stay back! Those women can't get up and walk! They're all of them dead!'

Aunt Epiphany's eyes opened even wider, and even more triumphantly, and she pointed the black leather head at Vanessa Slider and crowed out, 'So are *you*, my dear! You are passed away too! But you do not even have a body! Ha! ha! ha!'

Shem had backed away almost as far as the kitchen entrance, his eyes darting from side to side with fear and indecision. When Aunt Epiphany laughed at his mother, however, he brandished his cleaver at her in a show of false bravado, and called out, 'Get this, OK? These girls belong to us! We killed 'em, we cut 'em up. They're ours! You take 'em right back to the storeroom, you hear, else I'm going to do the same to you!'

Completely unabashed, Aunt Epiphany continued to walk toward them, until she was so close to Vanessa Slider that she could have struck her with the black leather head. Vanessa Slider was clearly unnerved, but she was defiant. 'Whoever you are, this is no business of yours! This is *my* business! This is my hotel! Just like my son told you, these girls are all ours! This is my day for retribution and you ain't going to interfere with it!'

The small figure in the black sheet had been standing close to the edge of Everett and T-Yon's blanket, but now it came over and clung to Vanessa Slider's left leg.

Vanessa Slider patted it on top of the head, and said, 'It's all right, *bebette*. This woman is going to take all of our girls right back to the cold store, and then she's going to go right back to where she belongs, which I hope is hell.'

'Oh, you think?' said Aunt Epiphany. 'You can talk all you like about getting your revenge, lady, but these girls want their revenge, too. They want their revenge on you, for what you did to them, and these are zombis, and there is nothing you can do to stop them. These are not zombis from the movies, my dear. These are not the living dead like you see in a George A. Romero picture. These are the children of Adjassou-Linguetor, brought to life with the walking powder. Look at them, and look what you did to them, and be afraid!'

The zombis said nothing. They stood behind Aunt Epiphany, swaying slightly, their flayed and mutilated bodies glistening with connective tissue and bodily fluids.

Vanessa Slider began slowly to step backward, gripping the black sheet that covered the small figure beside her. She turned quickly to see where Shem was, but Shem had circled around to stand next to the head chef, putting the kitchen counter in between himself and the zombis. He had picked up a large kitchen knife, as well as his cleaver, and he was holding them both up in front of him. He was trying to look aggressive, but Sissy could tell by the way he was grinding his few brown teeth together how frightened he was.

Aunt Epiphany crossed over to Everett and T-Yon and laid her hand on Everett's shoulder. 'Go,' she said, gently but urgently. 'Go now, as quick as you can. Go back through the wall and don't look back.'

Everett and T-Yon scrambled hastily on to their feet. Everett picked up the blanket and flung it around T-Yon's shoulders and scooped up his own shirt and pants from the floor.

Vanessa Slider was standing in the kitchen entrance now. Her face was taut with rage, her smudgy eyes even blacker than ever.

'You can't do this! You can't let them go! They have to pay!'

But Everett shouldered her aside and pulled T-Yon out of the kitchen. As they hurried away, heading for the elevators, Vanessa Slider let out a scream of pain and frustration.

'You can't go! You have to pay! Your mother killed my Gerard! Your mother destroyed my dreams, and all for you!'

Now, however, the zombis began to shuffle forward, lifting up their raw, meatless arms to seize her. Vanessa Slider took three deep breaths, as if she were about to scream something more, but then she clearly saw that these living dead wanted to punish her just as much as she wanted to punish Everett and T-Yon, and that they couldn't be stopped.

She pushed the little figure in the black sheet out of the kitchen ahead of her and started to walk as fast as she could

along the cinder-block corridor. But the little figure kept trip-
ping and losing its balance, and letting out little cries of dismay
as it did so, and she had to stop every few feet to renew her
grip on its sheet and tug it along.

Sissy hesitated for a moment and then went after her. The
zombis would never be able to catch her, and in any case they
had Shem to deal with. Sissy wished to God that she didn't
smoke so heavily, because she was wheezing after only the
first fifty feet, but the little figure in the black sheet tripped
again, and again, and it wasn't long before Sissy caught up
with them.

Vanessa Slider turned around and confronted her. 'Why did
you have to interfere?' she demanded, her voice hoarse with
hatred. 'This could all have been finished with by now, and I
could have gone to my rest.'

Sissy coughed, and coughed, but at last she managed to
catch her breath. 'Spirits like you, Vanessa, they never get rest.
Believe me, I've talked to more than my share, although not
one of them was anything like as troubled as you are. *You* –
you'll be tossing and turning until the end of time.'

'I'll have my revenge one day, mark my words.'

Vanessa Slider was about to turn around and continue along
the corridor when Sissy lunged forward and seized the little
figure in the black sheet. She pulled it back toward the kitchen
with all of the strength she could manage, and even when it
tripped she kept on dragging it. She would have guessed by
its size that it was a small child, about four or five years old,
but unlike a small child it didn't feel taut and robust. It felt
more mushy, under its sheet, and it gave off a faint but distinctive odor like bad chicken.

'*Bebette!*' shrieked Vanessa Slider. '*Bring me back my
bebette!*'

The little figure began to whine and cry, but Sissy refused
to lose her grip on it, and pulled it all the way back to the
kitchen. For all of her shrieking, however, Vanessa Slider didn't
come after her. She must have been more frightened of the
zombis in the kitchen than she was of losing her '*bebette*',
whatever it was. She didn't run away any farther, though. She
stood halfway down the corridor in her pale green evening

dress, her hand pressed indecisively over her mouth. Do I save myself, or save my *bebette*?

'Vanessa!' Sissy called her, when she had reached the kitchen entrance. 'Why don't you come on back? We can find a way to sort this out without killing any more people. I know about spirits, and how to help them to find peace.'

Vanessa Slider shook her head and stayed where she was. Sissy shrugged and pulled the little figure back into the kitchen.

Shem and the head chef and the kitchen assistants were all clustered close together, in between the counters. There were zombis now at both ends of the kitchen, so there was no way for them to escape.

Aunt Epiphany looked down at the little figure in the black sheet and said, 'Well . . . you sure have some nerve, Sissy! What do we have here?'

'You leave him alone!' Shem shouted at them. 'That's my brother you got there! You leave him be or I'll cut your tits off!'

'Your brother?' said Sissy. 'And so why does your brother always hide himself under a sheet?'

'You leave him be! You leave him be, or I swear that I will cut your tits off and push them down your throat!'

Aunt Epiphany said, 'You hush up, ugly boy. *You* in no position to be making no threats to nobody. Let us take a look at this brother of yours.'

She grasped the sheet and pulled it upward. At first, the little figure clung on to it tight, but then Aunt Epiphany twisted and twirled it, like a bullfighter's cape, and gave it a double-shake, and he had to let go. She threw it on to the floor, and there was Shem's brother, exposed for all of them to see.

As Sissy had guessed, he was around four or five years old. He must have been quite a beautiful child, when he was alive, but like Vanessa Slider he was obviously dead. He was wearing an all-in-one sleep suit that must once have been white, but was now patterned with green and yellow stains. His face was gray and his eyeballs were milky and there were green tinges around his mouth.

'*You bastards!*' Shem foamed at them. '*You bastards! That's my brother!*'

'He is decomposing,' said Aunt Epiphany. 'Look at the poor boy, Shem. He is rotting away.'

'That's because Momma couldn't take him to the mortician!'

At that moment, Vanessa Slider reappeared in the kitchen entrance.

'So now you know,' she said. 'Now you know why I cannot forgive.'

The little boy tottered over to his mother and she bent forward and kissed his forehead. 'There, *bebette*, everything will soon be well. Momma promises you.'

While she was standing there, however, trying to calm her long-dead child, three of the zombis had slowly but silently crept around behind her, and were now staring at her with their bloodshot, lidless eyes.

'Vanessa—' Sissy cautioned her.

But Aunt Epiphany laid her hand on Sissy's shoulder and said, 'No, Sissy. This has to be finished here tonight. Otherwise, it will happen again and again, and Everett and T-Yon will always be in mortal danger. This woman has stained the fields with the blood of innocent people. Now she must harvest the crop that has grown there.'

'But Epiphany, I can't just stand here and watch this. It's against my nature. I was put on this earth to help spirits, not destroy them.'

'If you cannot stand here and watch this, my darling, then with the greatest respect I suggest you leave, and go back through the wall, and I will meet you there when this all finished.'

Shem was shouting again, a hoarse barrage of swear words and sadistic obscenities. 'You're dead, you fuckers! I'll cut your fucking heads off and stick 'em up your fucking ass!'

The zombis were advancing on him and the rest of the kitchen staff from both ends of the kitchen and he could see that he had no way to escape. They glided forward, the zombis, their heads swaying hypnotically like cobras, and with their fleshless faces and exposed shoulder blades, Sissy found them utterly terrifying.

Vanessa Slider screamed. Two of the zombis had jumped

on to her back from behind and one of them was trying to bite into her neck. The little boy screamed, too, but the third zombi seized him by the wrist and swung him around, hitting him against the wall. She didn't let go, though. She pulled him back and swung him around a second time, and then a third, until his skull cracked with a sound like a breaking jug. His putrescent brains, as pale green as his mother's evening dress, were spattered in lumps up the wall.

'Oh my God,' said Sissy. 'Oh my dear God, this is just awful.'

'Remember that boy long dead already,' said Aunt Epiphany. Her tone was surprisingly ferocious. 'This zombi is doing him a favor.'

The zombi kept on smashing the little boy against the wall until his arm tore out of its socket, and he was little more than a shapeless lump of flesh in a green-stained sleep suit.

Vanessa Slider's eyes rolled as she saw what was happening to her *bebette*, but she couldn't speak. One of the zombis had buried her teeth in her neck, and was tearing the flesh away from her windpipe, while the other was ripping her dress off her back.

Between them, the two zombis stripped her down to her cream-colored teddy. She could barely stand, and so much muscle had been bitten away from her neck that her head waggled loosely from side to side. Her knees gave way and she twisted around and dropped on to the floor. As soon as she fell, all three zombis crouched down beside her and started biting at her. The only sound was the tearing of skin as they wrenched it away with their teeth.

'Remember this Slider woman, she is dead, too,' said Aunt Epiphany. 'It is only the dead, feeding off the dead.'

As she spoke, Sissy felt a deep tremor shaking the basement. Several pots and ladles dropped from their hooks above the kitchen counters.

'Earthquake?' she said. 'Do they have earthquakes in Baton Rouge?'

'No,' said Aunt Epiphany. 'It is the Slider woman. The zombis are devouring her spirit, and when her spirit is gone, all of this hotel will be gone, too. So you and me, Sissy, we must hurry.'

Shem was surrounded by a crowd of seven zombis. The head chef and his assistants were terrified, but it had become apparent to them now that the zombis had no interest in them at all. They may not have realized it, but Sissy knew that they were nothing more than Vanessa Slider's memories, and that they would disappear when the last spark of Vanessa Slider's spirit winked out, just like the Hotel Rouge and everybody in it – the revelers up in the lobby, the waiters, the jazz band, the arguing guests in the upstairs rooms, everybody.

Shem, however, was alive. Shem was flesh and blood, and that was just what these seven zombis craved, along with their revenge.

'Get the fuck away from me!' he screamed, and struck out wildly with his cleaver. He knocked the hand off one of the zombis, and it flew across the kitchen, but that didn't deter her at all. She kept coming at him with one raw hand and one bony stump.

Panting with terror and effort, Shem hacked and slashed at the zombis as they came close enough to tug at his clothes. He hit one of them diagonally, embedding his cleaver right across the middle of her face, but after he had levered his cleaver back out she continued to reach for him, even though her lips were hanging open at one side of her mouth in a leering double-grin, and one of her eyes was now an inch lower than the other.

'Gaston!' Shem shouted. 'Gaston, throw me over that can of cooking awl!'

'What you say?' the head chef shrilled back at him, in panic.

'I said throw me over that fucking can of cooking awl!'

Bewildered, the head chef picked up a two-gallon can of peanut oil, swung it backward and forward, and then heaved it in a tumbling arc so that it landed with a dull bang right at Shem's feet. Shem set down his cleaver on the counter and bent down to retrieve it, all the time continuing to jab his kitchen knife toward the zombis as they inched ever closer.

'Come on, then!' he challenged them. 'Come on, then! You're dead – let's see if you're ready to be cremated!'

He unscrewed the cap and then flung huge dollops of pale yellow oil all over the zombis, one after the other, until they were drenched in it. They didn't flinch, even when it splashed straight into their lidless eyes, and kept on coming. One of them seized his sleeve, and then another caught at his collar. He hit back at them furiously with the empty cooking-oil can, so that they had to release their grip. Then he reached across the counter for the kitchen blowtorch, lit it, and turned around to face them.

The sharp blue flame of the blowtorch was reflected in the zombis' eyes but they didn't hesitate. They snatched at Shem's shirt again, and one of them tried to claw at his face. He pointed the blowtorch directly at them, and the nearest zombi abruptly burst into flame. Then another, and another. Within a few seconds, all seven of them were pillars of rippling fire.

Shem yelled, 'Burn, you sluts! Burn! Got what you fucking deserved, yes? Hurt my momma, would you? Kill my baby brother? This is what you get! A preview of hellfire, that's what!'

But even though they were all blazing, their faces barely visible behind masks of flame, the zombis didn't cry out, because they had no breath to cry out, and they didn't show any sign of pain. They were dead, and their souls had long since left their mutilated bodies. Sissy knew that they were walking only because of Aunt Epiphany's walking powder, and the holy rage of Adjassou-Linguetor.

Shem tried to pull himself away from them, and his hand scrabbled across the kitchen counter in search of his cleaver. One of the blazing zombis gripped his wrist with her bony, fiery fingers, while another started to tug at his shirt, so that the cotton was scorched. Shem howled in pain, twisting himself around and trying to heave himself up on to the counter to get away.

'Gaston! Gaston! Help me here, will you! Gaston you *grand salaud*, help me!'

Gaston stayed where he was, on the opposite side of the counter, with his assistants clustered around him.

'Gaston! Give me your hand, you fucker!'

But there were seven fiery zombis, and they were over-whelming. Between them they all dragged Shem away from the counter, and down to the floor. Amongst the flames, Sissy could see his feet kicking, but the kitchen was starting to fill up with smoke as the last remnants of flesh on the zombis' bodies began to blacken and crisp.

'Oh God in heaven help me!' screamed Shem, as the zombis tore at his flesh. 'Not my eyes! Not my eyes! I never took *your* eyes! No!'

The basement trembled once again, more violently this time. A whole rack of saucepans and colanders fell from the ceiling and crashed on to the floor. Sissy looked around and saw that Vanessa Slider was lying motionless now, her arms and legs spread wide, her face dead white, although she was sure that she saw her blink. The three zombis were still crouched over her, biting the flesh away from her bones.

'How can they *eat* her?' said Sissy. 'She's only a spirit.'

'Of course she does not have real, living flesh, like her son,' said Aunt Epiphany. 'But her anger was so terrible that her anger gave her flesh, so that she could take her revenge. What she has is the memory of flesh, just like this hotel is just a memory. And even the memory of flesh is enough to satisfy these women that she killed and butchered and fed to her guests.'

The kitchen was completely filled up with smoke now, and the eye-watering smell of burned meat. The floor trembled again, and it was clear that Vanessa Slider's spirit had nearly gone.

'Now we must leave, and quick,' said Aunt Epiphany. 'It is all done now.'

The two of them hurried silently to the elevators. Sissy prayed that they would still be working, and that Vanessa Slider's spirit wouldn't be extinguished before they reached the second floor. Like everybody and everything else in the Hotel Rouge, they would simply cease to exist.

The elevator chimed and they stepped inside. The hotel shook again, and this time they heard a deep, threatening rumble, and the groaning of girders, as if the whole building were about to collapse around them. But Sissy pushed the button and the elevator began to rise quite smoothly, although now and again it shuddered a little and gave a disconcerting rattle.

A thought suddenly occurred to Sissy as they passed the first floor.

'Luther – what about Luther? Was *his* body down in that cold store, too?'

Aunt Epiphany nodded. 'He was there. I was not going to make him walk because of the way he was, cut open like that. And he was family.'

'But how are we going to explain what happened to him?'

'We do not explain. So far as we know, he was stabbed by some person unknown, and he was taken away in an ambulance, and we do not know where.'

'And you think that the police are going to believe that? What about poor Shatoya?'

'You know and I know, Sissy, that Luther is departed from the real world for ever. Nobody can ever find him. I will say prayers for him, and light candles.'

They reached the second floor and the elevator came to a jarring stop. For a very long moment, the doors remained closed, and Sissy started to think that she and Aunt Epiphany, too, would soon depart the real world for ever. Yet another deep rumble made the hotel shake, and Sissy heard glass breaking and people shouting. But faintly – very faintly – the sound of jazz. She recognized it: *Saint James Infirmary Blues*.

'*I'm goin' down to Saint James Infirmary . . . see my baby there . . . stretched out on a long white table . . . so cold, so sweet, so fair . . .*'

My God, thought Sissy. *How appropriate. A requiem for one woman's insatiable hunger for revenge.*

Then the doors opened.

Voodoo Doll

Sissy returned to The Red Hotel the following afternoon. It was a hot, glaring day, although a slight south-westerly breeze was blowing off the river which eased the humidity.

She found Everett and T-Yon sitting in the Showboat Saloon with Detective Garrity and young Detective Thibodeaux, drinking iced tea.

She had seen Everett and T-Yon last night, of course, when she and Aunt Epiphany had stumbled out of the wall on the second floor. T-Yon had told them that Everett had been champing to go back in to rescue them, but she had persuaded him not to.

'Well, you were wise,' Sissy had told her. 'Like Epiphany said, we're just two old ladies, while you have your whole lives in front of you.'

They had walked hand in hand back along the corridor, but as they had done so, they had heard another rumble – *felt* it, rather than heard it, through the soles of their feet. Sissy had hesitated and then walked back to the place where they had come through the wall. The others had waited for her as she placed the flat of her hand against the plaster. It had seemed to be solid again, so she had pushed a little harder.

She had walked back to join Everett and T-Yon and Aunt Epiphany.

'They're gone,' she had said, with a rueful smile, because she couldn't help thinking of Luther and Ella-mae and Detective Mullard, and all of those unnamed good-time girls. 'Vanessa Slider and Shem, they're out of your lives for ever.'

Today, Everett and T-Yon still looked tired, but they were both smartly dressed – Everett in a red-and-white striped shirt and slacks, and T-Yon in a white blouse and jeans.

Detective Garrity stood up as Sissy came in. 'Where you

at, Ms Sawyer? Gather you're leaving us today, you and Ms Savoie here, flying back to chilly Connecticut.'

'That's right. But I'll be back before too long. From what little I've managed to see of Red Stick, I like the look of it, and it would be good to get to know it better. I never even managed to have a gumbo.'

They sat down. Detective Garrity spooned sugar into his tea and looked across the table at her as he stirred it.

'Why do I have the feeling that our troubles are over and you know why but I never will?'

'I don't know, Detective. I may have a facility for telling fortunes, but I don't know everything.'

'It is something concerning this Vanessa Slider woman you kept going on about, isn't it?'

'Vanessa Slider is dead, Detective. Vanessa Slider is long dead.'

'OK . . . but why don't you leave me a contact number in Connecticut where I can get ahold of you. You know – just in case I have any more queries about ghosts or – what did you call them? – gone-beyonders. I still have more loose ends to tie up here than five plates of spaghetti.'

Sissy wrote her number on a paper napkin and passed it over. All the time Detective Garrity never once took his eyes off her.

'Just tell me one thing,' he said, folding up the napkin and tucking it into his pocket without looking at it. 'Just tell me that – so far as you're concerned – it *is* all over.'

'You're not a believer, Detective. You made that clear enough.'

'Maybe I'm not. But then I don't believe in God, either, which doesn't mean to say that I disrespect people who do.'

Sissy thought for a moment, and then she said, 'Since I've met them, I've grown very fond of Everett and T-Yon. They're almost like my own children. I wouldn't leave Baton Rouge unless I was sure that there was nothing threatening them any more, either from this world, or the next.'

'OK. I accept that. So what *did* happen between the time I left last night and this morning, when I came back.'

'What's your star sign, Detective?'

'My star sign? Sagittarius. Why?'

'I predict that you have a highly illustrious career ahead of you in the Baton Rouge police department, and I'm talking about Chief of Police. But this will only happen if you keep your sanity.'

'Pardon me.'

'It's like you said, Detective. *I* know what happened but you never will, and it's much, much better that way, for all of us. Especially for you.'

Before they left for the airport, Everett gave Sissy a squeeze and said, 'Thank you, Sissy, for everything. Without you, T-Yon and me – well, that would've been the end of us. Here, why don't you keep this? Let's say it's a souvenir of a hair-raising visit to BR?'

He handed Sissy a yellow envelope. She opened it up and slid out the photograph that was inside it – the picture of Vanessa Slider and Gerard Slider and Everett and T-Yon's mother, standing in front of the bar at the Hotel Rouge Mardi Gras festival, 1986.

'I'm not sure how to thank you,' she said, more than a little sarcastically. 'I'll frame it and hang it in my bathroom and scare myself shitless.'

She was sliding it back into the envelope again when her eye was caught by something that she hadn't seen before. The pretty black girl with the cornrows standing behind the bar had a tattoo on her right shoulder. She lifted up her spectacles and looked at it more closely. It was a tattoo of a serpent, swallowing its own tail. She knew that in mythology, it was called *ouroboros*, and that it symbolized the endless cycle of life. The eternal return.

She said to Everett, 'What time is our flight?'

'Seven fifteen. Why? You have plenty of time.'

'Is there a later flight?'

'I guess there's a red-eye. I'll have to ask Bella.'

'Please . . . see if you can book me on a later flight. There's somebody I have to go see before I leave.'

'Are you sure? Is there anything we can help you with?'

'No, no. Just call me a taxi. I shouldn't be too long, no more than an hour. I'll get back here as soon as I can.'

Sissy left the air-conditioned lobby and stepped out into the warmth of an amber afternoon. She told the taxi driver where she wanted to go, and as he drove her there he started up a long monolog about the LSU basketball team, and exactly what he thought of Trent Johnson. Sissy kept repeating 'really?' just to keep him talking, because her mind was completely fixed on where she was going and what she was going to say when she got there.

'Wait for me, please,' she told the taxi driver, when they reached the house on Drehr Avenue.

She climbed the steps up on to the porch and rang the doorbell. Almost at once, Shatoya opened the door. She was dressed all in black and she looked as if she hadn't been sleeping.

'Why, Sissy! I thought you went back home to Connecticut! That's what Epiphany told me, anyhow.'

'I have a flight booked for this evening,' Sissy told her. 'I just needed to have a last word with Epiphany before I left.'

'OK, come along in.'

Sissy stepped into the house and gave Shatoya a hug. 'How are you bearing up? I'm so sorry for your loss.'

'If they could just tell me where he is . . . Nobody seems to know.'

'I'll ask Bella. Maybe she could contact the hospitals for you and find out where they've taken him.'

'It's such a bad, bad dream. I've even lost his dear remains.'

They crossed the hallway and as they did so, Aunt Epiphany came down the stairs. She, too, was wearing black, a close-fitting crêpe dress with a glittering jet brooch.

'Sissy! I thought you would be on your way home by now!'

She came up to her and kissed her. She smelled of gardenias.

Sissy said, 'I would have been. But I wanted to see you before I left. Could we talk alone for just a minute? Shatoya, would you mind?'

'No, not at all. Would you like a cold drink, maybe? Lemonade?'

'I'm fine, thanks,' said Sissy. She walked into the living room and took the yellow envelope out of her bag. 'Take a look at this,' she said.

Frowning, Aunt Epiphany opened the envelope and drew out the photograph. She studied it for a moment with her hand trembling. Then she handed it back with an expression on her face that was both pleading and tragic.

'That's you, isn't it?' said Sissy, trying hard to keep her voice steady. 'And that was *you* I saw in the kitchen, when Luther and I first went down there. That was why I didn't see the girl with the cornrows amongst all of those zombis – you couldn't be in two places at the same time.'

Aunt Epiphany said nothing, but her lips puckered up and her eyes filled with tears.

Sissy saw the black leather head, which was still lying at the side of the couch. She nodded toward it and said, 'Adjassou-Linguetor. You're one of his children, too, aren't you?'

'It was my momma,' sobbed Aunt Epiphany. 'My momma came looking for me when I didn't come home. She found me somehow and took me away without the Sliders knowing. She disapproved so much of what I was doing, because she was so religious. But I was her only child. She loved me so much, she didn't want to lose me. She took me to the houngan.'

Sissy didn't know what to say. She thought of all the people that she had loved over the years, and lost, and who would never come back, no matter how much they smiled and danced and laughed in her memories. She took hold of Aunt Epiphany's hands, and it was only then that she realized why they had always felt so cold.